W9-BUF-009

Praise for Amy K. Sorrells

Then Sings My Soul

"Flashing back between the present and [the] past, Sorrells stitches together a beautiful story of family and belief that illustrates the importance of closure and the peace derived from faith. Recommended for readers interested in realistic fiction in the style of Kate Breslin, Kristy Cambron, and Chris Bohjalian."

LIBRARY JOURNAL

"*Then Sings My Soul* is the most phenomenal and heartrending story I have ever read. This struck my heart and soul and will remain in my memory forever. The horrific treatment of the Jews during the Holocaust will never be forgotten. Amy K. Sorrells could not have described the events happening with more authenticity . . . than she did. If this story doesn't 'get' you, no others will."

FRESH FICTION

How Sweet the Sound

"This book will turn your emotions inside out and grip your heart with a clawed fist before pouring acid—and then balm—over the wounds. You have been warned. Now, by all means, go buy this unusually edgy and entirely moving inspirational novel and read it for yourself."

SERENA CHASE, *USA TODAY*

"Debut inspirational novelist Sorrells opens her story powerfully . . . Sorrells will likely move many readers of faith, and she's worth watching."

PUBLISHERS WEEKLY ON

"You could read *How Sweet the Sound* because you love a well-told story, but Amy Sorrells delivers so much more. Here the depths of pain mankind can inflict meets the unfailing grace that waits to heal all who'll come."

SHELLIE RUSHING TOMLINSON, BELLE OF ALL THINGS SOUTHERN, AUTHOR OF *HEART WIDE OPEN*

"With poetic prose, lyrical descriptions, and sensory details that bring the reader deep into every scene, Amy K. Sorrells has delivered a lush, modern telling of the age-old story of Tamar. But that's not all. With a full cast of colorful characters and juxtaposed first-person narratives woven through, this story dives into the Gulf Coast culture of pecan orchards and debutante balls exposing layers of family secrets and sins. In the end comes redemption, grace, forgiveness, and faith, but not without a few scars carried by those who manage to survive the wrath of hardened hearts. Bravo!"

JULIE CANTRELL, *NEW YORK TIMES* BESTSELLING AUTHOR OF *INTO THE FREE* AND *WHEN MOUNTAINS MOVE*

"*How Sweet the Sound* is one of those books you want to savor slowly, like sips of sweet tea on a hot Southern day. Achingly beautiful prose married with honest, raw redemption makes this book a perfect selection for your next book club."

MARY DeMUTH, AUTHOR OF *THE MUIR HOUSE*

"Meeting these characters and stepping into their worlds forever changed the contour of my heart. Sorrells's words effortlessly rise from the page with a cadence that is remarkably brave and wildly beautiful."

TONI BIRDSONG, AUTHOR OF *MORE THAN A BUCKET LIST*

"Filled with brokenness and redemption, grit and grace, *How Sweet the Sound* is a heartrending coming-of-age debut about God's ability to heal the hurting and restore the damaged. Sorrells deftly reminds us that no matter how dark the night, hope is never lost. Not if we have eyes to see."

KATIE GANSHERT, AUTHOR OF *WILDFLOWERS FROM WINTER* AND *WISHING ON WILLOWS*

"A stirring tale of loss and redemption. Amy Sorrells will break your heart and piece it back twice its size."

BILLY COFFEY, AUTHOR OF *WHEN MOCKINGBIRDS SING*

"A daring and enchanted story, Amy K. Sorrells's How Sweet the Sound beckons readers to a land of pecan groves, bay breezes, and graveyard secrets rising up like the dead on judgment day."

KAREN SPEARS ZACHARIAS, AUTHOR OF *MOTHER OF RAIN*

Lead me HOME

a novel

AMY K. SORRELLS

Tyndale House Publishers, Inc.
Carol Stream, Illinois

Visit Tyndale online at www.tyndale.com.

Visit Amy K. Sorrells at amysorrells.wordpress.com.

TYNDALE and Tyndale's quill logo are registered trademarks of Tyndale House Publishers, Inc.

Lead Me Home

Copyright © 2016 by Amy Sorrells. All rights reserved.

Cover photograph of sky copyright © Dzulfiqar Zaky/EyeEm/Getty Images. All rights reserved.

Cover photograph of field copyright © Alejandro Gallardo/EyeEm/Getty Images. All rights reserved.

Author photo copyright © 2015 by Charlie Sorrells. All rights reserved.

Cover designed by Nicole Grimes

Interior designed by Alyssa E. Force

Edited by Kathryn S. Olson

Published in association with the literary agency of WordServe Literary Group, www. wordserveliterary.com.

Unless otherwise indicated, Scripture quotations are taken from the *Holy Bible*, New Living Translation, copyright © 1996, 2004, 2015 by Tyndale House Foundation. Used by permission of Tyndale House Publishers, Inc., Carol Stream, Illinois 60188. All rights reserved.

The Scripture quotation in the epigraph is taken from the Holy Bible, *New International Version,*® *NIV.*® Copyright © 1973, 1978, 1984, 2011 by Biblica, Inc.® Used by permission. All rights reserved worldwide.

Scripture quotations in chapters 6, 8, and 23 are taken from *The Holy Bible*, English Standard Version® (ESV®), copyright © 2001 by Crossway, a publishing ministry of Good News Publishers. Used by permission. All rights reserved.

The Scripture quotation in the author's note is taken from the *Amplified Bible*®, copyright © 1954, 1958, 1962, 1964, 1965, 1987 by The Lockman Foundation. Used by permission.

Lead Me Home is a work of fiction. Where real people, events, establishments, organizations, or locales appear, they are used fictitiously. All other elements of the novel are drawn from the author's imagination.

Library of Congress Cataloging-in-Publication Data

Names: Sorrells, Amy K., author.
Title: Lead me home / Amy K. Sorrells.
Description: Carol Stream, Illinois : Tyndale House Publishers, Inc., [2016]
Identifiers: LCCN 2015047359 | ISBN 9781496409553 (softcover)
Subjects: | GSAFD: Christian fiction.

Classification: LCC PS3619.O79 L43 2016 | DDC 813/.6—dc23 LC record available at http://lccn. loc.gov/2015047359

Printed in the United States of America

22   21   20   19   18   17   16
7   6   5   4   3   2   1

To Tucker, Charlie, and Isaac,

that you may be assured of and rest in his plans

The boundary lines have fallen for me in pleasant
places; surely I have a delightful inheritance.
—PSALM 16:6, NIV

Habitat loss, isolation of populations, combined with the
extremely small size of many of the remaining population, puts
[the Karner blue butterfly] at high risk of "winking out."

—UNITED STATES FISH AND WILDLIFE SERVICE

1

All at once, the Reverend James Horton understood why Frank Whitmore had killed himself. He pushed the manila file folder back across the desk of his office at Sycamore Community Church. Across from him sat George Kernodle, the sides of his burgeoning belly pressed tight against the arms of the old chair, the flesh of his neck falling over the starched collar of his shirt and striped silk tie.

"I'm sorry, James. I've done all I can to keep this from happening."

The red splotches on Kernodle's jowly cheeks and the sweat he wiped off his brow and upper lip did not seem to indicate much sympathy, and James's thoughts wandered back to Frank Whitmore. James had heard about the circumstances of Whitmore's demise through Charlie Reynolds, the pastor of the Methodist church, who had presided over the funeral and arrangements.

Whitmore's wasn't the first suicide among farmers in the area, the arrival of corporate farms having caused many already-ragged farmers to bend, break, and foreclose, unable to compete with the massive machinery, the demand for genetically modified crops that withstood weeds but sucked the life from the land, and the giant dairies that used heifers for two years and sent them to the slaughterhouse. What broke Whitmore, however, was not the nearby commercial dairy offering public tours and their own label of milk selling for eight dollars per half-gallon (compared to the $1.60 per gallon he received from the co-op), but rather a particularly nasty storm that knocked out the power on his farm. A widower of nearly a decade, Whitmore had isolated himself so much over the years that no one knew about his predicament. No one came to help him, and he did not ask for help. So when the power company indicated it would take over forty-eight hours to restore the power, Whitmore, faced with losing most of his milkers to the mastitis that would set in before then, shot thirty of his best cows and then himself, sparing them all from the misery.

The whole scenario bothered James for many reasons, not the least of which was that Whitmore had not felt like he'd had anyone to ask for help. The cows he hadn't shot were going to be moved to the Burden dairy farm across the fields from where James and his daughter, Shelby, lived. Though well aware that sowing seeds of Scripture and tending proverbial sheep did not make him a farmer, James had long watched the work and unpredictable nature of farming through the windows. Tucked between the Burden dairy and Stuart Granger's hog farm, James and his wife had been close to Laurie Burden and her two sons until time and seasons and tragedies came between them, until all that remained was an occasional smile and nod if they happened to see each other in the aisles of the IGA. Laurie's two boys were mostly grown and helped run things at the dairy, but they had enough of their own problems, and he was concerned about how they'd take on the added work of Whitmore's surviving herd. Then again, farmers had a way of figuring out and making do. Like barren fields each spring, just when he thought they had nothing left to give, they gave some more.

"The Lord gave me what I had, and the Lord has taken it away," James thought, reminded of the passage from Job.

"Are you alright?" Kernodle asked, jolting James back to the conversation.

Though he was seated, the room seemed to sway, and James gripped the arms of his chair. "How soon?"

"The auction will be Labor Day. That gives you about a month—"

"Less than a month. That's three weeks."

"Okay, three weeks. You have three weeks to tidy things up, notify your congregants, finish whatever you need to finish."

"How does one auction off a church? I mean, who *buys* a church?"

George struggled to shift his weight, and then he cleared his throat. "Might not be another church who buys it. Might be someone interested in using the land to start over. Build something new."

"And tear down over a hundred and fifty years of history? George—you have to know the carvings and stained glass alone are worth thousands. At the very least this building is a piece of history." James felt his throat thicken, and his eyes burned. He was determined not to become visibly emotional in front of Kernodle, but any warmth the two had shared over the years had long ago curdled under the strain of the loan applications and reapplications, the refinancing and now the default of the account.

"I'm sorry. I wish there was something more we could do." Kernodle hoisted himself up out of the chair, picked up the folder, and stuffed it into his leather attaché. Sweat began to discolor the top edge of his collar.

James knew he should stand and offer the man his hand, but in that moment he could not. Surely Seraiah and Zephaniah hadn't been exactly warm to King Nebuchadnezzar when he and his pals destroyed the Temple in 2 Kings. Granted, in James's case, there had been no forced famine, no siege, no one breaking in and scattering his congregants across the countryside. There had been no fires set, no plundering of the church's few possessions, no physical harm to blame for the church's demise. But after spending over twenty years in ministry, he couldn't help thinking up biblical parallels to situations he found himself in, whether he wanted to or not.

Though he felt the familiar urges of the Holy Spirit to love the enemy who sat before him, and to be kind, at the moment it felt a whole lot better to flat-out dislike George Kernodle. Although if he were honest, he'd admit Kernodle didn't deserve all the blame.

The decline of Sycamore Community Church was well under way by the time problems with the bank arose. A few years back, Gertrude Johnson noticed a small crack in the basement wall during the covered dish supper they'd had after the Palm Sunday service. By fall, the crack had grown into a fissure extending down to the floor and across the entire length of the room. Three assessments and estimates later from local foundation repair contractors declared the century-and-a-half-old foundation was not only cracked, but dangerously and precariously shifted. They'd pointed out bowed walls on the inside and extensive evidence on the outside, each symptom adding thousands to the structural repair required.

For generations, the building had been a trustworthy physical sanctuary, the sturdy brick and mortar taken for granted, so much so that James had been acutely aware of exactly where to step as he walked down the aisle each Sunday so as to avoid the creak of an ancient, warping floorboard. But even as he preached and they had their potlucks and weddings and baptisms and funerals, water seeped silent into cracks in window casings. Tree roots pushed and shoved through the soil and into the footings, weakening them. A shoddy roof replacement a decade before had neglected to upgrade the gutters and downspouts, so one whole side of the foundation had to be removed and replaced. One hundred and fifteen thousand dollars later, the church had a sturdy base and a generous, though ultimately insurmountable, loan from the bank.

What choice did they have? James and the elders knew debt was wrong, but the work had to be done. The elders pitched a fund-raising campaign to anyone they could think of—descendants of charter members, local and regional businesses, organizations supporting small-town churches. Molly, with the help of the vivacious Lizzie Bailey, had organized a community barbecue. A few children had tried to sell lemonade from stands on seldom-traveled country roads. But even with all that, they'd only raised $4,800. The bank had been willing to give them a low-interest rate and stretch out the payments, but contractors were not partial, not even to near-bankrupt churches.

The problem was not that people did not care about Sycamore Community Church. The problem was the same of any small town. The congregation, strongest in the Eisenhower era, had remained vibrant during the decades that followed. After James took over in the early 1990s, it had grown steadily for the first years he'd been there. But then, sometime around 2010 if he had to guess, attendance had been stagnant, eventually dwindling severely. The attendance the previous Sunday had been fourteen. It had started out as thirteen, which despite the fact he was not superstitious always made James cringe. Thankfully, Wilma Petticrew had shuffled in late, so the number rose to fourteen. There wasn't anyone to blame for this either, anyone except himself for not being more charismatic, not having the foresight to envision the postmodern pilgrimage of parishioners from the pews. Farms foreclosed. Families moved away. And the rest—if they hadn't given up on church altogether—were drawn like bugs to a streetlamp to the lights and sounds of the megachurch down the interstate. Congregants aged and died off until tithes—even from those willing to give their 10 percent—were nearly nonexistent, and the interest from a handful of aging endowments barely paid for the light bill, let alone allowed enough of a salary for James and Shelby to eat.

Even with the foundation fixed, the parking lot was full of horrendous chuckholes, and the velvet offering bags were threadbare to the point that just last week one busted open when a well-intentioned grade-schooler plunked in a plastic bag full of pennies he'd collected, and which had gone rolling every which way across the warping oak floors. And now, on the afternoon of September 4, he would be forced to pull the door of the church closed for good.

God's will and sovereignty aside, the loss of the church was one more death in James's life, creating the same sort of despair Whitmore must have felt when he shot each of the cows he'd raised between the eyes and then held the gun to his own head.

All that work.

All that blind trust.

All that faith in the weather bringing rain after drought and warmth after frost, of trying to be still and know somehow the Lord, Jehovah-Jireh, would come through at the last minute.

James wondered how the suicide rate of farmers compared to that of pastors.

He tried to force a congenial smile, but before he could extend his hand, Kernodle turned and ambled stiffly out of his office.

Moments later, Bonnie Thompson rushed in. "Are you alright, Reverend? Mr. Kernodle, he looked positively beside himself."

"Have a seat, Bonnie." James motioned toward the chair Kernodle had vacated.

Bonnie, the wife of Hank Thompson, owner of the local hardware store, never spoke ill of anyone. Besides the seasons, she'd been one of the few predictable things in James's life—and Shelby's, for that matter. Ever since Molly died, Bonnie had been there picking up slack when he was too depressed to make heads or tails of expense and budget reports, taking care of the weekly bulletin, taking care of most everything, really, so he'd have time to focus on what he did best, which was his sermons. She'd taken care of the accounting, too.

"There's nothing more the bank can do for us."

Bonnie sighed, then pulled her mint-green cardigan across

her chest as if bracing herself against a gust of wind. She had a plain face, softened further by a generous application of loose powder. She wore her hair rolled and set in a style that reminded him of his grandmother. Folks could easily pass by her in a store or on a sidewalk having no idea she was the sort of person the Lord used to help hold men together when their worlds collapsed.

"We've no more bonds, no more savings, and we owe too much already for another extension. And you know I can't possibly give another sermon on tithing. The few folks who are left don't have anything else to give."

A tear etched a trail down Bonnie's powdered face. "I know," she said as she pulled a handkerchief from her skirt pocket. "I can't believe it's come to this."

"Me either." James stood and walked to the window. The familiar *thump-thump* of a car woofer approached, and eventually Silas Canady's tricked-out late-model pickup truck appeared. The ginormous off-road tires turned slowly, and just in case someone might miss it coming down the street, bright-red-and-orange flame graphics gleamed on the shiny black paint of the hood and sides. As the truck rolled by, Silas tossed a cigarette butt onto the church's lawn.

In the park across the street, three mothers stood and talked while pushing their toddlers on the swings. Older children swung themselves across the monkey bars, slid down the slides, and he could hear them squeal as they spun themselves dizzy on the rusty merry-go-round. The park had been a popular place on Sunday afternoons when the church was in its prime, when the pews were filled in the morning and the picnics afterward lasted deep into the afternoon.

James put his head in his hands and let the tears that had threatened as Kernodle had sat in front of him flow freely. It wasn't the first time Bonnie had seen him weep. But it wasn't as if it was a usual occurrence, either. He was grateful she was not uncomfortable around a weeping man, that she would sit there and keep him company without trying to fill the awkward moment with pointless assurances.

This was a time to weep if there ever was one.

And he was grateful she allowed him that.

2

Nineteen-year-old Noble Burden wished for the thousandth time he were someplace else as he grabbed hold of the pair of slimy legs and pulled using all his strength and leaning backward to give added force with his body weight.

"Eustace? I could use a little help in here!" He called for his older brother, but the only response was the scuttle of mice and rats beneath the straw and the heaving sighs of Dolly, the laboring Jersey heifer. He'd expected her first birth to be a challenge since she was one of the smallest of the females, but he hadn't expected this much trouble. Most of the heifers took care of birthing on their own, and he'd arrive at the barn in the morning to find a new calf standing beside its mother and blinking at him like nothing remarkable had happened. Dolly was lucky Noble had shown up early for the morning milking.

Another pull on the calf's legs and Noble slouched down against the scratchy wooden planks partitioning the stall. His chest was heaving in the same rhythmic cadence as Dolly's.

"It's okay, girl. You're doing great." Noble thought he saw the cow blink in acknowledgment. She was one of sixty-three cows in the herd, which was the largest it'd ever been since their father had left them and all the work of the dairy a few years back. Soon they'd have close to eighty when they moved the surviving girls from Frank Whitmore's herd to their farm. A tragedy, what happened to Whitmore. But Noble didn't have time to dwell on that now.

"Eustace!" Noble called again, exasperated, as he leaned his head against the stall. He was sinewy, but this predicament needed the advantage of his brother's burliness and strength. Noble jumped to his feet as Dolly let out a long, deep groan, then grabbed the calf's bony legs again and waited until the cow's abdomen stiffened with the peak of the contraction.

He pulled.

"I always wanted . . . to grow up . . . to be . . . a midwife . . . to a crazy . . . progesterone-imploding . . . cow!"

The contraction ended, and both Noble and Dolly sank back into the straw again. "This isn't working, girl. I gotta find Eustace to give me some help here."

As he stood, the barn door slid open and Eustace appeared, his hulking frame filling the doorway, dirty white Purdue ball cap—the last thing their father had given him—set too high on his head of thick, wavy brown hair. Size was about the only thing going for that boy.

"'Bout time you showed up. I need the twine. May have to turn her over." A calf-pulling device was on their list of things to buy when they got the money, but they never had the money. Twine would have to do.

Eustace took in the sight before him, and his hands began to twitch, then his arms, until they flapped like a crazed chicken. Dolly was Eustace's favorite cow. He could often be found late at night sleeping out in the field beside her, the big, dumb cow seeming to draw as much comfort from Eustace as he did from her. Noble knew if anything happened to her, his brother would be even more of a mess than he already was.

"Cut that out now. Don't got time for your worrying. This'll all be okay if you calm down and help me."

Eustace's arms kept going and didn't show signs of slowing down.

"Eustace!" Noble shouted, causing Dolly to startle, and Eustace's arms slowed to a wide sway; then with his right hand he reached up and began rubbing the calloused spot of scalp behind his ear that didn't grow hair anymore. His expression was flat in its usual downcast, otherworldly way. "Dolly's gonna be okay. But *I need you to get me the twine.* Twine and iodine. Listen to me now. The twine's in the storeroom, beside the training harnesses on the bottom shelf. Iodine's there too. Quick now, go get 'em."

The storeroom, like the rest of the milking chamber, would be bright from a fresh powdering of lime. Noble heard glass bottles of iodine knocking to the ground and imagined the ruddy liquid painting a blood-like stream across the white, powdery floor. He prayed—though doubtful any of his petitions ever reached the Lord's ears—that Eustace would keep on looking, and sure enough, he returned to the stall and held up the twine in one hand and a bottle of iodine in the other like they were prizes at the county fair.

Noble took the twine. He poured the iodine over his hands and the hind end of Dolly. He wrapped the twine around the calf's protruding hooves, then gave one end of the twine back to Eustace. Together they secured the calf's legs, emerging from the exhausted heifer's hindquarters.

"We gotta turn you over, girl," Noble said to the cow, who huffed back in distress. "Onto your back now."

Noble nodded at Eustace. Together the two young men rolled Dolly onto her back, which would hopefully widen out her pelvis and allow the calf to slide through. Noble let go of the twine long enough to grab Dolly's harness and tie it to the metal rung in the concrete foundation of the barn. He secured it tight so she couldn't flip all the way over or try to get up, but Dolly acted too weak and worn out to bother fighting.

"We don't got much time if this calf's gonna live," Noble said.

With Dolly's next contraction, Noble and Eustace,

standing at Dolly's shoulders, yanked hard. The calf's front legs bent toward them, then slid farther up Dolly's swollen udders and belly.

"It's working!"

Eustace grinned slightly in acknowledgment and groaned with relief, sweat pouring down his face and neck.

"Here comes another contraction. Ready?"

Eustace nodded.

They yanked again with everything they had, Eustace leaning his broad shoulders into the work, and it paid off. The calf, in its entirety, stretched across Dolly's belly, then flopped onto the hay, moistened with blood and birth fluids.

Noble loosened Dolly's harness, grabbed a couple of old towels from the railing, and tossed one to Eustace. The two of them began rubbing the calf to dry it and stimulate it to breathe, Eustace's fingers, which were thick as sausages, awkward but gentle as he worked over the bony ribs and belly.

"It's a girl," Noble said.

The calf jerked and rolled its eyes back in its head, each new breath a shock and relief to its newly working lungs.

Dolly curved her neck around and licked her baby, smoothing the slime off its eyes so they opened and blinked back the glare of the early morning sun spilling through cracks in the old barn walls.

"Had a rough time of it, didn't you, little one? But you made it." Noble stroked the calf's neck and glanced at Dolly.

"You too, mama. That was a rough one, but you're gonna be alright now."

Noble watched as a lopsided smile spread over his brother's face. "You did good, too, Eustace. Glad you showed up when you did."

Without any indication he'd heard Noble at all, Eustace kept petting and rubbing the calf, cleaning its fur, and stroking the neck and head of Dolly until whatever thoughts went through his head seemed to assure him the two creatures were going to be fine. The calf jerked, its knobby knees pushing against the ground until first its hindquarters, then its front legs, lifted off the ground. Its moist nose nuzzled Eustace, the tender mouth searching, near frantic for something to suckle. A laugh, too loud and punctuated with gulps of air when he inhaled, rose and spilled out, muffling against the low-hanging roof of the calving stalls. He stood, muscles sinewy from the work of the birth, and wandered back outside the barn into the dewy morning without saying a word.

Eustace never had said a word.

Not ever.

Noble remembered being dragged along to doctors and therapists and special education meetings at the school back when Mama had tried to find help for Eustace. Some said he had autism, but he made too much eye contact and clung to Mama too much for that to be it. Some said Asperger's, but he didn't fit all that criteria, either. Some said he knew how to talk plenty and simply chose not to out of belligerence, which had caused their father to rage and try to beat a voice out of him on more than one occasion. Eventually Mama gave up trying to figure him out and fix him since nothing anyone recommended changed anything, and they all—except Dad—agreed to do their best and resigned themselves to accept him how he was.

As a result, Eustace grew happier, as much as they could tell from what emotion he did show. He smiled on occasion, belted out awkward and guttural laughter or anguish depending on the situation, and wandered off less—but frequently, all the same. Usually he roamed the pastures to find Dolly or a new butterfly to add to his extensive collection—one that would be the envy of any lepidopterist—or went to the barn to feed and dote on the calves. As he grew older, the wandering was still a problem, though not as frequent as it had been when he was younger. He didn't seem to mind he had no human friends to speak of. He was unusually strong and able to help Noble and Mama when they needed him. Years of farmwork had built his frame large and solid even as whatever ailed him seemed to have stripped his brain bare. And the dingy white ball cap, constantly perched crooked and too high on his head, topped it all off.

There had of course been moments when Noble felt plenty frustrated or ashamed of his older brother. Once, years ago when Noble had begun to notice their differences, he had thought long and hard about how to ask Mama about it. He'd been standing on a stool next to her as she worked on making a meat loaf. His job was to crush up the crackers to add to the lump of meat and other ingredients she kneaded.

"Mama?"

"Mmm-hmmm?"

He'd hesitated, almost deciding against asking as he poured the crumbs into her bowl. But then, "Why's Eustace the way he is?"

Mama'd pressed her knuckles into the meat, then folded and squeezed the crumbs through. She wiped her hands on her apron before taking a round white onion in one hand, holding it down on the cutting board, and beginning to chop. She'd brushed her hair—or had it been a tear?—away from her face. "The way he is. Yes. Well."

"Why'd God make him stupid?" He hadn't been sure she would answer, and as soon as the words left his mouth, he felt the shame of never being able to get them back, the sort of regret even as a child he'd known would change things he hadn't intended to change. He learned then some things hurt bad enough without saying them out loud.

She'd turned to him then, his beautiful mama, blue eyes rimmed in red, unaccusing, but spent. She'd bent down so her eyes were at his level.

"Maybe the better question, dear Noble, is why not?"

A question for a question. Noble didn't have an answer, of course, and after that, Noble knew Eustace was one more thing in their lives that couldn't be fixed, one more thing to tolerate, one more dream of "normalcy" dashed, one more thought of independence derailed. Growing up farming as

Noble had, as his daddy had, and his granddaddy before him, meant growing up knowing a lot of things were just plain left up to nature. Things like the yield of a crop. Coyotes taking down a calf born too soon out on the back pasture. The path of a tornado. The cheating heart of a man. Disconnected wires in a poor boy's brain. The death of a preacher's wife. A guitar that collected more dust than accolades. And the way a dreamer's heart grew restless.

3

"I hate you!"

Shelby, all of seventeen and too pretty for her own good, stood obstinate and irate before James. She looked so much like her mother with her long dark curls and freckles spattered across her nose, which—also like her mother—she tried to hide with makeup. The only thing she seemed to have inherited from him were his green eyes and height—she was five foot nine and he was six foot five.

"Just admit it. You wish it were me instead of her who died."

"Shelby, wait—"

So much for a gentle word turning away wrath. James

braced himself against the slam of the front door, the force of which popped the trim work off the casing again. He'd been mowing and putzing around the yard all day, trying to take out his frustrations against George Kernodle from yesterday. Molly's flower beds wilted quick under the heat of the August sun, even with the rains they'd been having. He'd watered the hollyhocks, tied up and restaked the tomato plants, and listened to C. S. Lewis's *A Grief Observed* on audio as he rode along on the riding mower, a gift from Molly for their tenth wedding anniversary still going strong. He often listened to audiobooks by the great theologians, and a handful of newer ones, while he mowed as a way to keep up with sermon research. He supposed he'd switch to fiction in a few weeks, maybe catch up with all the Tom Clancy novels he'd been wanting to read. Or maybe he'd listen to nothing at all except for the whir of the motor and the blades. When he'd finally come inside, he'd found Shelby in her bedroom primping to go out.

"Where you goin', hon?" He took a long draw from the glass of lemonade he'd brought upstairs with him.

"Out." She'd focused on the lit makeup mirror and patted more concealer on her cheeks.

"With whom?"

She evaded his questioning until things escalated to the fight, admitted to going out with Cade Canady, and ran outside to her old, two-tone blue-and-white pickup truck, splotchy with Bondo and rusted around the wheel wells. Whatever had happened between her and Noble Burden, whom she'd run around with for years, was beyond him. That she was chasing after Cade, who aside from being too short for her was also well known as the town bully like his father, Silas, was a true conundrum.

James followed her as far as the front porch and watched her peel the pickup out of the gravel driveway and spray up a plume of dust, which took its time settling over the quiet county road.

"Protect her, Lord. You know the troubles which surround her even better than I," he said softly.

He knew somehow he should rise above the emotion Shelby directed at him, that he should realize it was just a phase, an expression of the grief she was having to work through. But each time they argued or she left felt like one more failure. Dealing with the anger and disappointment of others—family in particular—wasn't new to him, but he never really had gotten used to it. When he was a young man going to college at Furman, his father, Orry Horton, worked in a tire factory and reminded James often that he worked his fingers burned and bloody to get James there. Orry had essentially disowned James when he decided to pursue full-time ministry. Church, let alone the work of ministry, were not high values in the life of a factory man and his family.

"I raised my son to work for his pay and for his honor, not to hide behind a pulpit," his father had said. "What'd religion ever do for anyone anyhow? You don't see Jesus comin' down from the sky and savin' us from this no-good life, do ya?"

His father-in-law, Dr. Henry Montgomery, was a plastic

surgeon and had been against James and Molly's union from the start, convinced James would never be able to provide her with the standard of living to which she'd been accustomed. Dr. Montgomery had sent Molly to Furman, too, in the hopes she'd meet a nice medical student from an old-money Southern family, but she'd wound up with James instead.

James trudged upstairs to the bedroom he and Molly had shared, and he sat on the stool beside her dressing table.

"Her absence is like the sky, spread over everything." Those were the words of C. S. Lewis on the loss of his wife, Joy, to cancer.

Yes, he'd thought as the words streamed from the audiobook. *That's exactly how I feel.*

James fiddled with one of the pearl earrings on the silver tray before him. He kept the table dusted but otherwise unchanged from the day she died. Hair ties and makeup brushes, perfume and jewelry were all neatly stored in little glass and silver containers she'd collected from antique stores. He picked up a frame with a picture of the two of them from their wedding day, her curls piled high and spilling around her creamy white skin and the freckles on her nose she had lamented so. Her head rested on his chest and their smiles were wide and unrestrained.

"Lord, I miss her so much. How long will my heart hurt this way?" he said aloud, running his finger across the photograph before setting it down. And yet he feared letting go of the ache would mean he was letting go of her.

Losing Molly, along with the impending loss of the church,

made James wonder over and over whether what he'd felt two decades ago in college was truly a calling to the ministry, or if it had simply been the blind idealism of youth. His roommate, Steve, had been a member of one of the last remnants of the Jesus People movement. James had gone to a couple of coffeehouse meetings with Steve, reluctantly at first. But soon, the campfire-like comfort of acoustic music and the poetry of the plain-language Scriptures swept him up into the world of evangelism. Until then, church had been a brick building where folks went on Sundays to feel shame about the things they'd done the week before, and the Bible—King James the only one he'd ever seen—read like a Shakespearean play everyone seemed to understand except him. By the time James had reached his sophomore year, a professor of New Testament studies—Dr. Ernest Wilcox—took him under his wing and believed in him in a way that made James believe in himself for the first time in his life. Wilcox convinced James he not only could be but should be the Lord's vessel, a man destined to save people, congregations, towns.

"So much for that," James said, half to God and half to himself, as he looked out the window and watched the dust from Shelby's truck still settling on the road. Waves of midsummer corn and soybeans swayed as far as he could see.

He'd had plenty of reasons to leave the ministry: the aging congregation, the devastation when he'd realized so many of the younger families were leaving for Higher Ground—the ironic name of the megachurch down the road. He struggled, too, with reconciling his ministry with his own natural propensity to doubt, not that he wondered whether or not God existed, but rather the fear that God is who he says he is, and James's own sense of inadequacy in light of that. He'd have left the ministry sooner were it not for Molly's encouragement to stick with it, the elders' beseeching him to stay, and the fact that something about the endless fields around Sycamore ultimately, at the end of a long day of ministry, steadied him. Swaths of crops reaching toward the sun were interrupted only occasionally by a chippy white farmhouse and a barn, or a rogue collection of grain dryers and silos. Despite everything, the seasons kept changing: spring followed winter, fall followed summer.

"If you're going to haul me all the way to the boondocks, you better buy me a place I can keep myself busy fixing up while you're off tending your sheep," Molly'd said to him when he secured the head pastorate position at Sycamore Community Church. They knew the town of Sycamore in west-central Indiana was home to less than five thousand people according to the last census, and that the closest major town with groceries and hospitals, fast food and other signs of modern civilization was over an hour away.

"Maybe we should wait for an offer from someplace closer to Atlanta," he'd said, even suggesting he work at a coffeehouse or landscaping company in the meantime.

But though Indiana wasn't her first choice, Molly had been up for the adventure of something totally new, a place they could call their own. "You won't know if it's where you're supposed to be until you give it a shot," she'd said.

So James had accepted the job and been happy to oblige her desire for a farmhouse. Being a pastor's wife was difficult enough, and he had been determined not to let the lifestyle or small-town life squelch her hopes and dreams.

"Would you look at that," Molly had said when they'd toured the clapboard home with the Realtor.

James had looked, and hard, at the peeling paint, the rotting places in the siding, the slight bend of the front porch posts beneath the weight of the sagging shed roof.

"I wish I'd had such a view growing up," she'd said inside, putting her hand up to the window, glass wavy with age. Her own parents' home back in Atlanta was a Tudor revival in Druid Hills, one of several breathtaking mansions in a row. She'd had views of precisely trimmed boxwood gardens, swimming pools, and rose gardens. By contrast, the 1880s Victorian farmhouse on the outskirts of Sycamore came with a wraparound porch and half a dozen acres of wide, untamed, open fields running alongside a sandy creek and covered in wild blue lupine, oxeye daisies, Queen Anne's lace, and pink joe-pye weed. Several hundred more acres belonging to Stuart Granger surrounded them. Granger'd been close to tearing the place down altogether and planting more corn and beans in its place—that is, until the Realtor had found it and James and Molly had made him an offer he couldn't refuse.

They had made a fine and cozy life for themselves within the aging walls, except for the sound of coyotes at night—which had disturbed Molly until he finally bought a gun, if not to actually shoot them, then at least to aim in their general direction and scare them off. The fact that Molly had been an artist, the intuitive, naturally gifted sort with no formal training and completely unaware of how much her work moved people, had helped ward off the initial isolation of the move. She'd always felt more comfortable in a hardware store than most men, and she had a knack for going to flea markets and roadside antique shops, finding something awful anyone else would toss into a junkyard and turning it into something marvelous. A rusty piece of iron fencing became a charming window covering. A weathered flower box became a sturdy container to keep towels neat and straight in their bathroom. Old shutters linked together became a screen for the fireplace. She enjoyed restoration so much she eventually had her own booth at one of the local antique stores and occasionally sold her pieces at seasonal art festivals. They'd bought the old blue pickup truck a few years back to haul her work to fairs and flea markets across the state, and sometimes beyond to Ohio or Illinois.

Once Molly settled in, she made quick friends with their nearest neighbor. At the time, Laurie Burden had a husband who was mostly absent and was expecting her first child. Dale Burden was a commercial truck driver, and Laurie confided to Molly she was glad for Dale's trips. Molly had voiced concerns about the way Dale treated Laurie over the years. Once their older boy, Eustace, was born, that probably added to the challenges of the marriage. Because of James's late nights getting to know his congregants, Molly was often alone and Laurie was lonely. The Burdens' second son, Noble, was born about three years later, and Molly spent as much time as she could helping Laurie with the two little ones.

And then Shelby arrived.

"I'm pregnant!" Molly had hollered at him from the front porch, waving a pregnancy test before he could even get out of his car, five years after their wedding. As soon as she'd gotten through the queasiness of the first trimester, Molly began work on the nursery, which she'd identified as such on that first day they saw the house. She'd built a window seat, valances, and shelving and painted the whole room creamy white before hanging framed pictures of vintage storybook pages on the walls. She refurbished a rusty, but exquisite, chandelier with pink-and-white glass to hang from the center of the ceiling, and she'd had a love seat with a heart-shaped back she found at a garage sale reupholstered in pink-and-white gingham.

"If this girl turns out to be a boy, what are you going to do?" James had laughed.

"I guess he'll have to learn to like pink."

Her intuition had been confirmed when Shelby hollered her way into the world and had not quieted down since, at least not until the accident two summers ago. Before that, Shelby hadn't minded at all the fact that she lived in a fishbowl of a world, on display for the congregation from the moment Molly and James had crossed the threshold of the giant, carved oak doors of Sycamore Community Church with her for the first time when she was only four weeks old. She cooed and gazed her way into the hearts of everyone, singing "Jesus Loves Me" a cappella with a microphone at the age of three and a half. From there, she sang whenever and wherever she could, whether at school and voice camps and competitions, or on Sunday mornings.

But when the accident happened, the singing stopped. And James was left with a dying church, a screen door banging shut, and dust settling over the road like sadness settling on his heart.

4

The whir of the cooling tank stirring the milk muted as Noble shut the door and secured the latch for the evening. A hawk circled over the high knoll that dipped down to the creek, past the Hortons', and soared over Granger's fields beyond. The bird's wings pushed silent against the invisible air as it searched for a vole or rabbit for its dinner. If Noble looked out over the cornfields, stalks high as his shoulders, he could imagine himself in Kansas or Oklahoma or anywhere besides Sycamore, imagine being so far out and so in the middle of nothing that no one would know who he was or where he was from. Nearby, most of the cows had finished their dinner of silage and were headed, single file, back to the pasture on one of a half-dozen paths of trampled grass, evidence of their mindless instinct to follow each other.

"Just like the rest of Sycamore," Noble said aloud. He recalled the times they'd gone to church and he'd heard Reverend Horton talk about God having a plan for everyone, something about a future and a hope. But if everyone in the myopic little town was content with following everyone else, how could any of them know they were living out God's plan? He might not know much, but he knew life was more than just following the leader. Besides that, the last thing he ever wanted to be was a dairy farmer or anything else remotely like his father. Sure, friends like Brock and Tiffany had been high school sweethearts, married a month after graduation, and made a decent living in town. But Noble had been—he realized now—foolish enough to want college and a real job in the city, where he could walk to the coffeehouse and read his books or the newspaper, and play his guitar for small crowds at the corner bar in the evening. He'd wanted to be a poet, a writer, a musician, dreams his truck-driving father hadn't hesitated to squash at every opportunity.

"You need to do something so you eat more than beans, Noble. Think I like driving a truck all hours of the night, being on the road, sleeping in the cab, coming home and milking those blasted cows? I don't, but it lets you and your big dumb brother and your mama eat, now don't it?"

Noble learned early on never to disagree with his father. Disagreement resulted in a beating with a belt, and a couple of those and a child learns quick to avoid it at all cost. He figured instead of belligerence, he'd prove Dad wrong with good grades, get a scholarship, and then he wouldn't be able to refuse Noble that. He was well on his way toward achieving his goal until the fall of his junior year, when instead of an 18-wheeler showing up at the end of the week, a set of divorce papers came for Mama.

Sometimes Noble sat late at night playing his guitar on the front porch, waiting for Eustace to fall hard asleep so he'd be safe and sure not to wander. He'd play the chords and imagine the corn an audience at the Ryman Auditorium or the Grand Ole Opry, familiar with them only from pictures he'd seen on the Internet. In some ways, he wished he was like Eustace, seemingly oblivious to the world around him. He had long imagined his brother speaking like a regular brother, the squabbles they might've had in the haymow, one-on-one basketball games played after dinner until all the sunlight faded and they could hardly see the rim before going inside, singing with him as he played his guitar, the syllables and sentences that might be rolling around in his head but never emerged.

He loved his brother. He really did. It was just that people were hard to love in general, and especially when they needed so much more than most. When they arose, Noble tried to push thoughts of wishing Eustace weren't around out of his mind. He tried not to let himself imagine the freedom of not being responsible for someone else's whereabouts, of coming and going like other kids his age who were out making a place for themselves in the world. He tried not to think about how much he hated Dad for leaving, hated the last three summers for their droughts, hated the fact that he had no say in the price they got for each gallon of milk, and hated small towns for the way they made a person who they were instead of the the other way around. If he was destined to care for Eustace and the farm the rest of his life, there wasn't much he could do about it. He'd learned a long time ago not to count on a father, whether earthly or heavenly, to get him out of Sycamore.

Daily bread was one thing.

But deliverance, well . . .

Deliverance was a whole other matter.

Noble trudged up the hill from the barn and saw Eustace's hulking frame out in the pasture, his old dingy white ball cap sticking out above the backs of the group of brown cows under the far grove of cottonwoods. He watched as Eustace doted on Dolly, hunching down with his bulky, double-jointed limbs at odd angles as he maintained eye level with her and the rest of the herd. Sometimes the way Eustace interacted with them—and they with him—reminded Noble of a preacher with his people gathered around him waiting, ears perked so they wouldn't miss a word of whatever silent wisdom Eustace imparted to them. When Noble and Eustace had been younger, their father's temper flared every time the cows came near the barn for milking time. Both boys would stand back and cringe as Dad whipped the cows, sometimes drawing blood, into the milking barn. His fence training was no less vicious. Eustace would begin flapping his arms, his mouth open as if he wanted with all his heart to scream, but no sound came out, and slowly he'd crumple to the floor and begin to sway back and forth, face still contorted until finally a velar cry filled the room. Noble had long before learned how to hold back the tears that throbbed against the backs of his eyes, and which if let loose would bring a beating to them both. But Eustace, he never could contain himself. And even Dad seemed to know a beating wouldn't wipe the misery from his son's face, so he just left him there to howl. Eustace could often be found on evenings like that curled in the corner of one of the calving stalls, or on warmer nights out in the field pressed up tight against the side of whichever cow had borne the brunt of their father's anger.

He couldn't talk, couldn't swim, couldn't find his way home if he walked more than a foot off their property, and couldn't even read. But Eustace had the astonishing brawn to lift and bale hay all day long, the patience to tame the most skittish of farm animals, and the ability to design unique contraptions, everything from his elaborate butterfly collection with handmade shadow boxes and delicate pins holding down the fragile wings, to battery-powered vehicles from Dad's old Erector sets, to a new and more efficient system of pulleys and lifts to transfer hay bales from the wagons into the highest parts of the haymow.

One summer when Noble was in middle school and Eustace in high school, Dad left for a particularly long trucking job. The boys and Mama handled the milking as they always did, the cows sauntering gingerly into the barn as if anticipating the sting of a beating at any minute. Eustace, always bothered by the fright in the whites of the gentle cows' eyes, began walking alongside them from the fields to the barn.

Noble watched Eustace use a stick to make marks in the muck along the way where a shadow or piece of fence or something caused any of the cows to startle. By the third day of this, Noble had grown annoyed with the obsession, which seemed vain at best and a distraction from the real work that needed to be done, especially when Eustace began collecting scrap wood and panels from wherever he could find them—the dump, or from someone they heard was tearing down an old barn.

Within a couple of days, Eustace had built a sort of chute at least thirty yards long, which smoothed over and eliminated the stressors and provided a sturdy boundary alongside them. At the next milking, Eustace shooed the cows into the chute, and they proceeded to the barn—to Noble and Laurie's amazement—without jumping or startling or balking at all. When Dad returned from his trip, he raged when he saw what Eustace had done. But after one milking, even he was impressed at how docile the cows had become, practically lollygagging into the barn.

Noble shook his head at the memory, took off his gloves, and wiped his hands on his work pants. Bringing Whitmore's surviving cows over shouldn't be too difficult. Eustace would make sure they felt at home. The worst would be training them to the electric fence, but even then, Eustace had a way of taking the barbarousness out of the process.

He looked up to see a plume of dust rising on the road to the north, and Shelby Horton's truck sailed past. He watched it until he couldn't see it any longer.

As much as he wanted to get out of Sycamore, that girl was the one thing capable of making him want to stay.

5

If it hadn't been for the fact that the only way to and from Shelby's house on the dead-end road was to drive past their dairy, and that she gave Eustace a ride to the Tractor Supply the days he worked there stocking shelves, Noble'd hardly know a thing anymore about the girl he grew up with and had come to love. The times he did see her working the registers, she barely acknowledged him, as if he was just another customer to ring up. Besides singing together at church until the accident, had she forgotten all the times they played as kids as their mamas talked and sipped cold drinks late into the evening? All the times they'd pretended to get lost in the corn rows, caught enough lightning bugs to make small lanterns igniting with alternating flashes of yellow, drank milk by the ladle straight from the cooling tank? She'd even seemed to forget they were each other's first kiss, giggling under the full summer moon the night they'd dared each other to let their lips touch.

The summer before the accident they'd snuck out of their homes after midnight to hike to the waterfalls, an unlikely and beautiful spot hardly anyone knew about at the far edge of Stuart Granger's property, before the creek turned and curved under the two-lane highway that led into town.

"Do you think we'll always be together?" she'd said to him, kicking her shoes off and tiptoeing across the edges of rocks poking out of the creek. Moonlight shone against her long, tan legs, and her tank top hugged the curve of her waist and hips.

"Don't know," he'd replied, following across to the place where they sat side by side, legs dangling over the edge of the wide, flat crag a few feet above the falls. He didn't know how to answer her, him faced with staying in Sycamore his whole life since Dad was long gone, and Shelby with a world of opportunities to choose from. She'd been wide-eyed and dreamy back then, unafraid to say things that shouldn't be said out loud like that since their child's play had quickened to a much deeper attachment. "Look up. You should see something if you're still."

They'd gone there to watch the Perseid meteor shower, happening at the same time as the Delta Aquarid meteor shower, since she'd claimed all this time growing up in the country she'd never seen a shooting star. The best time for watching was in the early morning hours before sunrise.

"If you don't see one tonight, you need your eyes checked."

She'd elbowed him, her eyes fixed on the sky filled with stars. "You shush. I'm trying to find one."

The air was cool and damp in that early hour, but his skin felt on fire next to hers. He knew then he wouldn't mind being with her forever, as much as a teenage boy can know such things. Besides being the prettiest girl he'd ever laid eyes on, being with her felt like coming home, the good kind of home he hadn't ever known but had imagined after the sounds and bruises of his father's beatings faded.

"There! I see one!" She sat straight up and leaned forward so hard he thought he might have to pull her back so she wouldn't fall into the creek below.

"I hate to tell ya, but that one's moving too slow. It's the space station."

She huffed, frustrated. "So how fast are they?"

"Some of 'em streak by in a second or less; sometimes you'll see a few at once. They're pieces of comets that enter the earth's atmosphere—"

"I know what they are."

"Okay, fine. Then you know that some are as small as a grain of sand." He leaned in closer to her and gently pushed a clump of dark curls behind her ear. "Happens in the blink of an eye. Like this." He felt the softness of her chin as he turned her to face him and brushed his lips against hers.

She did not turn away. "That one was too fast," she whispered. "Show me again."

He did show her, again and again and again.

She claimed she never did see a shooting star that night, and to his knowledge, she never got her eyes checked either. She lost her mom the following spring and hadn't let him close since. He knew the trauma had been unimaginable for her—the whole town was racked with grief, losing the preacher's wife. But he couldn't figure out why she'd acquired a distance and an attitude the size of a combine, especially from him. He didn't know how to fix that between them, either.

Shelby wasn't the only hard-hearted woman Noble had to deal with. He hung his hat and Carhartt jacket on the hook inside the mudroom door, kicked off his boots, and padded into the warm kitchen, where Mama was working on dinner. It wasn't the first time he'd wondered at how such a slight, diffident woman gave birth to two huge boys like himself and Eustace. Her shoulder blades poked from beneath her T-shirt like bird wings as she bent over the open oven and pulled out a pan of oven-fried chicken that made his mouth water.

He walked up beside her and kissed her on her soft temple. "Smells like heaven, Mama."

She wiped her hands on her apron and appeared to attempt a smile. "Wash up and tell your brother it's time for dinner."

The stairs creaked under the threadbare carpet, and the temperature rose exponentially as he reached the second floor, where their bedrooms were. The window air-conditioning units helped but couldn't keep up with the heat and humidity of August, not to mention the ups and downs of this summer's particularly stormy weather. Across the hall from his room, Noble saw Eustace at his desk, a trash can overflowing with snack wrappers at his feet, and his butterfly collection spread out in front of him. He hesitated in the doorway. "Hey, Eustace. Mind if I take a peek?"

Eustace didn't respond either way, so Noble dodged stray boots and comic books and piles of clothes. The old oak desk had been a teacher's desk in its better days, and it was covered with a large shadow box nearly half-full of butterfly specimens, as well as various butterfly-collecting supplies like tweezers and pipettes, small scissors, several small brown bottles of chemicals, and stacks of worn and dusty composition notebooks filled with notes and measurements no one but Eustace really cared about. The collection was exquisite, each butterfly preserved fully intact, organized by color and size, and aligned perfectly straight with the others. They were identified by scientific names he'd printed out with a vintage, dial-and-press label maker, no doubt something he'd found rummaging through their father's belongings: Nymphalidae and Libytheinae, Miletinae and Riodinidae, Papilionidae and Hesperiidae. Beneath those were common names like coudywings and duskywings, skippers and swallowtails, metalmarks and checkerspots, fritillaries and leafwings. He noticed an empty spot under the Nymphalidae column, beneath another label, Meadow Fritillary.

With a pair of tweezers, Eustace gingerly lifted a rust-colored specimen with black markings from the jar where it'd been softened and flattened between damp paper towels. He took it between his ample, work-worn fingers and squeezed the body of it, making the wings separate. Then he began to pin the butterfly to the board. Strips of wax paper held the wings flat, and he put the pins all around the front wings and hind wings, in the minute spaces between the antennae, and around the body. Most of the pins could come out once it dried and—though fragile—could hold its shape. The work was precise, measured, and, Noble thought, excruciatingly painstaking.

He wondered if this was how Mama felt, like the butterflies in Eustace's shadow boxes, after years of being beat down, literally and emotionally, by their father before he finally left them. Had each hit of his fist been like a pin holding part of her heart, then another and another, in place? Had each month, then year, then decade molded her into the doleful, fragile shell she'd become? In her prime, she'd been the Clinton County Fair queen. Her looks had gotten her most everything in her life, including their father. The giant portrait she'd received as fair queen hung in their stairwell for years, but she'd taken it down the night their father left. It had been there when Noble'd gone up to bed, and the next morning there was a big square of unfaded wallpaper in its place. She'd shown disdain toward anyone who'd offered help or friendship after the abandonment, and there'd been times they really could have used a casserole or a plate of brownies.

It seemed bitterness had rooted itself in her heart hard and fast like carelessweed, and except for the smiles she had for her sons, she limited her interaction with others to her sewing, making quilts, and doing alterations for folks around Sycamore. Even then, unless she had to measure someone, customers left their bag of fabric on the porch, and came to pick it up, without hardly interacting with her.

Noble and Eustace lumbered down the stairs and found Mama sitting at the table, milk already poured in their glasses and all the courses set on the table.

"Noble, would you say grace?" she asked as they pulled their chairs out and sat down.

"Sure." He elbowed Eustace to bow his head. "God is great; God is good. Let us thank him for our food. By his hands we all are fed. Give us, Lord, our daily bread. Amen."

"Amen," Mama said, nodding to them, as she had hundreds of other days, to begin eating.

Noble passed the platter of chicken toward Eustace.

"Dolly looks good out there." Mama passed the basket of rolls to Noble.

"I think she'll be fine. I'm calling the vet to put her on some antibiotics to be sure."

"Sounds wise. She's a lucky girl. Have you decided what y'all will name the calf?" Mama passed the green beans to Eustace.

They liked to name their calves thematically, and they hadn't decided on the newest theme yet. When Dolly was born they'd been using country music stars, and as a result

Reba, Carrie, Wynonna, Minnie, Loretta, and Crystal roamed the pastures. The year before had been women of the Bible, resulting in Deborah, Abigail, Sarah, Mary, and Tamar, to name a few. Each calf received a yellow tag in her ear displaying her name.

"What about nuts? This whole town's nuts; might as well name our calves to match," Mama scoffed.

Eustace laughed and sprayed mashed potatoes across the table.

"I guess that's a yes."

"I guess it is," Mama agreed.

"Peanut, Cashew, Walnut, Buckeye—is that a nut?— Almond, Pecan—"

Eustace slapped the table and laughed again.

"Pecan, eh? Pecan it is."

He was acutely aware in that moment how macabre to an outsider the three of them must look sitting around the chipped veneer table . . . Mama and her invisible scars, Eustace's hulking frame, the fact no one cared about mashed potatoes sprayed all over the table and the constant scent of manure hanging in the air. As strange and broken as they all were, for an elusive moment as the last ray of the sun crossed the room, he felt whole.

6

"Lord, bring her home," James prayed as he settled into his armchair and flipped on the evening news. He didn't have the energy to sort out whether he was more worried about Shelby being out with Cade Canady or about her being out in general. No matter how many times she'd left home since recovering from the accident two years ago, whether for school or shopping with Bonnie or work at the Tractor Supply, the silence of the house without her made the memories of the accident loud and sharp as ever.

That April Saturday had been the sort of spring day that gives folks hope after the bone-wearying ice and snow of an Indiana winter. The sort of spring day when mamas fling open kitchen windows, and the crisp breeze rustles long-stagnant lace curtains. The sort of day when the pointed leaves of hyacinths and daffodils finally poke their way above the mulch, gray and stiff. The sort of day when no one should have to die.

Molly, with Shelby beside her, had been driving southbound on Interstate 65, a road they'd traveled often on their way to and from Indianapolis. Shelby had been a finalist in a statewide voice contest. Their Honda Accord had been no match against the northbound, late-model Suburban, driven by another mother who lost control trying to avoid a deer and crossed into the oncoming lanes. To the mother driving the Suburban, that bright spring day must've felt like the middle of January as she stood on the side of the road. Perhaps she wore a sweater and pulled it tight around herself. Perhaps her arms ached from the strain of the car seat and the cooing infant within hanging from her elbow. Perhaps she wept as the emergency crews sawed through the bent, annihilated metal of the sedan, and the medical helicopter landed and took Shelby to the city hospital. Perhaps she turned away, unable to watch as the remaining paramedics at the scene covered Molly with a tarp and didn't bother to turn their sirens on when they drove her body away. James never met the woman, so he would never know for sure.

He put his beloved Molly in the ground on Good Friday, the day rainy and gray, and his life in the two years since had been a caliginous struggle to find the very direction and hope he would have otherwise preached about that Easter weekend. What he would give to have Molly sitting in the front row again, giggling at him like a schoolgirl whenever he missed a point or Jersha Pittman started snoring or Ella Cox ineffectively stifled a squeaky sneeze into her handkerchief. His life was divided into before and after the accident, and holidays were now marked as "the first time we've celebrated without her," and then, "the second time we've celebrated without her"; their wedding anniversary being the most dreadfully empty of them all.

As for Cade Canady, James had been worried about Shelby getting involved with that boy for weeks. Since the accident, Shelby had abandoned her singing, her friends, even her closest friend and next-door neighbor, Noble. James wasn't the only one who noticed the changes in her, either. The other morning he'd been deep in thought researching his Sunday sermon. Bonnie had come into his office, forgetting to knock, and he had been so startled he nearly spilled his coffee, ice-cold since he hadn't touched it for hours. He'd spun his chair around from his computer to see her standing on the other side of the desk, her forehead unusually furrowed.

"Reverend . . . James . . ." She cleared her throat.

"What is it, Bonnie?"

"Here's your mail." She leaned over and set the stack on his desk: catalogs with fancy curriculums, glossy postcards from church consultants offering the latest and greatest revitalization programs, brochures for church sound and tech equipment they'd never need, and bills—always bills.

"Thank you."

"I'm so sorry to have startled you, especially with all the stress you're under."

"It's okay, really. Would you care to have a seat?"

She fumbled for the arm of one of the chairs and sat on the edge of it, crossing her feet at the ankles. "Thank you. . . . Probably not the best time to tell you this . . ."

"Never a good time for anything lately, is there?"

"No, I suppose not . . . but . . . well . . . I'm worried about Shelby."

"Oh?" James removed his bifocals and rolled his chair closer to the desk.

"You know I don't like hearsay."

"I know."

"So you know I wouldn't repeat anything unless it was from a reliable source."

"I do."

She cleared her throat again before going on. "People have been talking awhile now about Shelby and that boy of Silas Canady's . . ."

"Cade."

"That's the one. I tried to believe the best, that Shelby wouldn't let herself get caught up with him or that group of kids he runs around with . . . that maybe—bless her sweet heart—she saw something good in him the rest of us haven't. But last evening, he and a couple other boys came into the hardware store as Hank was getting ready to close. They were goofing around in the aisles, so Hank stayed nearby to make sure to keep things in check."

"Go on," James encouraged as she glanced at him, hesitating.

"Well, Hank heard them talking about Shelby. He heard Cade bragging about how close he was to stealing . . . you know . . . My goodness, how am I ever gonna say this . . . ?"

"It's okay, Bonnie. I've heard it all."

"Yes. Well, you probably have. He said . . . Cade . . . he was bragging about how he was close to being the one to steal the pastor's daughter's virginity."

James sat back, crossed his arms, and rubbed his chin as he often did when he was especially bothered. He truly had heard everything in his career as a pastor, which of course doubled as a counselor, crisis manager, mediator, and mentor. But none of that prepared him for hearing painful things about his daughter. He leaned across the desk toward Bonnie. "I know they've been spending a lot of time together. I was hoping it was a phase. She hasn't been the same since Molly . . ." He slumped back into his chair.

"I know. We all know. I'm sorry, Reverend." She stood to leave the office.

"Bonnie?"

"Yes?"

He paused, struggling with whether to ask for advice, which he wasn't shy about asking for on other, lesser occasions. He looked up at Bonnie and said simply, "Thank you."

Initially when Shelby had started dating Cade Canady, James had been tempted to tell his daughter not to see him anymore. Apples don't fall far, as the saying goes. Silas owned the auto repair shop two blocks down from the church, and he had been overcharging and cheating folks out of money they didn't have for years. Cade was the sort of kid who wore his letter jacket in the height of the July heat and tried to make up for his vertically challenged blunders on the football field with fear and intimidation on the street. Well before Shelby had an interest in boys, Molly had read about the danger of setting harsh limits on teenage romances, as that would only fuel a *Romeo and Juliet* complex between the two. So for the time being, James had settled on trying—now clearly in vain—to find something to appreciate about the boy, while at the same time laying down an earlier curfew. He'd also insisted the boy come and meet him, figuring that would do the job, since such a requirement would scare off most questionable young men. The suggestion had resulted in yet another fight.

"No way!" Shelby appeared mortified. "I can't believe you don't trust me!"

"I trust *you*, Shelby. I'd just like a chance to get to know Cade."

"You can't tell me who to like."

"I'm not trying to tell you who to like. I know it's a little old-fashioned, but it's the courteous thing to do, for a young man to meet a girl's father and at least shake hands."

"Then what? You'd meet him and hate him. Besides, this is Sycamore, remember? Ain't nobody around here any of us don't *know*."

"I know *of* him. But I don't know anything about him personally. What's he like to eat, for instance?"

"Pizza." She rolled her eyes.

"What sort of movies does he like?"

"All the old *Terminator*s. *Rambo. Predator. RoboCop.* That kind of thing."

"I do know he likes rap." The recollection of the woofer booming from Cade's truck—which matched Silas's, including the flame decals on the hood—rang in his ears.

"There's nothing wrong with rap!" And with that, she'd turned and stomped out of the house to the truck.

James switched the television off, set his glasses on the table, and rubbed his eyes. *Molly, she needs more than what I can give her. She needs you.*

His dwindling congregation needed more, too.

Dr. Wilcox had told James that he'd save people, congregations, towns. Two decades later and he had a dead wife, a dying church, and a wayward daughter. He was supposed to be the caretaker of the flock and the lost sheep, the one who loved everyone despite their sins. But he needed Scriptures that spoke of what happens when the shepherd gets lost, what happens when a church is forced to close and a pastor can't find his way. "Waiting on the Lord," and Scripture's promises of the souls of the diligent being richly supplied, didn't comfort him anymore. The only words that felt true these days were those of his father, the tire-factory man, who'd said he'd never amount to anything.

Though warned by fellow seminarians and pastor friends

about the ebb and flow of faith in most everyone—including
and perhaps especially church leaders—he wasn't prepared
for his church to die. For a while, stories of the Israelites
in the desert, the widow at Zarephath providing for Elijah,
Ezekiel and the dry bones coming alive buoyed him. But
now, after losing Molly, he was near plain exhausted. His
own eyes and those of his congregants had long been glaz-
ing over with boredom as he delivered his sermons. Words
flowed from his mouth, the same stories he'd told before with
a different, dispassionate spin. Afterward, were it not for his
notes, he would often be unsure of exactly what he'd said. He
shuffled out to his car like the rest of them, shoulders weighty
with discouragement and an absence of inspiration, let alone
joy. If he were completely honest, he was cynical, skeptical,
and almost to the point of being perfectly fine with closing
the doors of the church for good.

For five years straight, when the elders met for his annual
review, he'd offered to resign. And yet each time they voted
unanimously for him to stay, refusing to accept it. After
Molly died, he considered moving back to her hometown
of Atlanta for Shelby to be close to her grandparents. But
Shelby had begged him to stay. Besides that, he knew a
physical upheaval so soon after the loss of Molly would not
help Shelby. Still, each time James woke in the middle of the
night and reached his arm around the cold side of the bed,
he wanted nothing more than to escape from that drafty
house, from the smallness of Sycamore that tightened his

throat, and from the calling he so often doubted he was worthy of anymore.

He tried to push all this, and the worry gnawing at him about where Shelby was and when she'd be home, out of his mind as he trudged up the creaky steps to his bedroom. Sunday was coming, and he still had a sermon to write.

7

Noble pushed three bales of hay down the ladder of the haymow, and they landed with a thud on the floor of the barn below. He was glad he and Eustace had done all the cutting and baling the week before since the unusually wet weather seemed determined to stay for a while, according to the weather reports. His arms burned from the work of moving bales, and as it wouldn't be milking time for at least another hour, he decided to take advantage of the quiet afternoon and sit for a spell in the loose hay. The rain fell soft and steady outside the hatch, and leaning against the side of it was one of the few places where the ache of the work felt worth it. The straight rows of the crops and the edges of the land appeared so distinct that the landscape looked more like a painting than something real that he'd worked and sweated over all day. He'd sown the seeds, and dirt caked permanently under his fingernails. The pads of his hands were thick and yellowed with calluses. Still, the gentle roll of the corn tassels and crisp lines he'd cut across the alfalfa field looked perfect enough to have been shaped by hands much greater than his and Eustace's. He'd almost forgotten how green the land could get, practically glowing, after the three years of intense drought that had caused all the bluegrass and even some of the toughest weeds to brown and go dormant.

At least it's not storming, he thought. As grateful as they'd been for all the rain this year, the storms that had come with it had been as intense as the drought. He thought about what was left of the Whitmore herd. From the mow, he could see the tops of the grain elevators and dryers a few acres away from where Whitmore's cows grazed. Though he knew they were fine alone in their pastures, he and Eustace needed to move them over within the next week or two. He stared up at the thick trusses and beams that held the barn together and wondered at how a tornado could knock them down in the blink of an eye, how things like a father leaving a family and a few cells of a child growing wrong in the womb could do the same.

Noble had realized the fragility of life for the first time in the mow years back, when Shelby used to traipse across the fields and the three of them—Noble, Eustace, and Shelby—played in the creek and hid in the mow and pretended the great loft was their pirate ship sailing across the ocean to places they only wished they could go. Places with sand instead of dirt and manure pressing up between their toes; places with palm trees instead of cottonwoods to nap beneath; places where princes escaped the awful, terrible rule of unfit kings and rescued orphaned princesses. Noble and Eustace ran around thrusting and swinging swords made of fallen tree branches, and Shelby flitted about in sundresses and rain boots. The three of them played in their otherworlds for hours, their adventures stretching into days. The cows became royal subjects over which they ruled (with kindness only), and the cats and their frequent litters of kittens became their serfs to protect from barn owls and raccoons, the villainous pillagers of their land.

A lot of barn cats roamed around the farm. Some they'd see once and never again, and others would hang around for years growing fat from barn rats and milk dripping from empty calf bottles and machinery waiting to be cleaned. As they did with the cows, Eustace kept track of all of them and Noble named them.

When they were young, no older than grade school, there had been an especially friendly black-and-white cat named Clyde, who quickly became Eustace's favorite. Eustace knew where Clyde slept, brought the cat pieces of lunch meat, and generally spoiled the feline until it had become a shadow following Eustace around at the heel wherever he went. One day when the three of them were playing in the mow, Clyde appeared, ears unusually flattened and groaning a low growl of annoyance. When they'd approached and peered over the bales of hay where the cat sat hunched and ready to pounce, the cat batted its paws at them and they understood why: Clyde had kittens. Correctly identifying the gender of a cat was not something they'd completely understood, and so they did not bother renaming her.

Eustace woke Noble early every morning so they could check on Clyde and her four babies—two black with white paws, one all black, and the fourth patterned like her mother—before they started their milking chores. They watched as the babies suckled at Clyde's milk-laden belly, coaxed Clyde into letting them pick the babies up and pet them as their fur thickened and their eyes cracked open for the first time.

Eustace loved on those kittens as hard as he loved on the cows. Once, Noble had caught him with one in his pajama shirt pocket when they were getting ready for bed. They'd had to wait until Dale passed out in his threadbare recliner, David Letterman and his audience making enough of a racket that he wouldn't hear the screen door click open and shut, so they could get the kitten outside and back to nursing at its mother.

Then came the rainy afternoon when everything changed. Noble remembered it like like an old movie, Shelby waiting for him on the front porch in a peach dress with puffy sleeves and blue ditsy flowers (he'd remembered because she wore a blue kerchief knotted on the top of her head holding back her black curls, and which matched the blue of her eyes), and the brown rubber boots caked in mud from their last excursion.

They figured Eustace had gone on up to check on Clyde and her kittens first. Wouldn't be the first time he'd beaten them to it. But as they headed toward the barn, they knew something was terribly wrong. The wailing sounded like a siren, louder and more awful as they ran toward it. By the time they reached Eustace in the mow, he was curled in a ball next to the bales behind which Clyde and her litter lived. He covered his head, his face with his arms, which muffled his moaning but not his distress.

Noble and Shelby looked at each other and back at Eustace, then at the bales of hay. Shelby stood fast by the hole in the mow up through which they'd climbed, her jaw slack with panic, and Noble peered over the bale.

Not one kitten—not even Clyde—had survived the attack, which must have come from one or more of the several barn owls that lived high on the rafters. It appeared as if Clyde had fought a good fight, her body limp and covered in open wounds as she lay over the remains of the four kittens, what was left of them that the creature hadn't plucked clean. The hay was a bloody mess from the massacre.

Thankfully Dale had been on the road, or he'd have smacked them around, Eustace especially, and made fun of them for their grieving. Mama had given them a boot-size shoe box and padded the bottom with a pretty dish towel. Noble, with Shelby's help, scooped Clyde O'Malley and her babies up with gloved hands and placed the lot of them in the box, and the four of them had a funeral for the family of felines out under the cottonwood tree on the hill that dropped down to the creek. Shelby brought her Bible and officiated, on account of her dad being the preacher and all. But she cried the hardest, too. And Mama hadn't cried at all, just stood holding Eustace's crazy arms to his sides and rocking him back and forth like she always did, even though he was already grown clear up past her shoulders.

He remembered Shelby, tears streaming down her cheeks, eyes red and swollen, which made them all the more blue.

He remembered putting a hand on Eustace's shoulder, gently so as not to start him into fits of arm flailing. "You know there's nothing you coulda done."

Eustace had only moaned and closed his eyes real tight as if trying desperately to block out the real.

"It's just the way things are, the weak being scooped up by the strong, the ones who aren't bothering anybody getting snuffed out for no good reason at all."

It wasn't the owl's fault he was doing what he needed to do to survive. But still, their belief, buoyed by the naiveté of childhood, in dreams and saving the weak ones was shattered and they were changed.

The whole incident had been like looking out the haymow only in reverse.

Everything beautiful at a distance looks pretty ugly up close.

8

James heard the screen door squeak and Shelby's footsteps padding up the stairs at 12:22 a.m. He'd fallen asleep with his cell phone on his chest and the house phone on his bedside table in case Sheriff Tate called, or worse. Feigning sleep, he listened as she settled herself, grateful for no sniffles or other sounds of possible emotional distress from her room across the hall. Her bedsprings creaked, and that was the last sound he heard from her until he woke her for Sunday services. He was grateful that she did not balk about going to church. Not that it would have mattered much, since there were only a few more left to fight over.

As the two of them left the house, James watched Shelby

rub her finger across the face of her smartphone, communicating more with her friends than the two of them had communicated in months.

"You have a nice time last night?"

"Mmm-hmm." She glanced at him, then back down at her phone, the pink case embedded with pink rhinestones.

"A little past curfew when you got back, wasn't it?"

"I guess."

"You guess?"

She did not move her eyes from her phone. "Fine, yeah, so I was about an hour late."

"An hour and twenty-two minutes."

"What do you do, stare at the clock the whole time I'm out?"

Determined to keep calm and not lose his temper, James focused on the country road ahead of them and the neatly sown fields of corn and beans on either side. "No, Shelby, I don't. But I do notice when you're late, and I do know that nothing good happens after eleven in this town."

"I wasn't doing anything wrong."

"What were you doing, then?"

The corn was way past knee-high. He guessed it would approach his shoulders if he stopped the car and stood alongside the stalks.

"We were just talking. We were on the swings at the playground in town. Ask Sheriff Tate. He drove by and waved. Did you send him out looking for me?"

His neck grew hot at the snark in her voice. "*No*, I didn't.

Shelby, look. All I'm asking is for you to respect your curfew. Can you do that for me?"

Her phone chirped with incoming texts and she grinned, but not at James. "Sure, Dad. Whatever."

"And about yesterday—"

She sighed and turned her phone facedown on her lap. "Look, Dad, I'm sorry. Sorry about the curfew. Sorry about our fight. Is that what you want to hear?"

He gripped the steering wheel harder. "You know I'm only concerned about your safety."

"Dad." She pulled a hair tie off her wrist and collected her long curls, twisted them, piled them on top of her head, and secured them. "You can't be scared all the time for the rest of your life. Isn't that what you tell me? About the peace that surpasses understanding? About trusting the Lord with all your heart and he'll make our paths straight?"

"Yes, but—"

"But what?" She picked her phone back up and rubbed the screen again, focusing hard on the soft glow in her hand.

It was his turn to sigh. "The accident aside, it's hard for a father to trust a boy with his daughter. I was a boy once myself, you know."

"Dad!"

"What?" He glanced at her, glad he'd caught her full attention. Wasn't it his job to mortify her?

"I'm *fine*."

"Remember what I said about hands-to-hands and lips-to-lips, and you won't have any trouble."

"Yes, Dad. I remember." She slunk down in her seat and pulled her phone closer to her face.

He noticed a hard blush in her cheeks.

Molly had been so good at anticipating Shelby's needs, responding to the ups and downs of the teenage girl's moods and angsts like a musician reading a score. Sure, there were difficult seasons, and Molly and Shelby had argued about the length of shirts and skirts, and on the reasons why she was not allowed to wear leggings without a tunic that covered her behind. But for the most part, the two of them had gotten along better than most mothers and daughters. While other parents complained of silent treatments and brooding moods, Molly and Shelby had attended mother-daughter retreats, shopped together, read books together, even crafted together, working for hours, sanding and painting and refurbishing, in the detached garage. Molly had explained to James that Shelby opened up to her when they worked on their art in ways she wouldn't at the dinner table or otherwise. And they'd been so grateful for that lifeline into Shelby's life.

Now that Molly was gone, James struggled to find a similar connection for the two of them. He had thought perhaps singing and church might be a possibility, but then Shelby stopped singing. He couldn't blame her. He knew she'd felt that her singing was the reason for the accident, even though the police, rescue team, and the whole of Sycamore tried to assure her otherwise. But once a person has decided to own the blame for something, the shame of that is a hard thing to shake.

James turned the radio to the pop station out of Lafayette, hoping to subtly show Shelby he was not only interested in her, but also that he cared enough to try to encourage her interests. Sweat trickled down his back before the car reached the outskirts of town, the morning was so thick with humidity. The sun shone, but the wind blew fierce, upturning the maple leaves, their silver underbellies a sure sign they were in for a storm sometime that day.

Sunday mornings in downtown Sycamore seemed the only thing unmarred by the technology and greed of the twenty-first century. The full width of the brick street, void of teeming weekend tourists and shop patrons, welcomed them. It was as if every building and every tree, every bench and every sidewalk had a chance on Sunday mornings to exhale, a chance to gird itself with the rest needed for the week ahead. Though the population was only a few hundred, Sycamore prided itself—in the spring, summer, and fall, especially—on attracting hundreds of folks from surrounding counties to its burgeoning farmers' market, antique shops, and boutiques.

As they passed the antique store, he noticed a dresser still for sale that Molly had refinished in robin's egg blue. James nodded toward the store. "I see they still have a piece of your mom's. Have you ever thought about selling some of your string art there?"

Shelby craned her neck to see as they passed.

"You're still making them, aren't you?" He thought about the one hanging over their front door that read *Home Sweet*

Home in bright-yellow yarn letters. The color of their siding. Molly's favorite color.

"Haven't for a while. But maybe."

"Think about it. I bet folks would buy 'em faster than you could make 'em." He felt her looking at him and turned to meet her gaze.

"Thanks, Dad."

He patted her knee and returned his focus to the street, where nothing stirred except the bricks shifting under the wheels of their car.

9

A *yellow butterfly* landed on James's windshield, fanned its wings a couple of times, and then flew off as he maneuvered the older-model Chevy sedan that had replaced Molly's Honda into the spot with the sign in front of it that read *Reserved for Reverend Horton.* No one would have threatened the spot anyway since there were plenty of spaces left empty in the crumbled asphalt lot, during service time and otherwise. Shelby lingered over her hair and lip gloss in the passenger-side mirror before following him inside the church.

That morning James had an odd feeling of being an observer rather than the orchestrator of the Sunday morning activities. He realized it was the same feeling he'd had as his friends guided him through the motions of preparing for Molly's funeral. No doubt Kernodle's baleful declarations two days prior were to blame.

He caught the comforting scent of lilac and cold cream before he stepped around the corridor and saw her, cardigan sweater and straight, gray wool gabardine skirt even in August. "Mornin', Bonnie," he said.

"Mornin', Reverend." She smiled, although her eyes carried a frown as she stood at her desk folding the fifty bulletins. They probably could've trimmed the number to twenty a long time ago and saved a few dollars, but they'd quit cutting the amount at fifty, more out of vain hope than any sort of optimism.

In his office, he set his worn Bible on his desk, a yellow legal pad thickened with prose stuck somewhere between Psalms and Isaiah and stressing the spine. Above the computer on the wall was one of Shelby's string art compositions, the word *Shalom* in a variegated rainbow yarn. Once his computer came to life, a stock photo of Indianapolis Colts quarterback Andrew Luck throwing a pass gleamed at him as he selected the morning's sermon from the collection of files on the screen's desktop. The printer hummed to life as it spat out the half-dozen pages. He stapled them before heading to the sanctuary, where Myrtle Worley was already warming up the organ.

"Morning, Reverend." Similar to Bonnie, Mrs. Worley could be counted on to wear the same thing in different color variations each week: a suit coat with a silk blouse beneath it which tied at her neck, a skirt with tight pleats that reminded James of accordion bellows, opaque hose, and thick-soled shoes. Molly never could get past the older ladies and their hose.

"Morning, Mrs. Worley."

The organ had been a gift of a parishioner back in the 1970s when the church was flourishing under the leadership of Tilman "Tilly" Icenhour. Tilly had been one of those pastors who had become a pillar of strength, hope, and light not only to the church, but also to the community during his fifty-year tenure. His bald head, encircled by a halo of white hair, solidified his iconic reputation, as well as the fact that he wore his billowy black robes trimmed with velvet long after all the other preachers had given them up for jeans and sport coats.

When James had interviewed for the position, Tilly had warned him of some of the joys and perils of ministry, the lure of becoming all things to all people at the expense of the less enticing road of patient obedience, the tension between caring for the flock and caring for family, the temptation of being the focus rather than being the angle of trajectory pointing people toward God, the balance of steadfast faith and truth in the midst of congregational demands for radical relevance. Each time they'd sat across from each other, James had felt like Frodo, wee and inadequate, under the tutelage of Gandalf carrying a Bible for a staff and that white ring of hair for a hat.

The congregation had been booming then, and looking

back, James wondered if he'd relied too heavily on the great wave of what Tilly had started. Should he have had the confidence to start his own programming sooner? Or should he have taken Tilly's advice for what some said it was—outdated—and adopted some of the more mainline initiatives like vision casting and technology, a band and cozy chairs instead of hard pews? Over and over he'd prayed and sought advice from Molly, his friends back at Furman like Dr. Wilcox, and the elders about what could be causing Sycamore Community Church to flounder the last few years. But no answers ever came. It was as if he was walking in circles in a desert like the Israelites, only there was no Promised Land . . . just a valley of dry bones, and he was not the Ezekiel they needed.

Tilly's optimism and encouragement for James had been unwavering, even when Tilly and his wife, Ann, had moved to Florida a couple of years after James and Molly had arrived. They'd found a place near Fort Myers where they could bask in the sun and anonymity after five decades on display on the stage of ministry.

"I didn't want you to argue with me about coming here today," Tilly had said to James, who'd been beside himself with surprise when Tilly appeared at Molly's visitation. His back was bent, his frame thin and rickety, but the gleam in his eye indicated he was mentally sharp as ever, despite his ninety-some years of age.

The next day, Tilly had delivered the eulogy, and James was further undone when Tilly's stalwart faith wavered.

"Christ overcame the grave, yes . . ." Tilly paused, gripping the sides of the podium as he tried, unsuccessfully, to stifle a sob. "Pastors' wives . . . aren't supposed to be put in boxes, lowered into a hole, and covered with dross and dirt. . . . None of us are. And though we have the hope of resurrection, we do not have answers sufficient to account for this day."

James learned that death had an air of contagion about it, that those paying their respects nodded awkwardly, their mouths thin-lipped and grim, resembling the reaction of folks when they learned you had the flu. Others, the older ones who'd had more experience with funerals, squeezed James's shoulder with shaky hands as they passed by, avoiding his eyes and preferring to gaze instead at the gaping hole over the side of the grave.

Later, Tilly reminded him that pastors' wives were, in fact, the buffer between the pulpit and the people, the soft middle where the grieving and needy found their place. And now James wondered if the vacuous space in his heart he had not been able to fill in the two years since Molly's death, despite everyone's best efforts to rouse him, was what brought them to this, the last month of not only his ministry, but of the generations-old brick-and-mortar church. In his widowhood, he'd felt that he'd become an untouchable, a leper in his own town. He'd dated, once. He admired other women from afar—Laurie Burden, for one. But circumstances and proximity that might have brought them together seemed to pull them apart. A broken parishioner was one thing. A broken pastor, quite another, and in the end, perhaps too much for a congregation to bear.

James set his Bible and notes and freshly printed sermon on the oak pulpit, edges rubbed shiny from the generations of hands that had rested and rubbed against its surface. He glanced at Shelby, still focused on her phone, sitting in the front row next to an empty space on one side where Molly used to sit, and an empty space on the other where Bonnie and Hank would soon join her. The worn pages of his underscored and bookmarked Bible crinkled as he double-checked that the lime-green sticky notes marking the day's Scripture references were in the correct places. A couple of early parishioners shuffled in, and the organ pipes reverberated with a peppy rendition of "Joyful, Joyful, We Adore Thee." Mrs. Worley's fleshy backside hung off the back of the wooden bench and rocked to the tune as Jersha Pittman—the oldest living great-grandson of one of the charter members of the church—hung the hymn numbers, last week's offering, $38, and attendance, 14, on the board.

At 9:43 on the dot, James addressed the congregants, which numbered eleven exactly. "Good morning!"

"Good morning." The congregational reply was muffled, out of sync.

"Join with me in this week's call to worship, printed in your bulletin." James was certain if he'd been closer to them, he'd have smelled the coffee struggling to take effect within them, along with freshly applied Brylcreem. He waited until the sound of shuffling papers subsided. "We come seeking Jesus, the Light of the World."

"We believe in the strength of God to illuminate dark places." The congregants' voices echoed against the bare wood of the pews, the rafters.

"The light shines in the darkness, and the darkness shall not overcome it."

"Lord, in this hour of worship, kindle in us the light of your love."

"Let your light shine through us, now and forever. . . . You may be seated." Though he'd been giving people permission to sit for hundreds of Sundays, the instruction felt strangely odd. Mrs. Worley began playing "Come, Thou Fount of Every Blessing," and James only half moved his lips to the lyrics as his mind wandered to baptisms and eulogies, sermon series and holidays celebrated and memorialized by the faint must of the red carpet that needed replaced, the oil soap that shined the pews and pulpit, the creak of floorboards as people shifted in their seats. Even as he delivered his sermon, he felt as if he were hearing someone else's voice. He looked out over the sanctuary as words about the faithful in Hebrews 11 fell from his lips. Except for one middle-aged couple he did not recognize, he knew without hesitation the name of every freshly coiffed, white-haired lady and thin-haired man nodding along—if not to sleep—before him. Another family sat near them, their young children clambering on and off the pew seat as the mother struggled to keep them occupied with coloring books and small toys.

He thought of the faces of those who used to fill the empty spots, the way a person can think about such things when they've been giving weekly sermons for so long. People had a habit of sitting in the same spot every week, so even if folks tried to be inconspicuous when they stopped coming, he knew they were gone. They left a shadow of themselves, a smile only they smiled during a favorite hymn, a giggle only they let out to certain jokes he told. His friend Jack McGee was one, still an elder despite his lack of attendance, but he had never been good about coming regularly anyway.

Raleigh Cox and his wife, Ella, had sat in the second row holding hands all the time except when James mentioned a Scripture and they let go to flip through the thin pages of their old, worn-out Bibles—bookmarks and bulletins floating to the floor every time—and he'd pause and wait until their scurrying to gather it all up subsided.

Gertrude Johnson, her thinning hair dyed persimmon orange, was known for her creativity as the owner of the town flower shop, as well as for her philanthropy, the result of a large inheritance. When she wasn't noticing cracks in the walls, she had sat in the first row directly in front of him and often scolded him afterward for what she felt were inconsistencies or inaccuracies in his sermons. Whenever they sang "Great Is Thy Faithfulness," she had dabbed at her eyes and blown hard into her handkerchief, often frightening Jersha Pittman awake.

Dr. Tom Lawson and his wife, Angie, who had seemed perpetually pregnant for ten straight years as she carried and bore their six children, had sat in the back row. Tom was a good man, sensible, someone James could count on for a solid handshake after the service. Angie was a dedicated mom, highly respected for her work leading school and parenting prayer groups.

Thelma Howard, an assistant professor at one of the nearby small colleges, had sat on the right in the fifth row back and had often brought a friend with her. Quiet and mousy, she would from time to time e-mail James during the week to ask for insight and clarification into the Scriptures, and he was impressed with her ability to cite—accurately, at that—the Hebrew and the Greek.

Behind Thelma, Laurie Burden had sat, mostly without Dale, and tended to her two boys, now young men, Noble and Eustace.

For the first few years of his ministry and then especially in the last five years of what he often referred to as the exodus of these and over a hundred other parishioners, he felt like he'd been punched in the gut each time a family left. A few of them told him in lengthy letters—occasionally with meal or gas cards enclosed—of God leading them to Higher Ground Church, needing to go where they were more fed, someplace more in sync with their postmodern problems and life stages, someplace where the music made them feel closer to heaven. Most of the time, though, they just left, the only indication that they'd done so being the empty spot in the pew, with the decision confirmed when he saw them at the supermarket and they avoided him, turning quick down the pet food aisle before he could have a chance to greet them or ask them gently, and with genuine concern, where they'd been.

After a while, he couldn't blame them. He couldn't—and didn't want to—compete with the mainstream movements in places like the enormous Higher Ground Church down the interstate. Rather than be constantly devastated by their departure, he decided to try to be glad for folks when they left. After all, didn't Jesus send out his own disciples in Luke 10? Who was James to say that the Lord was not leading people elsewhere to do different work for him?

Still, disappointment and self-doubt lingered as he remembered everything Tilly had warned him about: the Walmart effect of bringing in glossy graphics and program designers, praise bands with members wearing matching Buddy Holly glasses, fog machines, banners outside announcing the latest and greatest sermon series and building fund drive—everything Higher Ground had and then some. Higher Ground Church resembled the Taj Mahal rising above the cornfields where the interstate rounded a bend on the way to Indianapolis. The traffic getting in and out of the parking lots on the weekends prompted them to hire police, patrol cars with lights flashing as officers in uniform directed cars in and out before and after all three morning services and the Saturday evening service, too. There was no doubt that what the megachurches did worked. It was relevant; it was timely; it was, as those who'd left Sycamore Community Church had told him, fulfilling in more ways than a small, ragamuffin church that still used hymnals, recited the Apostles' Creed, sang the doxology after the offering, and typed and printed their own bulletins. He didn't doubt that they preached the same gospel. But he wondered why—and if he were honest, he resented the fact—so many were attracted to the loud and shiny places that made old places like Sycamore Community Church seem obsolete, even ignorant by comparison. On the days James felt most discouraged, all he wanted to know from God was: Wasn't the gospel supposed to be enough? Wasn't *he* enough?

His eyes settled on the back right corner of the sanctuary at Laurie Burden's empty spot. Her boys were grown now, and he rarely saw her since first her husband, Dale, left them and then Molly died, even though they were next-door neighbors. The acres between them and the loss of both their spouses had no doubt been part of what strained the relationship they'd had. He knew she probably had more reasons than most to leave the church, if not because of James's pastoral failures, then because she'd given up on God. He'd see her sometimes inside the coin-operated Laundromat or at the Tractor Supply or the drugstore, and she always looked cold and sullen—not far off from the way he felt on the inside. He wondered if she had the same questions he had, about whether the church in general was still a place for widows and orphans.

These thoughts lingered in James's mind as he stood, his back holding the front door of the church open after the service. The fresh air, though humid, was a relief since at least there was a breeze outdoors. The church had no air-conditioning, and this was the time of year when they all questioned the lack thereof. If heat and humidity came early as they sometimes did in the unpredictable Indiana springs, many a June bride fainted in the midst of her vows, and August weddings were out of the question since multiple attendants and guests were sure to hit the floor. But as soon as they got quotes for installing central air, a hint of fall would creep into the air and they'd decide it wasn't worth it to add to their loans.

As they exited the narthex, folks extended their hands toward James. He asked them about their recent surgery or wayward child, or how their gout was or when they were plowing or planting, or their recent delivery of livestock to the markets. The older ones hobbled and lurched down the cracked steps to their cars, most of them parked along Main Street, which ran directly in front of the church. Some of them moseyed down to the Percolator, which served hotcakes and coffee and a blue plate Sunday special.

"You alright this morning, Reverend?" Rich Orwell, one of the elders, grabbed James's right hand with both of his. "Didn't seem like you were quite yourself up there."

Most of the flock had left except Bonnie and Hank and Jersha, who, along with Shelby, cleaned up crumpled bulletins and stray hankies and other things parishioners left behind. James felt relieved to be able to let his guard down and talk to his longtime friend.

"Attendance is booming, Rich. I'm not sure where we'll put people anymore. Might have to invest in some folding chairs."

Rich seemed unfazed by James's sarcasm.

James ran his hand through his hair and focused on a passing collection of gray clouds. "Besides that, raising daughters is hard work."

"Don't I know it."

The two men chuckled more out of mutual sympathy than humor. Rich had raised three daughters, now scattered in all corners of the country and with a gaggle of grandbabies to boot.

"Anything Eileen and I can do? I'm sure she'd be glad for some girl time with Shelby, if you think that'd help."

"Nah," James sighed. "Just prayers. For wisdom and for her protection. And a phone call to Sheriff Tate if you happen to see Shelby parked at the end of a dirt road or in a cornfield with Cade Canady."

Rich raised his eyebrows clear up to his hairline. "Silas Canady's boy?"

James nodded.

"Shooo-eeey. I'll do more than pray. I'll beat the living daylights outta the kid if I need to."

10

"Stop! Make him stop!"

Noble felt his body jerk as the sound of his mother screaming in his dreams roused him awake. Rarely did a month go by that he didn't have nightmares about the horror that had been life with their father. He squinted at the clock on his nightstand, hands pointing to 2:50, and slugged down lukewarm water in the glass from the night before. He hated when dreams woke him like this. He needed that extra hour or two of sleep before he could face the morning milking and yet another day of chores. He'd especially hoped for a decent sleep since that evening he'd be playing at the Purple Onion. The fact that it was tenderloin night would only add to the crowds, which had been steadily increasing over the past year or so to come see him. Besides that, the folks who'd be there had put in a hard day like him and deserved a good song to wash down their whiskey. He'd been rehearsing a new set heavy with Johnny Cash songs and was excited to see what the crowd would think.

On his way back to bed, he checked on Eustace. Worry shot through him at the sight of his brother's bed, flatter than it should be in the glow from the barn's floodlights against the pitch black of the moonless night.

"Eustace?"

Noble stepped closer to the bed and confirmed his suspicion: Eustace wasn't there.

He checked the bathroom.

Nope.

He checked his own room. Eustace often came and slept there if a storm scared him.

Nope.

He checked Mama's floor, for the same reason.

Still no Eustace.

He cursed under his breath, a combination of annoyance and concern.

Mama stirred. "Noble? What is it? What time is it?"

"Eustace isn't in his bed. I'm going to check the barn and pastures."

"It's three in the morning. Wait—I'll come too." The light from the barn outside illuminated Mama's face, contorted with sleep and worry.

"It's alright, Mama. I'll find him."

Noble grabbed the high-powered flashlight from over the washer on the back porch, pulled on his work boots, and headed to the barn. "Eustace? Eustace! Where are you?"

Bullfrogs groaned and crickets clicked from the low area of pasture near the barn, which was more swampy than usual with this year's heavy rains. A random sparrow, apparently confused about the hour, chirped from the big cottonwood. The air was so still the tire swing hung motionless as if the stage were set for a movie.

Noble cursed again, knowing full well Eustace wouldn't answer him even if he were able. As many times as Eustace had wandered off like this, Noble never got used to the panic he felt. In the last six months, Noble had discovered his bed empty like this at least a half-dozen times. They usually found him in the pasture with the cows, and Noble hoped he'd find him there again this time. But he couldn't keep himself from thinking the worst as he trudged across the yard, nearly turning his ankle in a low spot hidden in the shadows of nighttime. Strange and frightening thoughts loomed and grew larger in Noble's mind with every moment that passed: Eustace wandered onto the road and got hit by a car. Eustace wandered into the pond near the reverend's place and drowned. (He never did learn how to swim too well.) Eustace climbed into the haymow to check on a new batch of kittens and broke his neck falling down the ladder. Noble felt a pang of guilt about his own increasing ache to do more with his music and leave Sycamore behind.

The problem was, he not only *felt* responsible, but he *was* responsible.

"Lord, why'd you let Dad leave? Why'd you leave me alone with this family, this life? And where are you?" Noble lamented aloud. A gaggle of bullfrogs singing like crazy near the water troughs stopped their groaning.

As long as he resented God, he figured he still believed ·in him. But why did it seem like whenever he'd needed God the most, he couldn't feel him at all? Seemed like God left the same day Dad did, a buxom stranger worth more to him than his wife, sons, and farm.

Who was Noble kidding, thinking he'd ever leave Sycamore? That he'd "get discovered" at the Purple Onion in little old Sycamore, Indiana? That he could go off and play his guitar somewhere that mattered, even if he was discovered? Not with an idiot brother like Eustace. That was the difference between him and his father—Noble didn't have the option to up and leave.

He slid the barn door open and checked the calf stalls first, figuring Eustace went and bedded himself down next to Pecan, or that he'd gotten up early, not realized the time, and would be there feeding all the calves their formula, the chore he liked to do best. But as Noble checked the stalls, the calves didn't stir.

"Eustace?"

He shone his light into each partitioned bed of straw but saw only sleepy calves, their bodies curled into little commas, except for one that struggled and wobbled to stand.

"Eustace?"

He climbed the ladder to the mow, but Eustace wasn't up there either.

He let go and landed with a frustrated thud on the concrete floor of the barn. He scratched his head, which was beginning to throb from fretting and being up too early without coffee. Though he wished he didn't, times like this Noble hated his brother for being born, hated him for making him assume the unwanted role of big brother, hated him for tying him down to this place. The resentment had been worse when he was in high school, when he was in the midst of discovering girls and kicking the butts of neighboring farm town teams when he played tight end under the bright field lights of Sycamore High, or pounding a ball against the hardwood trying to become the next small-town sectional basketball champions. Caring for "poor Eustace," as so many folks referred to him, was not a calling Noble would ever have chosen. But he was stuck with it all the same.

He went back outside and slid the door shut. The night was still, placid, and cool, humidity having ebbed with the sun. He walked toward the pasture, the same direction as the Hortons' pond. He wished Eustace was a little dumber so that he wouldn't know better than to step over the electric fence, that he'd respect his boundaries like the cows.

"No luck, eh?" Mama, breathless, approached him as he stepped over the fence. The bottoms of her sweatpants were stuffed into her rubber work boots, and the oversize T-shirt she slept in hung down to her knees.

"We're gonna have to get him an ankle bracelet or some kind of alarm. Think those dog collars would work on a human?"

"Noble, that's awful."

"No, really. This is becoming a regular occurrence. You want to keep doing this every couple weeks?"

"I don't know—maybe."

Noble glanced at her as she looked up at the stars, and for a moment he remembered what she'd looked like when she was younger, less hardened, her skin less ruddy from years of working on the farm. Mama was a stark contrast to Shelby Horton, pale and unaccustomed to hard work. But she was good and kind, and his heart felt heavy all of a sudden at the thought that his mama might not ever find someone to love her right. He wondered if that ever crossed her mind or if she told the truth when she proclaimed so often, "You and your brother are all I need."

The two of them hastened over the uneven earth of the pasture toward a small gathering of trees on the slope where the cows moved like shadows. Several of them lying on the ground looked like giant boulders in the darkness. Noble imagined they were annoyed at being woken before milking, too.

"Eustace!" Noble called.

They were close enough to make out the definition of eyes on the shadowy heads of the cows. He noticed a couple of tails flipping back and forth, and one of them mooed in protest.

"Eustace, if you're here, you come on out here now," Laurie called.

"Aha . . . hahaha . . ."

"Over there." Noble nodded toward the guttural cackle that only Eustace made and exchanged an exasperated eye roll with Mama.

They found him curled next to Dolly on the ground, his white ball cap pulled down over his eyes, clearly not caring a lick that he had scared them out of their minds yet again. Dolly turned her huge head toward Eustace, licked him with her thick, wet tongue, and nuzzled him. Eustace reached around and cradled her neck like an overgrown baby in his arms.

11

The shadows of Main Street's lampposts were long, and the low, angled sun reflected harsh off storefront windows as James walked to the Purple Onion. He was meeting the elders—Mike Crawford, Rich Orwell, Greg Howard, Hank Thompson, and Jack McGee—for a late-afternoon Thursday dinner. Along the way, he saw Gertrude Johnson arranging a new display of potted geraniums and fresh sunflowers in the front window of her flower shop, Fleurish. Through the plate-glass window of the Laundromat, he saw Ella Cox, along with a couple of other women he recognized, transferring loads from washers to dryers.

Well before he reached the door of the Purple Onion,

James smelled the cooking beef and fried onions. His stomach growled. He could never decline a good hamburger and onion rings, preferring that to their famous tenderloins. This sort of craving hadn't been a problem for him when he was younger, but his middle-aged paunch reminded him not to partake of it as often anymore.

Silas Canady rolled past in his truck, purple underbody lights gleaming. Irritation, fueled by what Bonnie had said about Cade and Shelby, pressed against James's chest, as well as the disdain he and everyone else in town felt for the man. With the only auto repair shop in town, Silas did enough fair business with some that he got away with swindling the majority of others, who continued to patronize the shop since the next closest one was farther than their broken-down vehicles could take them.

James and Molly had learned the hard way when the truck needed new brake pads and Silas had charged them over five hundred dollars. They'd paid the bill, not knowing anything about cars or car parts. Hank found out about it and said the pads cost about forty dollars and only took about an hour to replace. James had seen evidence of Silas's unfair practices again and again, as over the years folks had come to the church asking for help with their car-repair bills.

A man in a tattered military fatigue jacket limped toward him on the sidewalk.

"Hey there, Jack."

"Rev. You look terrible."

"Nice to see you too," James laughed.

"Wouldn't miss tenderloin night." Jack paused to lean on his cane and spent half a minute coughing and choking. "If Rosie's grease doesn't kill me, the cigarettes will."

Or the alcohol, James thought. A large poster announcing Noble Burden on guitar and Rosie's tenderloin special hung in the front window. He held open the glass door covered in Lions Club stickers and advertisements and inhaled the smell of grease and beer. His old friend gimped past him.

Jack was a Vietnam veteran whose leg had been blown off by a land mine, as he told anyone who looked at him funny. And if he didn't tell them what happened, he told them a joke about being able to get a pedicure for a discount. His favorite thing was to ask women at bars if they wanted to be his "sole mate." Sometimes they laughed. Other times they excused themselves and tried not to look at his missing appendage. He spent most of his time in his trailer home, but James had made a point to call him and ask him to come today, and after Jack heard about Kernodle's decision to close the church, he'd promised he would. Jack might not be reliable in many ways, but if he made a promise, he was sure to keep it.

"How can I help you, Reverend?" The teenage hostess, whom he recognized as one of Dr. Tom and Angie Lawson's six children, picked up a couple of menus. She was a pretty girl, one who, like Shelby, would no doubt be someone the boys would clamor over, if they weren't already.

"Bethany, how are you? How's your family?" Over her shoulder, James saw Mike Crawford wave from a large,

U-shaped booth across from the grill, and Jack hobbled toward them.

"They're good . . . fine, thanks." She hesitated, pulling the menus in closer to her chest.

James noticed a flush come to her cheeks, something that often occurred when he greeted people. It was the burden of a minister for normal, everyday interactions to be skewed by the common misperception that he could somehow read minds or sniff out their latest sin. "That's great to hear. If you don't mind, I'll mosey over to where the rest of our group is sitting." James nodded past her as Jack tumbled in next to Mike and Hank and the other elders sitting in the booth.

"Oh, alright, then. Have a nice dinner, Reverend Horton."

"Will do. Tell your folks hi. I miss seeing you all around." He looked into her eyes and squeezed her shoulder as he said this so she would know that he meant it, then walked past her toward the booth.

Hank stood and wrapped James in a bearish embrace. The other men extended their hands and scooted over to make room for him. He thought they all looked a bit nervous.

"So it's official, gentlemen," he said, trying to lighten the mood, even though he knew that was futile.

Mike wiped the sweat off his glass of iced tea with a napkin.

Rich rolled and unrolled and rerolled his silverware.

Greg leaned forward, crossing his arms on the table. "I'm sorry, James. I wish there was something more we coulda done."

Mike and Rich nodded in agreement as the waitress approached.

"Can I get you somethin' to drink?"

"I'll have an iced tea. Thanks." James had a nice view of the fry cook flipping steaks and burgers on the grill behind the bar. There was a rhythm to the way the young man slapped the beef on the hot surface and swiped his spatulas against each other to clean them, back and forth, flip the meat, swipe the metal, flip the meat, swipe the spatula.

So this was it. The end of his ministry. The end of his career. The end of another small-town church.

"You okay, Rev?" Hank asked.

He sat back and sighed, then ran his hands through his hair. "Good as I can be. I never thought it'd really happen."

"You're not alone," Mike offered. "You know thousands of churches are closing all over every year."

James surprised himself when he hit the table with his fist. "Yeah, but it shouldn't have been ours."

A hush fell over the restaurant, and the others looked at him, startled.

"I'm sorry." He sheepishly straightened his silverware and bent his head, lowering his voice. "I keep thinking about the last twenty-some years, what I've done wrong, where I messed up, what I did and didn't do that made this happen. I let the town down. I let the church down. I let everyone down. And then there's God, who's supposed to be *somewhere* in the midst of all this." He laughed a bit maniacally.

"Just 'cause you can't see him don't mean he's not workin'."

Jack hit his cane against the metal shaft of his prosthetic leg. "Loss don't mean the end, necessarily."

The waitress delivered James and the other men their drinks and took their food orders, giving him a chance to take a couple of deep breaths and try to settle down.

"Jack's right," Mike offered. "And like I said, you're not alone in this."

"The church belonged to all of us." Rich had lined his utensils up in a neat row on top of his folded and refolded napkin. "It was our church. The people's church. Sure, you were the leader, but a leader can only do as much as the people he's given to lead are willing to help. You can't make people stay—or leave for that matter. Every church has a cycle of sorts. Bigger ones handle the turnover better than small ones, and we happen to be a small one."

"There's churches who have less than we do who do stay together, though." James squeezed a lemon wedge into his tea.

"But they don't have George Kernodle and his fan club. Don't forget that," Hank said.

James considered this. Kernodle was the banker, the head of the town council, and he knew a group of townsfolk who wanted to see Sycamore become more of a tourist attraction, a town whose brick streets and ice cream stores and coffee shops beckoned traffic off the interstate and brought in more shops and money for taxes and schools. Churches weren't exactly helping to line the coffers of the town fund. Rumor was Charlie Reynolds and Mark Madsden from the Methodist and Baptist churches, respectively, had had their own run-ins and financial pressures, if not with Kernodle, then with one of his colleagues from the bank or town council. Kernodle had always had his eye on Sycamore Community Church in particular because it sat right on the corner of town square. Prime retail space.

"They can go to Higher Ground," Kernodle had the audacity to say during one of their recent conversations. "You know as well as I do the loans won't last and you'll be in the same position you are now in six months, probably less. Let what's left of your flock go, and let them go to Higher Ground. It's got more—" he raised his fleshy arms in the air—"*pizzazz.* More of what the younger folks are looking for and what the ones with families need these days. More color. More music. More technology."

James turned to Jack and the rest of his friends. "Do you think that's what our faith is coming to? A bunch of consumer Christians, people who leave when the music isn't right, when the stained-glass windows are out of style, when it's easier to go where you can be a number instead of someplace where you can't help but be known and accountable?"

"In some ways, I do." Greg stirred another packet of sugar into his tea. "But we can't change that. We can only go forward from here."

"Forward where?" James blurted. "I've never considered anything beyond Sycamore. I thought you'd have to take me out back and shoot me before you'd get me out of the pulpit. Guess Kernodle and his friends did it for you."

"Now look, James," Rich said. "It might be the end of this one particular church, but Charlie and Mark have already offered to take everyone in with open arms, whoever wants to come."

"But I'm a pastor. They've already got their pastors. What am I supposed to do with myself here in Sycamore?"

The waitress came and passed out the baskets of burgers, tenderloins, and fries.

"You ever thought about maybe takin' a sabbatical?" Rich stuffed a couple of fries in his mouth. "Take a few months to gather yourself, sort those kinds of questions out? Get Shelby through her senior year?"

"I thought about it. Thought about how miserable I'd be, nothin' to look forward to in my days besides sharing a meal with you hayseeds."

The men chuckled.

"I'll give you a job at my store, if you need one," Hank said. "Doing something completely different for a while might not be as bad as you think. I remember near the end of Tilly's tenure, he gave a sermon about the desert, how God works on us most in those times we feel like we're circling the drain—or the sand, as it was in their case."

Be still and know.

James fought the urge to roll his eyes at the familiar voice of the Spirit in his head. From the corner of his eye, he noticed Laurie Burden's younger son, Noble, come into the bar with his guitar in one hand and a backpack slung over one shoulder, his older brother following close behind. Not only had Noble grown up in the church, he'd played guitar for the youth group and for Sunday services, and he and Shelby used to sing together regularly for the congregation. The last time Shelby ever sang was with Noble a week before the accident. They'd organized one of their special gospel music services, where they played all the old revival hymns. The congregation—what was left of it—had loved it.

"Whadda you say we make the best of these last three services?" He nodded toward where Noble leaned against the bar, talking to Rosie Fancher, the Onion's owner. "Maybe ask him to play. Have a picnic and ask folks to share memories. I bet Shelby and Bonnie could put together a scrapbook of mementos if folks want to bring them in."

"That's a great idea." Mike grinned. "I got a few good stories from some of those men's retreats I could write out."

"Don't you dare." Greg shot him a playful, warning glance.

"Remember when the sparrow got loose in the sanctuary a few years back?" Rich said.

"Good night, if it didn't pull off Rory Pittman's wig that one morning and carry it up to the rafters," Mike laughed.

"And the time you dropped the fifth Lawson baby into the baptismal," Rich continued.

"And the time Sheriff Tate had to come and arrest Ray Donaldson for stealing from the offering. Man had no shame—he and Jersha were the only money counters. We thought for sure it was Jersha's counting, but no, it was Donaldson," James said.

"Yeah." Jack coughed. "The Baileys saw him down at one

of the riverboat casinos, and that's how we discovered he was addicted to gambling."

The men went on telling these sorts of stories and laughing until their bellies ached. On the way out, James stopped at the counter, where Noble was still talking to Rosie. Noble's brother, Eustace, sat next to him playing a game on his smartphone. James was struck by the way, up close, Noble had turned into a young man, wearing a goatee and the rest of his beard grown in enough to look scruffy, as seemed to be the style for his age. He resembled Laurie, pale-blue eyes, gentle smile, his light hair bleached even lighter by the sun.

Noble extended his hand. "Reverend."

"Nice to see you playing here tonight." He turned to Eustace and put a hand on his thick shoulder. "Nice to see you, too, young man."

Eustace didn't lift his eyes from the screen.

Noble shrugged and grinned, and James noticed a dimple, also like Laurie's, on the right side of his face.

"S'pose you heard by now about how the church isn't doing so well."

"I've heard rumblings of the sort, yeah. Sorry to hear that. Somethin' not right about a church closing."

"I won't argue with you." James raked his hand through his hair. "I don't suppose you'd consider playing for us these last few services? I know it's been a while—"

"I'd love to."

"Yeah? It's short notice . . ."

"Can't be easy, the spot you're in. I'll do what I can to help."

The two agreed to work out the details later, and James headed outside to where Jack smoked a cigarette and the others stood still laughing and reminiscing. He was grateful for their good memories. Grateful Noble'd said yes to playing so quick. But as he started his car and headed toward home, James began to feel a slow encroaching shadow of darkness on his own mind.

As he passed the Burdens' dairy, a red-winged blackbird darted in front of the car, flying alongside him for a second, long enough for him to see the bright yellow and red beneath its ebony wings before flitting off into the fields. He hung his arm out the window to feel the breeze press through his fingers. He saw Laurie sitting on her front porch, the low-hung sun glinting against an aluminum bowl on her lap and a pile of green beans on a newspaper at her side. If she looked up from her snapping, he would wave at her. But she didn't. He'd been driving past without a thought for so long, she wouldn't have had a reason to look up anyway. On this day, though, he wished that she had.

12

As Reverend Horton had spoken to him, Noble noticed the lines deeper than ever on the older man's face. He hadn't noticed before that the reverend's hair was at least half-white, especially around the temples, or the way his shoulders fell forward as if fighting against the pull of an overfilled backpack. Horton had grinned slightly when Noble agreed to play for him, but Noble thought it was a sad smile, the sort that you give a person when you're relieved to see them at a funeral.

"Well, it's settled, then," Horton had said. "I know you're preparing for your show here. We can talk later about the songs. You can pick whatever you'd like, really. No sense spending too much time discussing what's played, as long as it's something folks like."

"Yes, sir."

Noble could tell the man had things heavy on his mind as he walked away. He was halfway out the door when he turned and waved awkwardly. "Thank ya, Noble. Means a lot."

Noble turned his attention to the grill, where grease sizzled and the crunchy aroma of food cooking filled the air. Rosie simultaneously lowered baskets of tenderloins and fries into the bubbling oil of the fryers. She turned to where Noble sat, one elbow on the counter and the other arm holding his guitar case against the stool.

"Thanks again for having me, Rosie."

"One of these days, you'll listen to me when I say you don't have to thank me. Sold out of tenderloins and apple cobbler last time you played on a Thursday night. Heck, I don't even have to offer a special anymore. We have to turn people away every time you play. It's a mutually beneficial sort of thing."

"Thanks all the same."

Rosie pushed a glass of ice water his way and a Coke toward Eustace, who sat on the stool next to him and hunkered down over his smartphone. "Keep that pretty voice of yours hydrated."

"Will do." Noble finished the glass as Rosie shifted her attention to three men who had just ambled in. He recognized them as a few of the most respected farmers in the area, survivors of multiple droughts and lean times. They'd been born during the years following the Great Depression, the sort of dying breed of men who knew how to save and conserve and who were not lured by the dazzle of Big Farming, and whose values hadn't withered under the moral decline of subsequent generations. Their yes meant yes. Their no meant no. And you could pretty much guarantee they lived by the Good Book. Their plaid shirts were buttoned to the top notch under their dress overalls, dungarees saved for such outings, so they were still dark blue and free of mud or any other sign of the work they'd done that day. He knew without looking that their hands were calloused and fingernails stained permanent brown from decades of turning soil.

In the adjoining room where the bar and stage were located, a handful of folks gathered around three pool tables, a half-dozen video game machines, and a full service bar set strategically behind a partition so that underage patrons could come and have a safe place to socialize and enjoy the music. Eustace, who seemed to very much enjoy watching Noble play, sat at a booth by the front window, played a game on his phone, and sipped his Coke. Noble liked having Eustace there where he could keep an eye on him.

He made his way to the far back corner of the room and the triangular-shaped, elevated section of plywood that passed for a stage, featuring a drum set, three microphones, a small amp, and a couple of wooden stools. He centered one of the stools, opened his guitar case and attached the amplifier, then began adjusting the height of his microphone.

He played Thursday nights as often as he could, and occasionally he'd pick up offers to play in Lafayette or Crawfordsville, sometimes Lebanon, if the milking and chores allowed. He drew larger and larger crowds of locals and others from around the area, made good tips, and felt the pleasure of entertaining the crowd, which requested new and old country songs and a few rock and roll. When there weren't requests, Noble played older country covers of Waylon Jennings, Alabama, and always Johnny Cash, Mama's favorite. She'd rarely missed one of his gigs, sitting across from Eustace at the table he sat at now. When Noble played, he could see the tears of pride in Mama's eyes. When she came, she rarely spoke to anyone, crossing and curling her legs up on the seat of the booth, and sipping her Diet Coke. She hadn't come this night, but he wished she had since he was going to play a new Johnny Cash set. He'd be sure to play it the next time she came.

As Noble fussed with the equipment, a classic rock station out of Lafayette played on the overheads. At the sound board, he turned the radio down to test the mic and amps, leaning forward as he sang:

"Love is a burnin' thing
And it makes a fiery ring . . . "

He tweaked a few knobs and sliders and adjusted a couple of his guitar strings before singing the rest of the song.

Pete Moore, the bartender, nodded his approval as he

dried a freshly washed set of highball glasses. Noble turned the radio station back up, set his guitar against the stool, and sat at the bar waiting for 8:30 p.m., his official start time. The room glowed pink from the sunset, which he'd bet could outdo any on the ocean. Some said the brilliant colors were from dust kicked up by cars flying down gravel roads and plows tending fields. Whatever the reason, Noble loved Indiana sunsets. If he was gonna be stuck in Sycamore all his life, he'd at least be glad for those sunsets.

"'Specting a crowd tonight, Noble?" Pete asked.

"I'm not taking bets. Your Cubbies are on, though. And since Rosie's running a tenderloin special, you never know."

Pete was from "the Region," defined as anywhere within a couple of counties' distance from Chicago. In reality, he was from South Bend, which was a far cry from a farming community and, if you asked Noble, a little too proud of being the home of Notre Dame. But it was Indiana all the same. Pete was also one of the rare newer residents of Sycamore, having fallen in love with a small-town girl who insisted on settling down in the same town as her parents and returning from Saint Mary's College, also in South Bend, to be a teacher at the elementary school.

As the sky shifted from pink to orange to indigo and folks trickled in and out for dinner and then for cocktails, Noble began his first set of songs. He loved the connection with the crowd, the way an old farmer tapped his toes, the way that the longer he played, the more the countenances of the patrons relaxed. After nine, the crowd shifted from couples and older folks to younger adults and teens. Noble was well into his second set when Shelby came in, escorted by Cade Canady wearing his letter jacket, and three other couples, obviously older. They settled into a booth and made a ruckus ordering pitchers of beer, splashing it all over the table as they filled each other's mugs.

Noble tried to focus on his music even when Cade ran his hands up Shelby's thigh as they were squeezing into their booth. Cade took out his switchblade, which he twirled and flipped through his fingers, a habit he'd had since they were kids.

Too bad a switchblade can't make up for his deficiencies in the stature department, Noble thought.

One of the guys in the group came back from the bar with yet another pitcher of beer, and Noble glanced at Pete, who shook his head with obvious disdain. Another particularly skinny young man from the posse, whose teeth even from across the room appeared broken and stained, turned to face Noble. He buckled in half with laughter as he hollered, "Hey, cowboy. How 'bout you kick it up a notch. We're not here for a Hank Williams concert."

Noble feigned a smile and tried to ignore the obscenities that followed the kid's snarky comment. He finished the last chord of a George Strait song. "Y'all got a request? I'm happy to take it now."

The skinny guy started to speak again, but Shelby, who was sitting across from him, seductively squeezed herself out of the booth, chest brushing up against Cade's face. She sauntered up alongside Noble on the stage and whispered in his ear. "Don't pay them no mind. Country's fine with me."

The smell of alcohol on her breath was so strong he struggled to keep himself from coughing. He put a hand behind her head and whispered back, "You alright, Shelby? You shouldn't be drinking like this."

"I'm fine." The words slurred and she nearly lost her balance turning to face the crowd.

He shook his head. The Shelby he knew, the one who danced across the top of the waterfall at the far end of the creek barefoot, the one he caught singing into a broom handle on her front porch, the one who showed kindness to Eustace like no one else in Sycamore—she didn't need alcohol to have a good time. She'd seen what it'd done to Noble's father before he ran off, and she'd sworn she'd never taste the stuff. But he also knew that grief could do crazy things to a person, turn them into someone they never intended to be.

Still, as Shelby cleared her throat preparing to sing, Noble couldn't help noticing all over again the way her dark curls fell down her neck, the rise of her chest, the line of her chin, the outline of the lips he longed to touch again, to kiss again. Heat rose up inside him as she leaned a little too close to him and whispered the key and a couple of other technical specifics into his ear. He adjusted the frets on his guitar, strummed a few chords, and looked to Shelby for approval.

"That'll do," she said to Noble. As she was about to turn

back to the crowd, Noble could see tears rise and clear the haze of alcohol from her eyes. She stumbled into him. "I can't do this, Noble. I can't . . . I won't sing. Not without my mom."

He put his arm around her and gently pressed her head against his shoulder.

Noble saw Cade scowl as his friends in the booth sniggered. Beyond them, everyone in the diner had stopped, their attention fixed on the stage. Suddenly Cade jumped up, knocking over one of the pitchers of beer. He hurdled the booth, stormed the stage, and yanked Shelby away from Noble.

The amplifier wheezed and squawked.

"What do you think you're doin'? I've told you before— you don't *talk* to other men, you don't *look* at other men, and you sure don't make out with one on a stage."

"Hold on there, Cade . . . ," Noble said, stepping toward him.

Cade put his hand in his pocket. "Careful there, cowboy. Wouldn't want those strings or something worse to get cut now, would we?"

"I wasn't . . . ," Shelby choked out. "I was goin' to sing for you . . ."

Cade yanked her upper arm again, and she braced herself as if expecting him to hit her, the same way Mama'd braced herself against Dad so many times.

"Yeah, right." Cade clenched her arm so tight she gasped, then pulled her across the room and toward the door.

"Cade—" Noble called after him.

Cade paused and faced him. "Whatcha gonna do, cowboy? Stop me from leavin'? Like you stopped your old man from leavin', eh?"

At that, Noble started after him.

But Pete, who by this time, along with Rosie, had approached the stage, pulled him back. "He's not worth it."

"Maybe not," Noble said. "But she is."

He caught sight of Eustace with a look on his face that reminded Noble of the time he'd found the kittens dead in the haymow. Noble knew how much it disturbed Eustace when someone or something weak was taken advantage of by the strong. He was too docile, too uncertain about how to fight back to ever do anything, which was why Cade picked on him. Felt good to someone like Cade—shorter than a fence post but so full of pride he thought the sun came up just to hear him crow—to pick on someone like Eustace, too big for his own good and too kind to resist.

One of Cade's friends with blue-tinged hair and nickel-size earlobe expanders appeared somewhat apologetic as he handed Pete a fifty-dollar bill while the others left their mess and followed Cade and Shelby outside. "Sorry, man. Keep the change."

From the stage, Rosie offered free cobbler to the guests, and Noble struggled to regain enough composure to play on as the headlights of the cars reflected off the walls and they all drove away.

"Sorry, y'all," Noble said, taking a step backward as the

amplifier squealed again with feedback. "That'll do for me tonight."

From the booth by the window, Eustace erupted with laughter and clapped his hands.

As if on cue, Pete turned the radio back on to fill the awkward silence that followed.

Noble wound his guitar cord and collected his music charts, and the thought crossed his mind that it was a good thing Reverend Horton left when he did before he caught sight of how Shelby acted onstage and how Cade pulled her off.

"Noble?"

The man who stood next to the stage was unfamiliar and clearly not from Sycamore. His pressed khaki pants and navy sport coat, his salon haircut, and the way he held his shoulders back like someone with no worries about money were all dead giveaways.

"That's me."

"Cass Dinsmore." The man extended his hand toward Noble. "I was pretty impressed with your performance this evening."

"I appreciate that. Sorry about that last act there."

"No biggie." Dinsmore reached into the inside pocket of his sport coat and pulled out a business card, which he offered to Noble. "I work for the Lyric Group. I'm a scouter. I look for new talent to represent, and I'd heard good things about you from a couple of sources up in Lafayette."

"Yeah?" Noble took the card, forgetting for a moment his anxiety about Shelby.

"From what I've heard, and despite that little scuffle—" Dinsmore rolled his eyes—"I'm pretty impressed myself. My e-mail is on there, along with my phone number. Call me early next week. I'll be back in the office then. I'd like to talk to you about coming down to Nashville for a little visit."

13

The Sycamore Daily Ledger came out once a week on Fridays, and there it was on the front page:

Sycamore Community Church Slated to Close

The editor, Julie Shaw, had not bothered to contact James or any of the elders for a quote but instead relied solely on information from George Kernodle. Straightforward and without emotion, the article read like the church was any other business that had closed over the past decade, and in many ways, perhaps it was.

James wasn't sure what he expected, just something a little

more than the facts. They could have mentioned that the church had been the site of celebration for so many births and deaths and marriages, that it was built in 1857 by some of the original settlers of the town, and that it was the very first church building to be erected in Sycamore. They could have written about the floors, trim work, and pews, hand-hewn by a local carpenter who'd cut down ancient oaks from his own land to make them.

From her other work, James knew Shaw was a shrewd woman and no doubt wanted the story for the front page no matter how she had to get it, with or without fluff. He also knew there would be no feature article to come later. To her credit, she'd written the same way about the other six area churches that had closed in the last five years in the tri-county area, so it was an unbiased story. He could argue that few of those had the long-established history of Sycamore Community Church, but then again, a lack of history would not have lessened the pain of those congregations.

James slugged down the last of his grounds-laden coffee and flipped the newspaper to the sports section, which featured a story of two local football players—Cade Canady not one of them—being recruited by Indiana University and the University of Illinois. Hank would have something to say about why neither was looking at Purdue. A cross-country runner signed with Indiana State. The high school had big plans for this year's homecoming festivities. An editorial lamented the recent pay-to-play sports decision of the school district, and the threat of increased property taxes. Again.

Shelby, black curls sticking out all over, yawned as she padded into the kitchen, opened the refrigerator halfheartedly, then rummaged through a cupboard. "Don't we have any Pop-Tarts left?"

James pulled the front section of the newspaper over the top of an empty silver wrapper that had held the last of the Pop-Tarts, which he'd eaten. "Add them to the grocery list?"

Shelby groaned, shoved a couple pieces of bread into the toaster, and slunk into the chair next to him. She straightened when she saw the front-page headline. "So now everyone knows."

"Yep."

"So we have three more services?"

"Yep. I thought George Kernodle would let us go till the end of the year, but he's done giving us breaks. The building goes to auction—"

"Monday, September 5." She pushed the paper back toward him and tucked her rumpled hair behind her ears. "What are we gonna do? I mean, what about my senior year?"

"You can finish your senior year here. The house is paid for thanks to the in-laws . . . thanks to your grandparents. And I'll find whatever work I have to do, to keep you from having to leave. Who knows, I may join you at the Tractor Supply."

She frowned and toyed with a strand of her hair, twisting a piece around her finger. "I'm sorry, Dad."

"Me too." James felt tears prick his eyes.

This wasn't the way things were supposed to be. Not for him. Not for Molly. Certainly not for Shelby. He'd done the best he knew how with her, but he couldn't help but feel responsible for the way she hunched herself against the world as if bracing herself constantly for another tragedy. She'd been strong-willed long before the accident. He often wondered whether her most recent rebellious streak was the typical stance of a self-conscious teenage girl or the result of Molly's absence. Or was it the result of his ministry, which often left him preoccupied and unintentionally unavailable to her? There were undoubtedly a thousand ways he should or could father her better, but he hardly knew where to start. He hoped and prayed that his love—that God's love for her—would be enough, though he knew full well neither had been enough to sustain the church.

He tried to change the subject. "Working today?"

"Yeah. I gotta go pick up Eustace in a few."

"How's he been doing?"

"He's holding his own at the store. Does a fine job stocking. People come to expect him there now, so he doesn't bother anybody."

"Nice of Brock to give him the opportunity. Say, I saw Noble last night. He was playing at the Purple Onion."

"Yeah?"

It might've been his imagination, but he thought he noticed her face redden. "What ever happened between you two?"

"What do you mean?"

"You and Noble. You used to be pretty close, didn't you? Before . . . Well, anyway, I know the boy-girl thing can get awkward sometimes, but he's such a nice kid. Hard worker."

"Mmm-hmmm." She didn't look at James and instead focused on the newspaper. "Guess we're both busy, is all."

"By the way, thank you for being home at a decent hour last night. I appreciate that." She'd been home by ten thirty, early for a change. He'd been watching the news when she came in, and she'd hurried past him and said good night before he could ask her about her evening.

Shelby didn't reply as she grabbed her toast from the toaster.

"What sort of plans does Cade have for next year? Has he heard from any colleges about football?"

"I don't know. It's still early, I think."

"Look, Shelby, I know I'm not any good at this dating thing. I just want you to be safe."

"You've said that before. I'm *fine*." She kept her back to him as she stood at the counter and slathered chocolate hazelnut spread over the toast.

"I'm glad to hear that." James paused, trying to find the least controversial way to say more. "It's just that . . . well . . . whoever you choose to date should treat you with respect."

She nibbled the crust off the toast before eating the middle.

"And I know I'm a guy, but if you have questions about physical boundaries—"

Shelby jerked her head toward him. "Dad!"

"Okay, okay. But if you want or need to talk about stuff like that, I'm not embarrassed. And I won't get mad."

"Cade's not like his father, you know. He's *nice*." She glared at him now.

"His father . . . yes, well . . ." He felt himself losing whatever composure he had. "I guess I *don't* know that. Especially since he hasn't even bothered to come to the door once to shake my hand or meet me or walk you to the car. I don't know a thing about him except that he drives that truck and gets an occasional write-up in the paper about a football game or traffic ticket. That, and what I hear about him in town."

"What'd you hear about him? Talk in town's gossip anyway, and you know what the Bible says about gossip. 'A gossip goes around telling secrets, so don't hang around with chatterers.' Proverbs 20:19, right?" She threw the rest of her toast and the butter knife hard in the sink and started out of the room. "Besides, I *told* you, he's *shy*."

"'A wise child accepts a parent's discipline. . . .' Proverbs 13:1."

"Cut it out, Dad."

They'd gone around and around many a time throwing Bible verses back and forth at each other. She always had been good at memorizing Scripture. Maybe better than him. "Oh, and, Shelby, one more thing."

She continued to stomp toward the stairs without turning around.

"You might want to wear a scarf to work today."

She stopped and put her hand over a round, raspberry-colored bruise on her neck the size of a quarter and blushed bright red before pulling her hair over it and taking the stairs two at a time to her room, slamming the door behind her.

14

Noble poured the last of the syrup over his stack of
pancakes and kicked Eustace playfully under the table.

"Hey. Chew with your mouth closed, 'kay?"

Eustace chewed louder, stuck his tongue out, and grinned.
A half-chewed piece of pancake fell out and landed on the
paper towels bunched up and stuffed in his collar like a bib.

"Yeah, I know. *See-food.* Good one. But if you look outside, you'll see we ain't nowhere near the ocean. So close your
mouth."

It was the same conversation they'd had every day for
years. Same joke about "see-food" he'd learned from some
kids' cartoon. And he never did close his mouth.

Mama leaned down and gave Eustace's white ball cap a tug down farther on his head and pulled him close to her. He kept poking at the game on his phone screen as Laurie wrapped him in her arms and planted a kiss on his cheek. "You be good at work today, Eustace. Mama's proud of you."

Sounds of Mama clearing the table came from the house while Noble and Eustace sat on the front porch steps waiting for Shelby. Eustace sat like a schoolboy, feet together, hands folded in his lap. The job was good for him, even though it took time away from him helping with the farm. The hours allowed him time to help with the morning milking and left plenty of time for Noble to help him get ready, and for Mama to make sure he'd showered with soap since he had a hard time with hygiene. She made sure his pants and shirt were ironed and that his shoes were free of mud and manure since he never paid much attention to where he stepped.

Eustace suddenly fixed his attention to the spot on the porch where the railing was missing a couple of spindles that had rotted away. Noble realized Eustace was focused on a butterfly, blue and not too large, lying so still it had to be dead. Noble knew enough about Eustace's collections to know there weren't too many blue butterflies in this part of Indiana, and that there was one particular endangered species he'd been trying to find for years. He even had a label already made above the spot he was saving for it.

"Is it a Karner blue?"

Eustace looked at Noble, then back at the butterfly, then back at Noble again, and he nodded.

Noble caught his breath. It was a small thing to most, but he knew it was an extraordinary discovery for Eustace and that extraordinary was rare and to be celebrated. "That's great! Keep your eye on it while I go get you a jar."

When he returned, Eustace was holding the butterfly in the palm of his hand. The Karners were small, only a little wider than a quarter, and it wouldn't have been right to capture a live one and kill it since it was already on the verge of dying out. But since this one had already spent its life, it would be perfectly acceptable for Eustace to add it to his collection. Together, they tenderly scooped the creature into the jar and tilted the glass slowly upright until it came to rest on the bottom of the jar.

"I'll take it in for you, since Shelby will be here any minute."

Eustace was already distracted from Noble's assurance and moseying toward the side of the barn where a patch of dandelions grew. He stooped down and began to pick them.

"What are you doin'?" Noble called, but Eustace didn't pay him any mind. "Don't be getting your pants all grass-stained. Mama just pressed them."

Eustace went on picking dandelions. When he heard the engine of Shelby's old truck, he ran to her, holding the pitiful bouquet out in front of him, his face deadpan except for rosy patches of bashful on his cheeks.

"Aren't you the sweetest thing, Eustace! Thank you." She held her arm out to take them and smelled them as if they were a bunch of long-stemmed roses.

"Go on and get in the truck now, Eustace," Noble said. He turned to Shelby. "Sorry about that."

"Sorry about nothin'. Don't you apologize for him. Your brother's the sweetest man around these parts."

"If you're comparing him to Cade, then my manure-covered boot's sweeter than him, too."

"Noble Burden, could you be jealous?"

He raised his eyebrows at her and stepped back, crossing his arms. "That's a little presumptuous, don't you think?"

"Look, Noble, I know what you're trying to do here. But I don't need protecting."

"That's not what it looked like to me, him yanking you offstage like that."

"We'd all had too much to drink."

"Shouldn't have had anything at all. You're far from twenty-one. Besides that, ain't your father been through enough?"

She sat back and slammed her hands against the steering wheel. "My father? What about me? Haven't I been through enough? I think if I want a little drink now and then, why, God'll forgive me for that."

Noble took his red Chevy hat off and scratched his head, searching the horizon for clarity, for something wise or smart or even halfway charming to say to her before she took off. "Your father tell you he asked me to sing these last few Sundays at church?"

Shelby's countenance softened. Her voice was barely audible. "Yeah."

"I haven't sang at church since—"

"I know."

"Since we sang together on that Gospel Sunday."

"I said I *know*."

"Be nice if maybe—"

"Buckle up, Eustace." She threw the truck into reverse and floored it out of the driveway, kicking up dirt and gravel so Noble had to shield his face. "I know what you're gonna say, and I ain't singing with you again, Noble Burden. You can forget that! I ain't never singing again!" She hollered at him and kept hollering at him until he couldn't see the truck anymore.

Noble had once enjoyed playing his guitar for the youth group and occasionally the whole congregation back when he and Eustace and Mama still attended. He'd loved playing while Shelby sang, too, watching the way the old hymns roused even the most elderly or inattentive person in the sanctuary. Besides that, there was something about knowing those same chords had been echoing across the same ceiling for so many generations, the way even Eustace's head bobbed steady to the mostly quarter- and three-quarter-time rhythms.

When they were little boys, Mama'd taken great care to straighten his and Eustace's bow ties, tears streaming down her face as Dad slept on, unwilling, as always, to go. The Sunday school teachers told stories of ancient, robed heroes, the droopy felt characters straightening to life as they smoothed them into place on felt boards. He'd been so eager to stick the baby Moses in the felt weeds along the felt river, or felt palm leaves on the road into Jerusalem, or Jesus onto the smiling donkey. It had been a safe place for Noble, the ritual of fruit juice and animal crackers, Mrs. Bennington and her nylon hose and dress and the smell of drugstore perfume , and the paste on sticks as they made their crafts, which Mama stuck on the refrigerator in vain. Sometimes her efforts to make the lessons stick with them worked, the ones Noble felt mattered anyway, about not stealing or killing and honoring your mama and caring for the least of these like a broken brother when all you want to do is leave. And the part about not committing adultery, which in a strange way helped ease the sting of their father leaving, since he'd broken that commandment clean through. At least God would be mad at him too for that one.

The Gospel Sunday Noble'd mentioned was the third of its kind at Sycamore Community Church. He and Shelby and a handful of other kids from the youth group had gone to a summer camp a few years back and learned a bunch of old gospel songs. There was something about the old-fashioned harmony and the vintage lyrics of songs like "Down to the River to Pray" or "I'll Fly Away" that made them want to share what they'd learned with the congregation. No one else had her voice, the ability to harmonize with Noble without either of them having to try. He doubted there was an eye that wasn't glistening when she sang, her voice rivaling Carrie Underwood's, in his opinion. Everyone enjoyed the event so much they decided to make Gospel Sunday happen more often, every couple of months, in fact. And the last one had been the Sunday before Shelby's mom died in the wreck.

Noble had stood across the casket from her and Reverend Horton at the graveside service, seen the tears on her face, her shoulders shivering from the cold rain falling around the tent. He had vowed that day to always look after her, but their friendship had grown awkward after that. Instead of pulling closer to the ones who loved her most, she'd started distancing herself from most anything that resembled her life before the accident. No more singing, no more of her old girlfriends. She'd started dressing in tight clothes that were too revealing. She'd started running around with Cade and his group of losers. It was as if she wanted to pretend like her life with her mama around never existed. The only thing she seemed to still have room for was making sure Eustace got to and from work.

Back inside, Mama sat at the table with a fresh cup of coffee and an unfolded copy of the *Sycamore Daily Ledger*. She read out loud the headline about the closing of the church. "Wow. I didn't know it was getting that bad."

"Yeah. Reverend Horton was at the Onion last night and told me a little about it. Asked me to play at the last three services." He poured himself a cup of coffee and sat down at the table with her.

"Did he now?" She looked over the newspaper at him.

"Figured I'd help him out. Must be rough, losing everything you've worked for. Raising Shelby without his wife. I feel bad for the guy."

Laurie sighed and refolded the paper, then gazed out the window in the direction of the Hortons' place. "Me too. . . . Speaking of which, how are things with you and Shelby?"

"Same, I guess."

"Give her time. She'll get back to her old self."

"I don't know. She seems so . . . out there." Noble shook his head and turned the cup of coffee in his hands. He looked into her eyes. "Pain changes people so. Changed her. Changed the reverend. Changed you."

She ran her hand through the hair she used to use to hide the bruises Dad left on her face, pushed back her chair, and went to the kitchen sink. "Yes, I suppose it has."

"Why?"

Noble watched his mama wash a white bowl she'd used to make a cherry pie the night before. She rubbed and rubbed at the rosy stains. "Time doesn't always heal things, 'specially when someone dies . . . or leaves. Makes you feel like you can't go back to the way things were. And you can't, really. Like trying to get creek water back that's already run on past."

"Reverend Horton sure won't have much left now that his church is shuttin' down."

"Maybe not. But sometimes when God takes away, you end up with more than you had to start with."

"That's not what's happened with us."

She bowed her head and rubbed her temples. "I know."

He thought about Cass Dinsmore and Nashville and the faintest of hopes that maybe whatever he had to offer could get them all out of Sycamore. Maybe this was finally the plan, the future God had for him. There might be opportunities for all of them in Nashville—better support for Eustace, less hard work for Mama. He could bring in enough money to support them and pay the bills on time for once. "Don't you ever wonder if God has more for you, Mama? More for us?"

She straightened and crossed her arms. "I stopped wondering that a long time ago. I got all I could ever want and all I care to handle right here in this house. And in the fields and the barn out there. Ain't nothing more for me in this world besides what we can see in front of us."

Noble took the jar with the small blue butterfly, flat and lifeless, and set it on the desk next to the rest of Eustace's collection. He poked at the box of pins that would soon be used to dry and set and mount it next to the rest of the specimens.

There's gotta be more than this, he thought to himself and headed back to his room, where he picked up his guitar and plopped down cross-legged on his bed. He sorted through and plucked out the chords for songs he thought he might play at the Onion, a couple more he thought he might play if he really went to Nashville, before pulling out a couple of familiar church songs to play on Sunday at the service.

From downstairs, he heard the door to Mama's sewing room shut. The walls were thin. Her machine began to whir and pause, whir and pause. He pictured her as she turned and worked the fabric of whatever project she was working on and wondered if she had really been telling him the truth or if she was settling for the little she thought she was worth.

15

Noble and Eustace finished in the barn Sunday morning with just enough time before the service to clean up and stop at the Percolator for coffee and donuts and a Sunday version of the *Indianapolis Star* with all the coupons Mama liked to collect. As they drove toward town, the corn and bean fields alternated and gave way to ranch homes and then the high school, then Main Street and the square, lined by boxy buildings with chippy, forlorn architectural details that had once made them look distinguished in their day. Sunday mornings felt like a farm convention at the Percolator, one of the few times during the week the beef farmers mingled with crop farmers and swine farmers with chicken farmers and dairy farmers, the only noticeable difference between them the seed or tractor logo on their caps. Otherwise they all had the same dirt on their boots, halfway up their knees, drying and cracking and crumbling off onto the tile floor as they slapped their knees in laughter or shook them out of nervousness as they spoke about the latest market prices or crop developments or governmental subsidy battle raging at the state assembly.

Noble got a carryout order of donuts and coffee, and the three of them sat shoulder to shoulder across the front bench seat of the pickup as they drove down Main Street toward the church. Noble glanced at Eustace, poking at a video game on his smartphone. "Turn that thing on silent before we go in so at least no one will hear you playing with it, 'kay?"

Eustace didn't take his eyes off the screen in his hand as he lolled out of the truck after Noble parked.

"Okay?" Noble asked again, a little louder.

"Turn it off, Eustace," Mama said.

Noble couldn't remember the last time he'd seen Mama in a dress, and he admired the way the pretty floral cotton had transformed her from the disheveled, worn-looking woman who sat at her sewing machine or worked in the garden or barns most of the day to someone younger he hardly recognized. As she walked ahead of them, he smelled the scent of lavender shampoo in her blonde hair, which shone in the sun.

The three of them walked up the steps of the church. The wrought-iron railing wriggled in its crumbling concrete base, the steps craggy from another season of ice and thaw and salt sprinkled on them. The parking lot held a few more late-model cars than usual, no doubt because of the news of the closing, since plenty of folks were way more interested in local gossip than the gospel.

"Take your hat off, Eustace." Noble elbowed him as they entered the gathering space.

Mama and Eustace picked their old spot in the back row of the church and Noble carried his guitar case to the front. The reverend had called him yesterday and explained the song set, which he'd be playing along with Mrs. Worley on the organ. "Praise to the Lord, the Almighty" would be the call to worship. In the chancel, Bonnie Thompson straightened an arrangement of altar flowers: a spray of sunflowers, tiger lilies, and daisies. Myrtle Worley sat at the organ filing her nails. Adam Russell, who had taught him music and history in high school, straightened the Bibles, hymnals, and offering cards in the pews. Before folks began arriving, they had time to run through the songs three times, and Noble was careful to keep eye contact with Mrs. Worley and let her lead. Wasn't anything worse for a guitarist than a passive-aggressive pianist—or in this case, organist—and he wasn't about to give her reason to resent him or feel like he was intruding on her stage.

Noble recognized nearly everyone who came that morning. Old friends of his grandparents sat near the front, and behind them the Orwells, Crawfords, the Howards, Stuart Granger and his wife, the Baileys, and Sheriff Tate and his family. And Julie Shaw, editor of the paper.

Shelby sat in the front on the far side, pressed against the arm of the pew as she stared into her phone. As much as she drove him crazy, he wasn't about to give up on her. Not yet. Not even with the small hope of Nashville now. He ached for the time they'd shared, for the way they could simply sit and look at each other and without saying a word know that all the world was right. When she did look up at him, he winked at her. She blushed and focused quick back on her phone.

"Welcome to Sycamore Community Church," Reverend Horton said from behind the pulpit. "It's a fine day to be together and worship the Lord. Let's start by greeting whoever's sitting around you."

The congregants obeyed and shook hands and grinned and laughed amongst themselves.

"You may have seen the headline in the paper," Reverend Horton began. All the coughing, throat clearing, and bulletin crinkling quieted, like a child about to be scolded, allowing the words to travel over the parishioners scattered sparsely in the pews. "After today, we'll have two more services left before we're forced to shut our doors."

Many heads nodded.

Reverend Horton appeared to Noble to be on the verge of tears, something Noble imagined was unusual for him from the way the parishioners shifted uncomfortably in their pews.

"Since I've been here . . ." Horton fumbled for words and gripped the sides of the pulpit to steady himself. "I've been here twenty-some years now, and never before have I . . ."

From his spot, Noble could see tears running freely down

Horton's face, ruddy with emotion. He held the pulpit as if steadying himself, then hung his head. "I'm sorry . . ." The words seemed to Noble to be for a larger failure than breaking down in that moment. Mike Crawford, Rich Orwell, then Greg Howard got up from their seats and walked up beside Horton, who'd backed away from the pulpit.

Hank Thompson approached the microphone.

"Don't let 'em close us down." Lizzie Bailey's voice quaked as she stood to deliver her plea from a few rows back. Her husband, Dan, tugged at her sleeve in a vain effort to get her to sit back down. As the town beautician, she was not a person whom anyone, and certainly not her husband, could keep quiet.

"Don't let 'em, Rev."

Noble couldn't identify the man's voice ringing out from a pew across the room.

George Kernodle sat with his arms crossed in the second row, his wife, Susan, sitting stoic, expressionless, next to him, and their two teenage daughters next to her, eyes focused on their smartphones. Several more congregant pleas and offers of support rippled across the room before Hank rapped on the pulpit gently to regain everyone's attention.

"It's okay, everyone. Calm down a minute." Hank looked back at Horton, who nodded approvingly and wiped his nose with a handkerchief. "What the reverend was trying to say is he—we all—have been feeling the strain of decreased attendance the last few years, this year in particular. The elders have long been meeting and praying to try to find the Lord's leading in trying anything and everything to keep this church from dying."

"Alright now," someone hollered.

"Tell us more."

James stepped up to the pulpit again, his face as red as ever. "I think the best thing to do would be to introduce George Kernodle. He knows the details of the state of the church and why ultimately this had to happen. George?"

Noble watched a look of horror flash across Kernodle's face, followed by a flushing of his jowly cheeks. His features hardened as he hoisted his huge body up to the pulpit, and he pulled a handkerchief out of his pocket and wiped the back of his neck and forehead.

"Thank you, Reverend." Kernodle paused and scanned the people in the pews before him. "I'm afraid it's true. We've done everything we could to help the past few years, but it's come down to closing. The bank was generous in its loans and low interest rates, but at the end of the day, the board . . . the bank . . ."

He crumpled into a fit of coughing, and Noble was sure the corpulent man was going to have a heart attack right in the chancel. Greg produced a bottle of water. Kernodle nodded with appreciation and appeared to gather himself.

"As I was saying," Kernodle continued, his voice strained and belly heaving with each breath. "The bank has exhausted all its options. The building and property and contents go up for auction on Monday, September 5."

The audience gasped and whispered amongst themselves

as Kernodle waddled toward his seat but then, at the last second, turned and walked down the aisle and right on out of the church. Mrs. Kernodle, mouth open with what appeared to be horror, gathered her purse and Bible, grabbed their two daughters, and they followed hurriedly after him.

"What can we do?" Lizzie stood, voice trembling and mascara running down her face. "Surely we can do something, Rev."

"Yes, tell us. Can we save it?"

Horton returned to the pulpit, with Hank and the other elders still at his side. "We've looked at everything and every which way. There's nothing more we can do. But listen. I've been thinking. Just a few months ago, the fields around my house were bare. Not a sign of last season's crops. But today when the sun came up, the rows of corn and beans stretched green and tall for as far as I could see. Sometimes what looks like the end becomes a new season. A new day."

Noble shifted his guitar on his lap and wondered if Horton might break down again. The crowd seemed intent, focused on every word. In the back of the church he could see that Eustace had resumed playing a game on his phone. Noble felt out of sorts being there as an onlooker to such a seemingly major event, like a Peeping Tom in on a family meeting.

"In John 12:24 Jesus said that unless a grain of wheat is planted and dies, it remains only a single seed. Alone. But if it dies—"

His voice echoed across the room, through the rafters.

"If—it—dies—"

He paused.

"Its death will produce many new seeds. It will bear much fruit. It will produce large crops."

This was the Reverend Horton Noble remembered. His presence filled the room as much as his voice, each syllable building pressure waiting to be released. Reminded Noble of storms blowing into town, the ones that sent you running through the house to open windows to even out the pressure.

"The doors of this building may close, but the doors of the Kingdom, no one, no bank, nothing can keep those gates from closing. So while this is not what any of us want, I have to trust—we have to trust—that the Lord has greater plans for those of us who are losing a building. That he has greater plans for this town. Because he is bigger than a building. He is more sure than bricks and mortar. He cannot be shaken, though the ground give way and the earth may tremble—though we may tremble. He is here, in the midst of this . . . of us."

"Go on," Lizzie Bailey said.

"Alright now," Jersha Pittman said.

Noble watched as with each phrase Reverend Horton stood taller, appeared more confident.

"Isaiah 54:10 says, '"For the mountains may move and the hills disappear, but even then my faithful love for you will remain. My covenant of blessing will never be broken," says the Lord, who has mercy on you.'" Horton turned to Noble and Mrs. Worley. "'Jesus My Lord'?"

They answered him with a nod, and Mrs. Worley mouthed, *Key of C* to Noble. He adjusted his guitar, and when she nodded, they began to play.

"Stand with me now, will you?" Horton said, lifting his arms.

Noble strummed the opening chords, and as he did, he wondered if God had bigger plans for his life, too, and if Cass Dinsmore was more than a chance meeting, but something God might finally have that was going to be good for him. He exhaled the words to the song, feeling them as he hadn't in a long, long while:

"Have you seen Jesus my Lord?
He's here in plain view."

Noble watched Shelby fiddle with her phone screen as she and the rest of the parishioners stood, joining in slowly, until eventually their voices rose in unison. Surely she knew she belonged up here with him. She had to remember how good they'd been singing together. She had to.

"Take a look, open your eyes,
He'll show it to you."

Noble crooned into the microphone, and when he looked toward Shelby again, she glanced quick away, and he could see a flush color her cheeks. He grinned and sang on.

"Have you ever looked at the sunset
With the sky mellowing red,
And the clouds suspended like feathers?"

That morning, he had been taken with the way the sunrise had colored the sky above the farm in much the same way as this song described, the clouds suspended, the trees, the breeze, everything more hushed than usual. Even the cows had been more docile as they moseyed in from their spots on the quiet pasture.

"Then I say . . .
You've seen Jesus my Lord."

Noble felt tears prick at his eyes and feelings he hadn't realized were wound so tight inside him began to unravel. Memories of holding palm branches on Easter morning flashed through his mind, of coaching Eustace down the aisle next to him, of Christmas candlelight service, of Mrs. Bennington telling them about the Resurrection while beading key-chain crosses, of a whole week of vacation Bible school and filling a chart with gold stars for every verse he recited by heart, of the smell of hair gel Mama used to slick his and Eustace's unruly hair to the side and how she'd rubbed the scuffs out of their school shoes with polish, and the feel of the hardcover Bible in his arms.

In the chaos of Dad's rage and beatings, church had been a sanctuary, a home away from home, a place where kindness smoothed his unruly heart and rubbed the scuffs off his soul, if only for a morning. The rest of the week, if he thought about God, it was often an argument, and he wondered what his Sunday school teachers might think of the way he talked back to God, the way he shook his fist at him when Dad beat on Mama; the way he told God *he better protect Eustace.*

It was in these conversations that Noble felt God taking his punches and then embracing him like a boxing coach. It was in the wrestling and holding tight and trying to pin him down that Noble had come to know God as true, though he still had a hard time trusting him.

After the service, Mama and Eustace waited near the chancel while he put his music and guitar away. "Thanks for coming, Mama."

Instinctively he placed his hand on Eustace's upper arm as they walked down the center aisle of the church toward the doors where Reverend Horton still stood shaking hands with folks as they left.

"Thanks for playing on such short notice, Noble."

Noble took his outstretched hand. "Thanks for asking. Still want me next week?"

"If it's no trouble, we sure would."

"No trouble at all."

"And, Laurie, so good to see you and Eustace here. I've missed you both in your spot in the back row."

Noble thought Mama looked a little flustered but only for a second before she straightened, shook the reverend's hand for a moment so brief it bordered on rude, and hurried down the steps.

Noble still had his hand on Eustace's arm when Shelby brushed by him and began to whisper in her father's ear. The sweet smell of her still-damp hair undid him until Eustace's movement toward the steps distracted him.

"See you next week, Reverend." Noble looked into Shelby's eyes as he said this and would not, if he could help it, let her look away.

16

Monday, James took his lunch to the park across from the church as he often did when the weather was nice. From there he could see the courthouse, the Percolator, the Fleurish flower shop, and the gas station. He sat in the gazebo, which smelled of fresh paint, and he munched on a peanut butter and marshmallow sandwich, something Molly had introduced him to. He'd made fun of the concoction—even more so when she called it a "fluffernutter"—but now it felt like comfort food. Raleigh Cox filled his car with gas while Ella adjusted her makeup in the passenger-side mirror. A gaggle of kids in cutoffs and flip-flops—if he had to guess, he'd say they were in middle school—went into the station and emerged several minutes later with Slim Jims tucked in their back pockets and cups full of slushies.

Truth be told, James wasn't sure he believed a word anymore of what he'd said during his sermon the day before. Maybe God couldn't be shaken, but he sure could. He preached what his head knew to be true, even as his heart struggled very much to reconcile the Jesus who saved with the Jesus who let Molly and then his congregation die, and the Jesus who let Silas and Cade Canady flash their fancy cars through town with the Jesus who let lonely, hardworking Frank Whitmore's power go out.

The trouble with being a pastor these days was that he was human, and quite possibly a worse human being than many who sat in the pews in front of him. To be sure, Jesus guaranteed they'd have trouble in this world, but James didn't have to like it.

At least he would not have to worry about being publicly ambivalent about these things once the church closed. But in the meantime, James felt like he had a terminal disease, that everything involving the church was a countdown until it was the last time he'd do it: last lunch in the park; last prayer time in the sanctuary; last time he'd hear the clock behind his desk chime; last time he'd say, "Mornin', Bonnie," as she came and brought him coffee and the morning paper from Indianapolis. And then the last time he'd shut and lock the door of Sycamore Community Church.

What now, Lord?

He strained to hear a whisper of hope or peace or for

something to fall from the sky and land on his head to tell him what direction to go. Verses that usually clogged his mind were absent. Not a thought, not even the thump of his heart—which he felt, along with a slight bit of nausea, each time he envisioned turning off the lights, putting his key in the old latch for the last time, then dropping it off at the bank for George Kernodle. He pulled out a package of antacids he'd been keeping regularly now in his pocket and winced at the chalky taste. He stretched, hoping to alleviate the ache in his gut and wondered if the ache wasn't a Molly-size hole in his heart he'd never ventured near enough to fill, except with busyness and the needs of his congregants, however few.

He pulled a golden apple from the bottom of his lunch bag and took a bite. Across the park, Susan Roberts, dressed in a pencil skirt and a lightweight blouse that hugged her shape in the breeze, walked into Fleurish. He and Susan dated briefly about a year ago. He was several years her senior. She was widowed, her husband a Marine who'd died in Afghanistan. They'd gotten along fine enough. Susan had made him and Shelby dinner after church on Sundays. He took her into Lafayette on a couple of Fridays for the latest movie. She'd been more than patient with him, until the night they'd gone all the way to Indianapolis for the symphony. Afterward, he'd pulled up to the curb in front of her home to drop her off.

"Well?" she'd said, leaning against the inside of the car door with apparently no inclination to open it.

"Well, what?" He'd honestly had no idea at the time.

"Are you gonna kiss me, or what? It's not a sin to kiss a woman who's a widow, you know. Might do you a bit of good."

He'd looked at her, dumbfounded, feeling like a middle schooler on a bike with no brakes—a feeling he knew, in fact, because his mama'd bought him one at a garage sale not knowing it was broken until he'd taken it to the fishing hole and landed in the lake after it had careened down the hill and he'd been unable to stop. Six stitches to his head and a cast on his arm for the rest of the summer. He rubbed the place on his forehead where the skin was forever puckered from the scar.

"James, did you hear what I said? We've been keeping company for months now, and I understand you are a gentleman with a reputation to maintain. But I am not without passion, and I don't believe you are either."

"No . . ."

"Then what are we doin'?"

He looked at Susan then, perhaps the most intently he had in the few months they'd been seeing each other. At least he thought that's what they'd been doing, seeing each other. She was beautiful, in her early thirties with a great figure she maintained by running five miles every morning out to the old covered bridge and back. She'd tried to get him to join her, but he was well aware of his physical limitations and had refused. Her hair was the color of honey and near drove him crazy when she wore it up in a messy bun, and she had legs that could, as Jack McGee had said, launch a thousand ships.

Now that he thought about it, he really didn't know why he hadn't kissed her yet. He and Molly had kissed all the time, and the sex—well, they'd had that every chance they could and then some. So he knew he was not necessarily a celibate sort of man. But he also realized, as he watched Susan's breath steam up the inside of the front window that evening, that he'd buried that part of himself out on Mill Run Road in the cemetery on the hill along with Molly, that somewhere in his subconscious he'd determined that because he'd failed to keep her as Molly's father predicted he would, he would never again deserve to keep anyone else, whether physically or matrimonially. It was as if he'd finished that volume of his life and shut it tight.

He'd put both hands on the steering wheel and watched the bugs fly into the fluorescent light of the lamp at the corner of Susan's street. "I guess I don't really know."

Susan had let out a long sigh before pulling open her door and getting out. She shut it gently and walked around to his side of the car. He rolled down his window, and she leaned over and rested her elbows on the door. "You can't let yourself die along with her, James. Shelby deserves more. Heck, you deserve more. Try listening to some of your own sermons for a change. There's a time and season for everything."

He turned toward her, intending to tell her he was sorry, to try to explain, but he didn't have a chance. She grabbed his face and pulled him toward her and kissed him firmly. When she pulled back, she wiped the lipstick off his lips the way a mother would wipe jelly off her son's face. "I'll see you around, James."

She turned and he watched her walk up the steps to her house, and as he did, he regretted not touching her, mostly because he knew now he'd never have the chance again.

>>>> ————— <<<<

James tossed his paper lunch bag into the rusty metal can and avoided the cracks in the sidewalk as he walked back to the church. As he approached the old brick building, he regarded it closer than he had in a long time.

When James and Molly moved there to take the position of the popular Pastor Tilly, the congregation had numbered in the three hundreds, which made for really nice potlucks and holiday celebrations and made things like a children's ministry—rather than just a babysitting hour—possible. The building had in fact a half-dozen Sunday school rooms, and one side of the basement had a special teen room painted purple and electric blue with a red-and-white checkerboard tiled floor reminiscent of a set from *Saved by the Bell*. Now only one room was used for infants and fussy children, or more often, for Myrtle Worley to pat her upper lip and dry her armpits while she waited for James to finish his sermon, after which she would play her closing hymn.

James knew of this habit of Myrtle's because Shelby had stumbled in on her one time when she'd come in to retrieve a diaper for someone with a newborn. They'd both been more than startled, because Myrtle was standing in front of the window air conditioner, her dress unzipped and hanging on her wide hips, her arms extended like Christ himself. She'd nearly had a fit of apoplexy trying to pull the dress back up when she heard Shelby come in, and for weeks neither had been able to look the other in the eye.

A mourning dove sat on the edge of the bell tower, which hadn't worked since well before he'd arrived there. He mimicked the dove's cry and grinned as it sang back to him again, "Who-WHOOOO-who-who-who-who."

"Who, indeed," James said aloud. Who was he, and who was he to become?

"Hey there, Rev."

The voice came from the park as he was about to cross the street to the church. He turned and saw Dr. Tom Lawson coming toward him. He recognized then that Tom's youngest son and a friend were playing in the park.

James extended his hand. "Good to see you, Tom. Nice day to spend here."

"It is."

Instead of letting go of his hand, Tom kept hold of it and grabbed James's arm. "Haven't had a chance to talk to you about the closing. Angie and I are real sorry. Is there anything we can do?"

He considered how Tom and Angie, though they hadn't been around the church much recently, had donated so much—money, yes, but beyond that, too. Angie had led so many Sunday school programs, and both of them had been key parents for the youth. And of course they'd supported him and Shelby after Molly's accident. "You've done so much already, Tom. Heck, if it weren't for your generosity, we'd have closed a long time ago."

Tom watched the boys play catch in the grassy part of the park. "I'm sorry we stopped coming to services."

"It's alright."

"Let me explain. The walls, they felt like they were closing in on us. Angie, especially. She needed space, someplace away from the church where she felt constantly guilty about Sara Beth."

James's eyes widened, then narrowed with concern. He knew that Tom's oldest daughter, Sara Beth, had been the talk of the town a year ago when she'd given birth to a baby girl and no father had been identified. She was nearly the same age as Shelby; they'd been in many classes together over the years. Teenage pregnancy in Sycamore was not an anomaly—on the contrary, many girls brought their children to their graduation ceremonies. But it was an anomaly for one of the Lawson children. Tom was a successful cardiologist and one of the doctors who had invested the most in a new hospital in Lafayette, so he had more to spend than most, if not all, the residents of the town. Angie was a stay-at-home mom. Their house was a restored nineteenth-century beauty, a three-story Georgian brick building with original architectural detailing in crisp white, with black shutters and a wraparound porch they'd added. For generations it had been the first house anyone saw coming into

Sycamore, the last house folks saw when they left, and the one house everyone envied. Tom and Angie were envied too, walking up the sidewalk to church with their six children like stairsteps following them into the sanctuary. The children sat still, unusually still compared to most of the other children in attendance.

"Did someone say something to you? To her?"

Tom turned to face James, looking hard into his eyes. "No, no, it was nothing like that. Nothing that hadn't been happening around town already. There were—still are—the disapproving stares, rumors, the usual. But as far as church goes, we haven't felt able to go anywhere since she had the baby."

"You haven't gone to church anywhere?" He thought for sure they'd been going to Higher Ground.

"Angie can't bring herself to go. She thinks everyone knows about Sara and that everyone thinks we failed."

"But that's ridiculous."

"Is it? Think about it, James. Where and in what church is it really okay to be broken anymore? Especially around here? We could go to Higher Ground and try to be anonymous, but that wouldn't last long before people start asking questions. And then once they know, well . . . the staring starts all over again."

James rubbed his temples and searched for something to say. An image of Professor Wilcox flashed through his mind, referring over and over again as he had throughout James's training to Ezekiel 34. Pastors are supposed to go after the lost sheep of their flock, to find the ones who wandered. He'd been so wrapped up in grieving Molly, in trying in vain to pick up the pieces of his and Shelby's lives, that he'd left his flock to fend for themselves. He was supposed to strengthen the weak and bind up the injured. He was supposed to search for the ones who were scattered. "I'm so sorry I never came looking for you all."

"You could have come, and sure, there were times I did wonder why you didn't at least call. But, James, you lost your wife. And besides that, no one in their right mind can blame only you for the hundreds of reasons—valid or crazy—that people have left this church over the years. Anyway, if you'd tried to convince me and Ang to come back, we wouldn't have listened. I'm not saying we'll never go back to church, but right now we need to shelter ourselves and get through this the best we can."

James straightened and looked hard into Tom's eyes. "This church might be dying and part of me along with it. But I'm still enough of a pastor to tell you that you are not supposed to go through what y'all are going through alone. Not you, not Angie, and especially not Sara Beth."

Tom looked out at the two boys playing baseball and sighed.

Smack went the ball into one glove.

Thwack went the ball into the other.

"If only it were that simple." Tom seemed to be measuring his words for a moment, the red-and-yellow merry-go-round spinning in front of them. "I imagine the two of us aren't much different, really, feeling like we let down the people we love most."

"Maybe so. But that doesn't mean we can't start doing better." James just wished he knew how.

17

Noble flipped Cass Dinsmore's business card between his fingers, still red from the usual scrubbing he gave the barns and machines after milking. He pictured Dinsmore at the Onion the night they met: expensive clothes with pressed, tailored pants; hair styled with "product," as Mama would've said; and those shoes. When you've never had fancy shoes—or any without mud and manure on them—shoes are the first thing that make an outsider stick out. He'd bet money on Dinsmore living in a suburb. The guy probably lived in one of those mansions with cool clean tile under his feet after a shower, a giant flat-screen TV hanging above a fancy trimmed-out fireplace, a three- or maybe even four-car garage. He imagined a swimming pool with manicured grass and edged sidewalks instead of his own gravel drive, which bled into a yard full of clover and dandelions.

Why shouldn't Noble want at least a taste of that sort of lifestyle? Too many friends he'd grown up with were stuck like him: third-, fourth-, even fifth-generation farmers, destined to produce more children who grew up to be farmers, if they weren't bought out by the big corporations or bankrupt because they couldn't compete with the farms that used GMO seeds and got GMO yields. Others lived in town, or tried to, on minimum-wage jobs at the Walmart or the TA or the big hardware store out by the interstate. Many of them seemed happy enough, but they probably had no idea what they were missing. Didn't know how to dream. Didn't even consider they might have a choice.

Now here was his chance, about as likely as winning the lottery, but real just the same. To make a living playing music, he knew that'd mean selling the farm. There was no way Mama and Eustace could run it for long without him, no matter how strong Eustace was and no matter how well trained the cows were. But what would be so bad about that? Surely they'd get over it and eventually Eustace would forget about the cows; his mama would be grateful for intact countertops and clean, new carpet and easy access to the grocery. He already felt so bone tired. Not yet twenty years old, and his hips ached when he finally lay down at night. His knees cracked in the morning when he woke. How was he supposed to till the fields, bale the hay, raise cows up and put 'em down, watch over a brother who was supposed to be watching over him if nature had worked the way it was supposed to, and do all the other work their father abandoned him to, for the rest of his life? Why didn't God birth him into a family that was more predictable, in one of those suburbs where folks got up every day and went to work and got paid time off and sick days, with a small perennial garden to tend, where the worst problems folks had were aphids on their container tomatoes and a tick on the butt of their house dog?

He caught himself imagining more and more often walking the neon-lit streets and playing the smoky bars of Nashville he'd seen on the Internet. When his fingers touched the guitar strings, when his wrist moved to the rhythm of a song, something happened within him, like the notes spelled freedom and he ached to sing out that word until his lungs burst— something milking cows day in and day out never came close to. It's not that he was naive enough to believe music wouldn't be work, too, that the recording life would never become repetitive and the people he'd meet there would be perfect. He'd spent his whole life working, so he wasn't about to pretend any career would come without sweat and the digging in of a shoulder to the wheel of it. But at least there'd be music in Nashville. And more than that, it'd be his choice.

He sat on the front porch steps and kicked some of the manure off the bottoms of his boots. In front of him was a field of corn taller than his shoulders. The breeze blew the tassels so they looked like the waves and swells of an ocean, and he imagined casting a boat out across it as he dialed the Nashville phone number. His stomach clenched as he waited for Cass Dinsmore to pick up.

"Cass Dinsmore's office. This is Michelle. How can I help you?" The woman on the other end of the line sounded kind, put-together, successful.

Noble cleared his throat. "Uh, hi. My name's Noble Burden and—"

"Mr. Burden, of course. Mr. Dinsmore's been hoping you'd call. Can I put you on hold for a moment?"

"Sure." A couple of swallows chirped and chased each other up and through the branches of the walnut tree that stood between the house and the road. In the pasture behind him, he heard the cows lowing.

"Mr. Burden!" The man's voice boomed on the other end of the line.

"Mr. Dinsmore?"

"Hey, I've been looking forward to your call. Say, what would you think about coming down to Nashville and playing for a few folks? I have a couple of bands looking for a guitarist. A couple of record labels, too."

Noble's stomach clenched, and he tried not to sound too excited, too desperate. "When would you want me to come?"

"How's next week sound? Say, Thursday morning? We'll pay for a flight from Indianapolis and for your hotel accommodations, of course, so you can fly in on Wednesday. My assistant will e-mail you about those arrangements."

"Next Thursday?" A week and a half. He considered

whether that'd give him time to settle Whitmore's herd and find someone to help Mama and Eustace milk. That would cut it close. But who was he to argue? "That's great. Yeah. Thank you, Mr. Dinsmore. Thank you so much."

"Noble, please, call me Cass. And you're welcome. It's not often I see such natural talent as yours."

"Thank you."

He ended the call and jumped as high as he could off the front porch and hollered until Mama ran outside, followed by the familiar creak of the screen door behind her. He'd be sure to add oiling the door to his list of things to do before he left.

"What is it? What's happened?"

"They wanna hear me play! They're bringing me to Nashville to hear me play!"

She cocked her head, clearly confused.

In that instant Noble remembered he hadn't told her anything about Cass Dinsmore. There was no getting around it now. "Last week, there was a scouter from Nashville at the Onion."

"Yeah?" Mama said, looking skeptical. She shifted her weight and crossed her arms. Never a good sign.

"He told me to call him. I just got off the phone with him."

"Nashville? As in Tennessee? You want to go play in Nashville?"

Worry rose in her voice, the sort Noble had found in the past was difficult to calm. "It's only for a visit for me to see what it's like and for a couple of his friends to hear me play."

"Noble—"

"Mama. It's my dream. You know I love the guitar. You said yourself you wished I didn't have to stay around here. 'Sides, what if Nashville has something for all of us?"

"Me and Eustace in Nashville? You gotta be kiddin'." She laughed, a high-pitched sound that meant anything else Noble said would be counted as ridiculous.

"They say I have talent."

"I know you have talent. The whole town and half this side of Indiana knows that. I don't know what's so wrong with you using it here."

"Really, Mama? Here? You don't know what's wrong with just here?"

"Here works, Noble. Works for me. Works for Eustace. Works for you, too, if you'd learn to accept the fact we can't leave."

"And you know that for sure?"

"What?"

"That we can't leave? You know that's not ever gonna be possible? How do you know that, Mama, if you ain't never left here yourself?"

She stepped back and tensed. He knew he'd crossed the line, and while she never had struck either of her sons, he could tell she was fixing for this to be the first time. Still, he couldn't help himself.

"If we don't have to scoop manure the rest of our lives, wouldn't you like to know that? At least know it for sure?"

18

Sometimes James ran into his congregants by happenstance, like Tom Lawson at the park. Others sought him out as the day neared for the church to close.

Stephen and Olive Lee lived out on the two-lane highway in a ranch home, their front yard filled with every sort of concrete sculpture and yard ornament imaginable. James knew this because he and Molly and Shelby had been out there for dinner years back. The displays were such a spectacle that cars rear-ended each other regularly as drivers rubbernecked or took photos with their cell phones. James ran into Olive at the dentist's office, where she'd peered at him uncomfortably for some time over the top of a *People* magazine. When the hygienist called her name, she'd paused before going back and said in front of the half a dozen others in the waiting room, "It was the music, you know."

"Pardon me?" he'd said.

"The day you let that boy onstage with the guitar was the day Stephen and I knew the devil had arrived. It's a good thing that church is closing. Ain't no room in Sycamore for a church of the devil."

George and Clara Bogan, whom he only vaguely remembered because Clara had been one of Shelby's teachers in grade school, wrote him a letter telling him they'd left a long time ago when James had decided to quit wearing the heavy black robe and began wearing khaki pants and a sport coat. "We couldn't bring ourselves to stay in a place where the pastor is so egotistical he feels he can disrobe in front of his congregants," they'd said.

Frank and Viola Dean had stopped James in the condiment aisle of the IGA to explain why they'd left. Frank occupied himself studying the various brands of pickles while Viola, dressed in a purple housecoat with a single pink foam curler on the front of her head, had leaned in close to him, patted his hand, and whispered, "There's always been too many old people in the church. We couldn't stand being around all those old people. They're all sitting there waiting to die. The church was dying with 'em. We needed some pep, didn't we, Frank?"

Frank had placed a jar of kosher pickles in the cart and rolled his eyes apologetically at James after Viola continued on toward the mayonnaise.

Others, like Jack McGee, gave James hope that not all his years at Sycamore Community Church had been in vain.

Jack McGee had invited James out to his trailer to talk about the church closing over some apple pie, to which James had happily agreed. Truth be told, McGee's church attendance tenure had peaked on three consecutive Sundays: the one when he got saved, the next week when he got baptized, and the following week, as Jack had said, "to seal the deal." After that, Jack came sporadically and then hardly at all, although the two of them met regularly at the Percolator or the Onion or the TA out by the interstate. Jack was only an honorary elder, the others agreeing to the status after James had convinced them it'd do them good to have a unique, outside perspective.

James stepped up the ramp to his old friend's trailer home. Far enough from town that it wouldn't be an eyesore, but close enough to walk to, Jack's trailer was one of about a dozen set up on blocks and divided into two sections by a gravel drive running through the middle. The piece of land the trailer park occupied was admittedly pretty, set in a shady dell with giant oaks and cottonwoods creating a shelter overarching them. It was almost as if nature somehow figured if life wouldn't give the folks there the solid shelter they needed, maybe it could. He noticed the sound of a stray cicada, a couple of feral cats wrapping themselves seductively around the cinder blocks beneath the trailers, and birds flitting and chirping in the branches above. Thistles, tall with full purple blooms, and fat, fuzzy carpenter bees buzzing and pausing occasionally to sip nectar, framed the sides of the trailer.

James felt sweat run down his back, the sun and humidity already sweltering even before noon. Rust stains resembling the path of tears down a ragged face striped the sides of all the trailers and Jack's in particular. The whole trailer rattled as he knocked on the door and more so when he heard the uneven thump of Jack's gait moving toward the door.

"Morning, Rev."

Years before he'd tried insisting Jack call him James, but he never had. He followed Jack into the hole of a home, which reminded him of a Hobbit's without the charm—low ceilings, cramped and dark. One couch, a crooked bookshelf, and a TV on a metal stand that appeared to have been acquired from a 1980s high school audio-visual department were smashed against two of the walls. Veterans' magazines and Louis L'Amour novels lined the shelves, along with a few others by Brad Thor and the worn copy of *Mere Christianity* James had given him at one of their coffee shop meetings. He was happy to see that the book was thick around the edges from frequent flipping.

James sat on the ragged couch and rubbed his knees as Jack rifled around in the kitchenette. When he returned, he handed James a mason jar, and James realized that the apple pie McGee was referring to was homemade moonshine. He should have known.

"Just for you, Rev. Take a nip. It'll take the edge off all this talk of the church dying." He sat next to James and took a long sip from the liquid in a faded NAPA Auto Parts store mug. "I'm real sorry 'bout the church."

James thought about replying with what had become his standard, "Yeah, me too," but the words didn't come. He felt the moonshine warming his head already.

"You're prob'ly wonderin' why I asked to see you."

"I am." James tried to smile as he took another sip and winced as the liquid burned his throat.

"Fresh from the oven, that apple pie." Jack laughed. "Well, Rev, it's simple. All these years you been preaching to me, albeit a bit unconventionally, kept me from whackin' myself. Led me to Jesus. I figured I could at least try to give a bit of that back to you. See, the way I see it, now anyway, is the spot you're in, bein' a preacher, it's a lot like bein' a soldier."

"Oh?" James considered Frank Whitmore's plight again, how faced with losing his best milkers and watching them die, he shot them and then himself instead. He thought about the recent attention in the news given to preventing suicide in soldiers, a horror all too common among them.

"Yes sir. Preachin's got to be a lot like war. You fight for those people, you see the enemy take some down, you watch some of 'em die, help some of 'em live. You lose a part of yourself in that war, you know, the fight between the angels and demons and all they talk about in the Bible that we can't see but that are all around us fighting all the same." Jack rubbed the stump of his leg. "Aches like the devil when part of yourself goes missing. It's tough learning to find a way to live without it. . . . I'm lucky I just lost this here. Preachers lose a part of their hearts."

"I don't know that I'd compare it to all that—"

Jack held up his hand to stop him. "Now wait and hear me out. I know you're too humble a man to think preacherin' and pastorin' could be compared to a war wound. But the way I see it, it sure is."

James settled back into the couch and rested the jar of moonshine on his knee. The room seemed to tilt slightly.

"Did I tell you 'bout how I got this or rather, lost this leg?" Jack stood and hobbled on his cane to the window facing the woods behind his trailer.

"Stepped on a land mine, if I remember correctly."

"That's right. But did I tell you where I was goin' when that happened?"

"You and the other guys in your platoon were headed back to base and it was nighttime so you didn't see the mine."

Jack kept his back to James. "We were headed back to the base eventually. But we were . . . well, we were takin' a detour, you might say. We'd seen 'em that morning, on our way out to scout for the 'Cong, but we was too busy to stop then, and besides, they couldn't have gone where we were goin'. There were three of 'em, little girls, T-shirts for dresses, faces stained from dirt. Their eyes, big and brown like baby deer caught in a thicket. As scared and starved-lookin' as they was, we knew their mama or daddy were sure to be dead, so we made a pact to bring 'em back to base. Couldn't help all the kids but we figured we'd help these ones. So after we was done with the scoutin', my buddy Dave and I, we separated from the group and set out to come back the same way, which we wasn't supposed to do. The 'Cong, they'd be waiting for us to do that. We were always s'posed to take a different route. And sure 'nuf, I could see the hut when I stepped on it. 'Cong planted it." He cursed.

"What happened to the girls?"

"Dave, he went to check for them in the hut . . . we told him not to, but he wouldn't listen . . . he was careful, but mines don't care 'bout careful. He got to the threshold and the whole place blew. A piece of one of the girls' shirts landed right next to me. Pieces of them . . . The 'Cong used them to trick us. Place was so *messed up*." He kicked the wall next to the sliding-glass door and the whole trailer shook. He turned on his cane and faced James, and his face was red and soaked with tears. "I wanted to save them girls. If I'd done nothin' else over there all those years, I wanted to at least save what kids I could. I don't care about losing this leg. It's the girls I dream about at night."

"You couldn't have—"

"Oh, don't give me that pastor bull. I beat myself up for years over it and still do. You can't convince me I couldn'ta done somethin'. No one can. I'll only rest when I see their little faces on the other side. That's the only thing gets me through the days. That I'll see them girls healthy and smiling when I get to heaven."

"I'm sorry, Jack. I had no idea."

"No one does. You're the first person I ever told. Dragged myself back to the base with Dave's tags around my neck." He lurched closer to James. "So I got a question for you, Rev."

"I'm listening." James tried not to react to the smell of Jack's teeth, which were in desperate need of a cleaning, or his body, which was in desperate need of a bath and a clean set of clothes.

"What are you gonna do to heal your wound?"

James felt Jack's eyes bore into him. He was right, if he allowed himself to think about it. He was exhausted. As if he wasn't still in pieces from losing Molly, he felt like a whole part of himself had been blown off the day George Kernodle came and delivered the news of the closing and auction. "I don't know, Jack."

"Rev, you got a bad case of combat fatigue if I ever saw it. Best cure is to get off the front lines for while. Rest up. Take some time to do somethin' you like or to do nothin' at all."

"I won't have a choice but to do nothing in two weeks." James twirled the glass of moonshine in his hands. "Can I ask you a question?"

"Sure. Ask whatcha like."

"Why did you stop coming to church?"

Jack thought a bit and put his hands through his long, peppery hair. "Look, Rev. I'm not a churched man. You know I found the Lord late in life. Don't mean I don't believe in going to church, just means that's probably the area I need to work on in my life. Humans are hard for me, Rev."

"I can understand that."

Jack pivoted on his cane and headed toward his bedroom. "Be right back," he said.

James studied the Marine Corps flag hanging above the couch, a framed picture of a group of war buddies on some unknown battlefield hanging crooked above the TV, and a couple of shotguns in their cloth cases propped in the corner of the room.

"Who's that?" James asked, pointing to the photograph.

"That's my platoon." Jack shifted his weight and took the picture off the wall, then pointed to a clean-shaven young man kneeling with his rifle in the front row. "Would you believe that's me?"

"Hardly!" James laughed.

"And that one there—" Jack pointed to the young man standing behind him—"that's Dave."

They were both silent for a moment, James not wanting to break the silence that seemed appropriate at the mention of the deceased soldier's name. "'There is no greater love than to lay down one's life for one's friends.'"

"John 15:13," Jack whispered.

"You know, God meant for us to have fellowship, to suffer alongside one another. I'm sure it's hard for you to go to church, but we need the church. That's one of the hardest things about all this for me. If God designed us for fellowship, then why would he allow one of his churches to close?"

Jack chuckled. "I don't think I'm the one you want to ask such serious theological questions. But if I had to say, we probably won't get an answer from the good Lord about any of this. And if there's anything I've learned, it's that we can't hold on to the whys. The whys are what made me want to put a bullet in my brain. We have to keep moving on, with or without the limbs we've lost."

"That was a better sermon than I've preached in months. Maybe years." James laughed. But it wasn't far from the truth.

Jack put a box in James's hand and covered it with both of his. "I want you to have this. Don't argue with me about it. Just take it."

James turned it over and read the words on the top. *Purple Heart.*

"I can't—"

"You can and you will. Can't take it with me and got no descendants to give it to. Be honored to give it to another soldier."

"I'm not—"

"You are to me, Rev. Saved my life. You give up a part of yourself for a brother in combat, you get a Heart."

James couldn't keep the tears from coming.

"Take it. The stuff that makes someone worthy of a Purple Heart needs to be passed on."

James's hands trembled as they held the box, and he ran his fingers across the raised relief of the image of George

Washington, the etched words on the back, *For Military Merit*. He pulled a handkerchief out of his pocket and wiped his face. "If I can't argue with you, then I guess all I can say is thank you." He stood and threw his arms around his friend, and the two embraced in the hazy room broken up by shafts of light gleaming through the dingy windows.

19

"Ceeeee-ow! Here, ceee-ow!" Noble stood at the door of the barn where the herd entered, eight at a time, for milking. Most of the cows lined up on their own, but there were a few who lollygagged out in the pasture and always had to be called. The sun rose over the far hill and the ripples on the creek glimmered as the cows who'd been lying on the ground rose slow onto their sleep-stiffened haunches. As he waited for them to file in, he shooed a couple of flies away from his face and watched a monarch butterfly flitting around the milkweed growing against the corner of the barn. George Strait crooned from the radio in the milking parlor.

A few hundred yards out in the pasture, Eustace meandered

in the Gator with a couple bales of alfalfa in the back, bringing up the rest of the herd lumbering toward the barn, their enormous, swollen udders swaying between the angled bones of their hind legs. That dingy white hat was perched too high on his head, and the grin on his face—same no matter how many times Eustace drove the Gator—made it look like he was a grade-schooler given permission to drive it for the first time.

A grade-schooler. That's what Eustace was. A big, giant grade-schooler. Aside from the time he asked Mama what was wrong with him, Noble couldn't remember when he first realized he would be the caretaker of a big brother that should've been able to take care of him. It probably wasn't a moment, just a slow happening like everything else at the Burden Dairy. More likely, he realized it when he was the only one—since God hadn't seemed to have been there then either—who actually tried to defend himself when their father came around wanting to beat on them. Dad beat them when he was sober; he beat them when he was drunk. He just liked beatin' people. Including Mama. The worst was when they were younger and someone'd come around when they weren't expecting it, like the milk truck or Molly Horton, the days when he and Eustace were still young and before Dad realized he'd have to be more careful about when—and where—he used his fists.

Often in the summer when school was out and they had nothing else to keep them busy, Mama had doled out old baby-food jars to him and Eustace and Shelby so the three of them could run off to play and make butter. They'd take a ladle to the milk tank and fill the jars three-quarters full, seal them up tight with the lids, and skedaddle out of there before Dad could catch them. They'd run to the creek shaking the jars the whole way, then sit on the mossy banks and stick their toes in the water and shake and shake the jars. Eventually, a clump of butter appeared in the bottom, sitting in a puddle of buttermilk. Sometimes Mama put a pinch of salt or sugar in the jars ahead of time—cinnamon, if they were really lucky. They'd scoop the butter out with their fingers, sweet cream cool and smooth on their throats.

Once, Dad had found them out there and not noticed Shelby was with them. He was coming at Noble and Eustace hard with an old piece of barn wood, rusty nails still sticking out the ends. When he'd seen Shelby, though, he backed down.

"He always act like that?" Shelby had asked, her dark curls falling over her ivory skin.

"Pretty much," Noble admitted, hot with the shame of realizing all over again something was broken in their family.

>>> ———— ⋘

Eustace was nearing the end of grade school when he made one of his biggest mistakes. He and Noble had cleaned all of the milk collectors and tubing and hung it to dry. They washed out the barns and did all their chores. But as they washed out the room where the milk tank was, they

unknowingly knocked the plugs loose that powered the cooling and cooling alarm system for the milk tank. The next
morning Dad checked the tank temperature and it was way
too warm. The tank truck was coming to empty it that morning, and half a dozen rounds of milking were unfit for sale.
Noble could still remember the way the purple rose in his
father's face. He could still feel the chill that ran through him
as all the blood drained to his feet and he and Eustace stood
there, weak-kneed and waiting for their punishment.

The beating lasted only a few minutes, but it'd seemed
like an hour. Mama'd heard it all the way from the house
and ran out to try to stop him, but she, too, got Dad's wrath,
right on the side of the face where she ended up with half a
dozen stitches. Eustace got it worst, though. He always got
it worst. Dad broke one of his ribs, and the punch he took
to the face swelled his eye up so bad the doctor had to lance
it so the swelling wouldn't make him lose his eyesight, it was
pressing up against his eyeball so tight. He had a scar from
that and one that matched Mama's that took a dozen stitches
to close.

Noble remembered standing in the corner of the emergency room watching the white-coated doctor give Mama
and Eustace shots and then sew them up with a curvy needle
while a kind-faced nurse dabbed at the still-oozing blood
with clean gauze. Every so often she'd glance at Noble and
smile at him, but her eyes gave away her sadness. Noble kept
his face still and tried not to cry, which was what he wanted
to do. He wanted to cry and run into the clean and kind arms

of the nurse, to steal a bunch of that gauze that looked so soft for the next round of beatings, and some gloves, too, for the heck of it. But Dad sat in the chair across from the exam tables and glared at him, a warning he knew meant he had to keep his mouth shut and his hands at his sides.

"Heifer went crazy." Dad cursed as he told the young doctor who smelled like soap and had extra-neat combed hair. "Never seen nothin' like it. The wife here and Eustace, they got in her way and she wouldn't have it. Woulda trampled over Godzilla to get outta that barn. Gonna have the vet come and make sure she ain't sick."

Dad shook his head like he was right sorry about the whole thing. He kept his hands shoved deep in his work coat pockets so nobody'd see the swelling and bruising on his knuckles. "Never seen nothin' like it."

Noble had tried to get in front of Eustace to help him fight back, and Dad had thrown him against the wall so hard the wind came out of him and his back ached for days from the impact. He hadn't said anything about his own pain, and he wouldn't as long as Eustace couldn't say nothin' about his. He remembered that day from all the others because of the look he'd seen on Eustace's face, his big brother lying on the limed-up floor, his hands held up to his face to protect himself. Strange thing was, Eustace wasn't wincing, though he knew what was coming. He was focused on something in the corner of the room, something far beyond and behind Dad and his rage. Like the male calves when the noose was wrapped around their soft necks, their wet noses nudging up to the hand that led them as they were sold to the butcher for veal, Eustace's eyes were calm. And that had filled Noble with a rage he never got over. Not even now.

Like everything else Dad did, his leaving them came unannounced. He did what he liked and didn't care what anybody thought. Noble was sixteen at the time and had heard Mama and their father fighting plenty from their bedroom. He'd heard his father's harsh demands for sex before he knew what sex was, and the banging of the headboard against the wall, and the slam of the door and Mama crying herself to sleep afterward. He'd heard Dad blame her for the money never being enough, for him having to be on the road all the time, for her forgetting to pick up his beer at the store, and for Eustace coming out of the womb stupid.

So when he left for a trucking job like usual one Monday morning and didn't come back that Thursday like always, they felt relief more than worry as they picked over the brisket and potatoes Mama always made on the nights of his return. And when he didn't come back Friday and then Saturday and then the whole next week and the one after that, it felt like the world turning from gray to Technicolor, the air changing from heavy to sweet and light.

Mama quit crying at night and started cleaning, opening windows and washing them outside and in so the sun came in and filled the new white kitchen she'd painted and the milk jar full of zinnias she'd weeded back and cut fresh. And when the papers came from a lawyer out in Kansas, she signed them and took them right back out to the mailbox and then baked Noble and Eustace and her a cake. "We're having a birthday."

"Ain't none of our birthdays," Noble had said.

"It's this family's birthday. We're starting new." So she blew up balloons and let them have as much ice cream as they wanted and turned up the oldies music station, which was what her own daddy, who'd gone to his grave hating Dad, always played when she was little. She threw away and put away and gave away anything that reminded any of them of Dad, and whatever was left she threw in a heap and they had a bonfire and danced around it like those tribal folks in Africa he'd seen in the *National Geographic*s he borrowed from school. None of that took away the hate Noble had for his father, but it sure did help. And for the first time in a long time, he remembered the story of Moses begging Pharaoh for freedom, and he felt like God was there with them.

>>>———<<<

Noble went back inside the barn to switch out the cows and the automatic milking devices. He turned up the radio.

I keep a close watch on this heart of mine
I keep my eyes wide open all the time . . .

From George Strait to Johnny Cash. Not bad. An old wives' tale said the cows gave more milk when they listened to music, and he'd trained them all up on country and western. Helped pass the time, too. Eight cows at a time meant about eight rounds of milking, each round taking about fifteen minutes by the time he got through cleaning all the teats beforehand, hooking them all up and unhooking them, and dipping the teats in a protective Betadine and lanolin mixture when they were done. The rhythmic sound of the machines reminded Noble of a candy factory as the pulsations mimicked in mechanical form a suckling calf.

Of all the farm duties, milking time was his favorite, especially since Dad had left. The cows were happy, he and Eustace were happy, and they all relaxed into the hum and whir of the milking and the sway of the cows as they gave up their milk. If Dad had done anything right, it had been to maintain the Jersey herd. Jerseys were the gentlest, most trusting of the milking breeds, and the extra richness of the milk allowed them to get enough more cents per gallon to keep the farm going with a smaller herd than some of the other breeds like Whitmore's Holsteins.

They could ride a Jersey cow, too.

He remembered the first time Shelby had been brave enough to let him help her ride Marcia, one of the older cows named after the *Brady Bunch* girls.

"Where's the saddle?" Shelby had asked.

"Ain't no saddle for a cow."

"You expect me to ride this thing bareback?"

Marcia stuck her huge tongue out and reached it up to lick the dripping snot off her snout. Noble had fixed a bitless bridle to her head.

"Yep." Noble grinned. He leaned down and laced his fingers together for Shelby to step into.

Gingerly she did and pulled herself up. Marcia sidestepped, and Shelby leaned her whole body flat against the cow's back. "I don't want to do this!"

"Too late now," Noble said, taking the reins and guiding Marcia out toward the pasture, where he led them in a big circle before bringing her back around to the barns.

By the time they got back, Shelby was laughing so hard she was in tears.

"So I guess you had fun then, eh?" Noble asked, holding her gently under her arms as he helped her down.

"I surely did."

Shaking off the memory, Noble fixed his attention back on Eustace, who was shooing Dolly into the barn with the last of the girls. She'd recovered nicely from the traumatic birth of Pecan, who was still relegated to the barn with the other calves being weaned from their mothers.

Before Dolly, Eustace had other favorites, but none like her. She'd been born shortly after their dad left them. She was a little weaker than the other calves from the start, the sort of calf Dad would've let die or shot if he'd still been around. Her suck was weak and uncoordinated, and her tongue kept lolling out of her mouth as she ate, making everyone wonder if perhaps she'd lost some oxygen in the birth process, something Pecan so far seemed to have avoided. Then Dolly ended up with severe diarrhea—the scours—and had to be monitored constantly for dehydration and progress (or lack thereof). When she ate, Eustace stood patiently and held the enormous bottle as she struggled with the nipple, her eyes rolling into the back of her head she was so crazy for something to fill her belly, which was no doubt aching from the disease. Even the vet, who'd come to give her intravenous fluids when she'd been at her sickest, suggested they let her go. But Eustace had been relentless in his dedication to keeping her alive. He'd paid so much attention to her that he'd saved her life, really. Since then, she'd acted more like a dog than a cow, the way she ran—as much as a cow can run—to the fence whenever Eustace came around.

Noble eyed Eustace as he attached Dolly to the shell and claw of the milking apparatus. "What would you think about your little brother going to play guitar in Nashville?"

Eustace walked past without looking at him and grabbed an armful of alfalfa. He tossed a bunch in the trough in front of each cow.

"That's what I thought," Noble said, a pang of guilt washing over him.

20

Sunlight angled through the stained-glass windows of the sanctuary. The six two-story stained-glass windows had been made and installed by one of the church's charter members. The windows portrayed well-known images from the New Testament: the Good Samaritan, the Farmer Scattering Seed, the Lamp on a Stand, the Lost Sheep, the Prodigal Son, and the Wedding Feast.

The pew squeaked, feeling the release of James's weight as he stood. He hadn't exactly been praying, as had been his routine before heading back to his office each morning. Aside from finding it hard to pray in general, he was distracted with apprehension about his upcoming nine-thirty appointment.

He heard the clock on his office wall chime nine o'clock as he walked back that way. Bonnie had yet to arrive—she usually didn't get there until about nine thirty, which would give him some time to look through the folder of some of Tilly Icenhour's earliest sermons he'd found while cleaning out his office.

He was struck by one dated August 18, 1957, which would've been the heat of the summer. The sermon's title was "Wondering as We Wander." James knew from the church's history that 1957 had been a rough year, with many people wanting a new church building to match all the other more modern-style churches popping up in places like Lafayette and Indianapolis, but Tilly had bucked against their requests. Decades later, when Tilly had explained the situation to James, he said he had not been against growth and evangelism, but that he'd been against a giant (at least for Sycamore) campaign that would have stretched them financially and distracted them from the many existing needs within the church congregation.

"It's about balance, James," Tilly'd told him over one of the many coffees the two had shared at the Percolator before Tilly and his wife moved to Florida. "That's the hardest lesson a pastor has to learn. The world's gonna tell you to always have something big you're working on, some new and shiny vision to captivate and motivate your congregation, to keep it going, to keep it fresh and afire. But programming, new-fangled music and technology, that's not what keeps a church alive. It's depth, James. It's the gospel. And whenever you choose the depth of the gospel over new and shiny, you're gonna have a battle on your hands. The battle will be worth it, but it'll be a battle all the same."

James skimmed through the typed, stapled pages that spoke in plain, yet poetic prose about the beauty of finding God not only in the spectacular and new, but in the plain, in the uneventful, in the desert.

No one knew this boring, steadfast sort of faith like the Israelites as they wandered for forty years. God saw to it that they had everything they needed, but in my opinion, he let them wander until they got the "wants" out of their system.

They were blinded by the lives of the Egyptians, their captors, and no doubt thought that once they were freed, riches and the perceived blessings of material things would be theirs. But God wanted more for his people than possessions. He wanted to give them a land, a home, where rest and peace were the outpourings of a Promised Land centered on him.

This proposal for a new building has distracted us from many things, from each other, and from God. And while new buildings are often needed, as the leader of this church, the elders and I can assure you it is not needed for us—not right now. We're a culture built on working toward something, and we become uneasy when that goal is contentment with where we are and what we have.

Contentment in a capitalistic society can feel like a desert, like a place dry and flat, barren and lonely. But God tells us in Hosea 13:5, referring to the desert wandering of the Israelites, that he took care of them in the wilderness, in that dry and thirsty land. And again, in Deuteronomy 2:7, he reassures us that he has blessed us in everything we have done. He says that he watched the Israelites' every step through that great wilderness. During those forty years, the Lord was with them, and they lacked nothing.

"James?" Bonnie knocked softly on his office door.

"Be right there," he called. He paused to straighten his tie in the mirror on the back of his door before opening the door. He couldn't remember the last time Gertrude Johnson had attended a service, and he'd only really seen her when he went into her flower shop, which was a rare occasion unless he was buying a bouquet for Shelby for her birthday as he had always done since she was a preschooler.

As he grasped the door handle, Gertrude pushed the door open, shoved past him, and sat down in the chair in front of his desk, her purse squarely on her lap, and her hands folded over the top of it as if she'd been the one waiting for him. She was one of those women whose eyes always seemed to bug out slightly—even from behind her glasses, or perhaps because of them—as if she were ready to verbally pounce on whomever contested her opinion. She wore a leopard-patterned cardigan and had a feathery fuchsia scarf tied around her neck despite the ninety-degree weather forecast for that afternoon.

"I'm here about the church closing."

"Good morning, Mrs. Johnson. It's been a while."

"It has. Frankly I'm surprised you noticed."

"Noticed what?"

"Why, that I'd been gone, that I'd left the congregation. It was some time ago, you know."

While he knew she hadn't been there, he didn't know she'd officially left, nor could he remember whether her departure had been recent, a matter of months, or years ago. "Yes. About that. Would you like to talk about it?"

"Would I like to talk about it. Pshaw." She pushed the *pshaw* through her lips like a little sneeze and peered at him over the top of her glasses as if he should know precisely why she'd left.

Still unaware of her reasons for being there, he tried to approach the conversation another way. "This closing has been hard on all of us. If there's anything I can say or do, or anything that needs to be said between us, I want to end things well here, for everyone."

"It's a little late for that, don't you think?"

James sat on the corner of his desk in front of her, trying to keep things casual, unassuming. He remembered Gertrude from many of the potluck dinners and from Sunday mornings, but beyond that he could not recall ever having a conversation—at least one of any length—with her. He tried to remember if they'd had a row, or if she'd had a fracas with someone else in the church, but he couldn't remember anything involving her.

She sighed without attempting to hide her impatience. "It was the service time."

"The service time?" he asked, puzzled.

"Yes," she huffed. "Of course. Don't pretend you don't know what a problem the service time causes." With obvious disdain, she looked over the top of her bifocals at him.

James leaned forward, puzzled. "I'm sorry, but I really don't know what you mean, Mrs. Johnson."

She let out an overly loud and long sigh. "It's the Methodists."

"The Methodists?" He tried not to grin as he repeated the name of the church across the town square from them and which she'd nearly spat out at him. "You mentioned the service time—"

"I know what I said," she interrupted, rolling her eyes. "It's the service time and the Methodists. They dismiss fifteen minutes earlier than we do."

She tossed a photocopy of a letter across the table at him, and when he read it, he vaguely recalled receiving it some time earlier. He and Bonnie had gotten a good chuckle about it at the time. He ran his hand through his hair. "Ah yes, I do remember this now."

"By the time we get to the Percolator, all the best tables—all the tables in general—they're taken. Filled with Methodists. We either have to wait, which no one wants to do on a Sunday especially, or we have to go to the TA for brunch, which is no place for a lady or a family, and you know that." She sat back, her puffy cheeks red beneath the smudges of pink rouge, her frown lines deeper than he'd noticed.

"I am sorry for your inconvenience—"

She interrupted him again. "Inconvenience! I'll say. My gastroesophageal reflux syndrome burns like you can't imagine if I'm late for a meal, and antacids won't stave it off any longer. I couldn't wait to eat, and the TA food, why that made it all worse, too. Not to mention Mike's bowels."

James raised his eyebrows and pulled out a handkerchief so he could feign a cough to cover his amusement. "Mrs. Johnson—"

"He has to move his bowels after lunch, after church. Same time every Sunday. If he doesn't, we have to start in with the milk of magnesia, then—"

"Mrs. Johnson. Please. I really am sorry you found the service time, which has been the same since long before I arrived, to be such a trouble for you and for Mike. What I'm most concerned about, though, is whether you've found another place, another church, for you and Mike to call home."

She sat up straighter in her chair and studied her manicured fingernails, which were painted bright red. "We have."

"Outstanding. Maybe the Lord used the service time

problems to help you find a place that better suits you all around. He can work in all kinds of mysterious ways. Even lunchtimes."

James's attempt at cheerfulness did not dampen Gertrude's apparent resolve to make him feel as though he ought to repent of the longstanding error of his ways. He considered folks like the Bogans, the Deans, and the Lees and their complaints and reasons for leaving. Stephen Lee had gone so far as to refer to James and the rest of the parishioners who'd joined in singing the guitar music as pagans, and cited Matthew 6:7's exhortation against "vain repetitions" in a letter announcing his family's departure. James wasn't sure where that left many of the great hymns, not to mention Paul and Silas, who sang on and on while imprisoned, and David, who danced half-naked around the campfire with plenty of instrumentalists standing around as witnesses.

"He's mysterious, alright," Gertrude said, jolting James back to the conversation. "We've gone from evangelical to Baptist. Found a little church off of 52 near Colfax. There's a place in town serves catfish and an all-you-can-eat brunch buffet on Sundays, and there's never a crowd. It'll do."

"The church or the restaurant?" The question slipped out before James could stop himself.

Gertrude cocked her head slightly. "The restaurant. We're home by one fifteen every Sunday now and back to feeling regular."

"That's great to hear. Really great." James stifled another laugh as he extended a hand toward Gertrude. "Is there anything else I can help you with, anything else you'd like to say about the church closing?"

"If you should find a way to stay open or reopen, consider that start time for the services. Could you do that for me?"

"I don't think that's going to happen."

"I wouldn't be so quick to doubt, Reverend. The Lord works in mysterious ways, remember?"

21

Eustace was not in his bed when Noble woke up the next morning at 4:15 a.m. He pulled on his work boots and a dingy white T-shirt from the wash pile and headed toward the barn, where he hoped Eustace would be feeding Pecan and the other calves. The cows lay in the fields, shadowy and still in the darkness.

He slid open the door to the barn and was grateful to see that Eustace was there with Dolly's calf, Pecan, who was sucking on the oversize bottle as if it was the last one she'd get in her life. Pecan nosed frantically against the bottle nipple, legs knobby and hip bones jutting up from her tiny hindquarters, all angles and awkward. Thankfully, she'd avoided the scours and any other complications from the traumatic birth, and she had been gaining weight nicely.

Relieved by Eustace's whereabouts, Noble went out to the front loader and drove it down the gravel road to where the hay was stored to pick up the usual load for the morning milking. At the sound of the engine turning over, he knew the cows would start making their way in from the pasture, and sure enough, by the time he came back, nearly all of them were waiting for him at the trough, into which he shook the hay. Back inside, he turned on the radio, got the bucket of lime out, and began spreading it on the surfaces of the milking parlor. He slid open the door to Eustace's homemade corral and the first eight cows loped into the room.

"I'm countin' on you to give me a break this morning, ladies." He shoved Florence, who was balking, stubborn, into the first stall and shut the stanchions around her neck. "I'd like to be done before it's time for your second milking."

Well, she seemed all right by dawn's early light
Though she looked a little worried and weak

"A little Martina McBride for your listening pleasure." He playfully slapped the hindquarters of the cow named Pearl as she moseyed into her stall.

He closed the stanchions around the necks of Pearl and the other six cows, threw some clumps of alfalfa into the concrete trough in front of them, and turned on the pulsator.

Let freedom ring, let the white dove sing

The claws with teat cups hung above each stall, and Noble pulled them down, one by one, and attached the cows.

Let the whole world know that today
Is a day of reckoning

Milk flowed and swirled through the claw on its way up and through the rest of the system to the milk tank in the next room.

Let the weak be strong, let the right be wrong
Roll the stone away, let the guilty pay
It's Independence Day.

He repeated the process eight times until all the cows had been milked, while in the next room Eustace continued feeding the babies. Weaning a calf from its mother was hard on all of them. They had to be separated soon after birth so that the calf wouldn't get used to sucking on the mother's teats and then wind up sucking the ears off other calves in her absence. The mother cow had to have a time to grieve the loss of her calf, too. Once, they'd driven the Gator to the back field where a calf had been born early the night before. After placing the calf in the back of the Gator and pulling away, the mother ran after them. Her instinct and determination to stay with her calf had moved even Noble to tears.

There were times like that in the tediousness of the job that nature surprised and captivated him—the perfection of the life cycles, the seasons, the rainfall.

Mama used to run after Eustace's school bus, too, waving until they could no longer see the bus, while tears ran down her face. On the first day of sixth grade, Noble got to ride the same bus as Eustace for the first time. Noble finally understood Mama's tears.

Since the junior high and high school shared the same campus, the middle schoolers rode the bus with the high schoolers. The upperclassmen looked enormous to Noble, football players in jerseys for game day, their shoulders so broad it seemed at the time they already wore their game pads. And since he and Eustace had been in separate schools for a few years, Noble wasn't aware of the gauntlet of shame the ride was for his older brother.

"Hain't you learned to talk yet, *Euuuuuuustace?*"

Noble, who sat on the aisle, could smell the scent of cigarettes on Ricky Richard's breath as he leaned up from the seat behind them and drawled into Eustace's ear. Eustace pressed his face against the cool glass window and kept still.

"You know they can't fix *stuuuupid*. So why do you even come to school, *reeeee-tard?*"

A few of Ricky's buddies nearby chuckled while girls in the seats around them shifted uncomfortably and looked away. Ricky flicked Eustace on the back of his head and Eustace still didn't move.

Noble felt the heat of shame and anger rise within him.

He'd been too young, too naive, perhaps, before that, to feel ashamed of his brother's differences or to realize others noticed them. Noble had looked up to Eustace, his stacks of books, the way he took time to play chess with him when Dad never did, all his butterfly collections and equipment. He'd been aware that Eustace was different, but he didn't realize shame could be associated with that, that somehow those differences would make Noble feel like he needed to hide the fact they were related or avoid Eustace when his school friends came around. So on this day, Ricky set off a powerful instinct that kicked in an anger that made Noble forget the fact that he was half Ricky's size.

Noble turned around in his seat and stared at Ricky, the boy's face pockmarked and splotchy from acne, and a glop of something—syrup, maybe—on his T-shirt. He could see the veins in Ricky's muscular arms, the stubble of a mustache above his top, sneering lip, the mean in his gray eyes.

"What are you looking at, punk?" Ricky gibed.

A chorus of laughter erupted from Ricky's friends.

The girls around them stared, eyes wide with dread.

"Not much, donkey breath," Noble said.

"What did you call me?" Fury filled Ricky's face, making his acne look ten times worse.

"Donkey. Breath. I could add pizza face, scumbag, jerk wad, and I could spell all those words out for you too if you need me to."

Ricky's face turned rigid and a strange shade of purple and he was silent as his posse continued to laugh even harder, almost as if they were laughing *at* Ricky now instead of *for* him. Anger and feelings of protection over his brother overshadowed any fear Noble might've felt.

Then it happened.

Ricky leaned forward and Noble pounded his sixth-grade fist square into the center of the sophomore's nose. Ricky crumpled into a ball and writhed with pain.

"You broke my nose! You little punk! You broke it!" Ricky sat up, his hands full of blood, which continued to pour out his nose. Noble sat back on his haunches and stared as the bus pulled into the school lot. He heard the bus driver talking into the walkie-talkie, and out of the corner of his eye he saw a teacher and the principal coming toward the bus.

Mama said nothing to him on the way home, just patted him on the leg and turned up Waylon Jennings on the radio. She didn't tell their father. She didn't cry anymore at the bus stop. Ricky never bothered Eustace again.

And Noble had never punched anyone again.

But that was about to change.

22

Lunchtime at the Tractor Supply was always busy. Many farmers, like Noble, finished their morning chores and came into town for lunch and market talk and whatever needed replaced or fixed. Noble was there because a belt on one of the tractors broke, and he wanted to get some more calf starter before they got too low. Besides that, he wanted to see Shelby, to find a reason to tell her about Nashville.

Shelby was working the cash register, which was right in front of the entrance, so Noble couldn't avoid her, and she couldn't avoid him.

"Tough to be stuck inside on a nice day like this, Shelby?" He tipped his Purdue cap at her as he and Eustace passed.

"Hey, Noble. Eustace." She smiled slightly.

"Been waiting on some calf starter to come in. You know if it has yet?" He asked this knowing for sure she wouldn't know since his buddy Brock was in charge of special orders and refilling stock when it ran out. But it gave him something to talk to her about, a reason to linger an extra moment.

"No idea. Ask Brock. He's back there." She nodded toward the back of the store without looking up at them again.

"Thanks." He left Eustace in his favorite section in the front of the store with all the miniature trucks and plastic animals. Noble pushed a cart toward the back of the store, stopping to pick up a tractor belt and look at the display of porch swings. He ran his hand along the fresh, smooth pine and wished there was a way to bring one home for Mama. Hers was chipped and showed signs of rotting and would have to be taken down or replaced soon.

The swing was Mama's favorite spot. He recalled sipping Coke out of a bottle and sitting next to her as they waited for Eustace's bus to come over the hill on spring and fall afternoons. Maybe he could get a couple extra gigs at the Onion or someone would hire him to play in Lebanon or West Lafayette, especially with students returning to Purdue and looking for hangout venues with live music. He could hope. And he could see what Cass Dinsmore had to say in Nashville.

"How's the music, Noble?" Brock asked when he found him in the stockroom. "Heard y'all raised the roof at the church last Sunday. Word is the Baptists are jealous."

He and Brock were the same age and had been friends since preschool. Brock hadn't gone to college either, mostly because he hadn't wanted to go into debt, but also because he had a wife already—his high school sweetheart, Tiffany—and both of them were content to stare into each other's eyes in Sycamore the rest of their lives.

"Whatever. It was a favor, on account of their closing. It was nice, though. I'd sorta forgot how it felt to be in church."

"Ain't so bad, is it?"

He knew Tiffany never let Brock miss a Sunday service at the Methodist church. Brock typed a few things into the computer, then led Noble outside to where a new shipment of calf starter sat on pallets still wrapped in plastic.

"I'm going to Nashville next week."

"Brown County? I love that place."

"No, Nashville, Tennessee."

Brock stopped what he was doing and eyed Noble. "You called him? That guy you told me about?"

"Yep." Noble felt himself stand taller. "He wants me to play for some of his friends. Record-label friends."

"Yeeee-awww! You're kiddin' me!" Brock came around from behind the computer and high-fived and embraced Noble.

"What's goin' on back here?" Shelby leaned against the doorframe of the stockroom.

Noble had noticed the way Shelby was dressed—or not dressed, really—when they'd arrived, leggings and a tight T-shirt so short her abdomen showed, and in her navel, a little silver piercing with a crystal stud that glinted when she moved.

"Noble's goin' to Nashville!" Brock blurted.

Shelby crossed her arms and frowned. "Yeah? What's in Nashville?"

"Agents and record labels, evidently," Brock said.

"After you left the Onion with Cade the other night . . . turns out a scouter was there . . ." Noble felt himself flush and fumble for words as he watched a look of disapproval come over Shelby's face. He knew Nashville had been a dream of hers at one time. Maybe it still was. "They're paying for me to come down and play."

"Well, ain't that just fine, Noble. Fine for you." She glanced over her shoulder toward the front of the store, where Eustace was fiddling with miniature backhoes and combines.

"Nothin's even happened yet. Probably nothin' will," Noble offered.

"Not like you ever cared much about what happens around here in Sycamore. Not like anyone else ever leaves."

He coulda sworn he saw tears beginning to puddle in the bottoms of her eyes before she turned and left abruptly. Why did she care what he did? She'd made a point to make sure he knew she hadn't cared for a while now. Besides that, she had Cade.

"Still got it bad for Shelby, eh?"

Noble whipped his head toward Brock.

"What, man?" Brock said. "It's not like it ain't obvious or anything. Been obvious since she was in kindergarten."

"You know she's hardly talked to me since her mama died."

"I know she's hardly talked to anybody—least of all her old friends—since her mama died. Tiffany said she pushed all her old girlfriends away months ago. She's hurtin', Noble."

"We all got somethin' to hurt over." He handed Brock his bank card. "If I can do something to change my life, to get us all outta this town, don't you think I should?"

His normally vociferous friend frowned, appearing to measure his words. "I'm thrilled for you, for Nashville and all. Really. But sometimes . . . well, sometimes leaving ain't the answer for our pain. Sometimes the dreams God has for us, the biggest difference we can make in the world is right where we are."

Noble threw the bags of calf starter and the tractor belt back in his cart. "Don't see what kind of difference I can make turning the same dirt and shooing the same cows around for the next fifty years. And I don't see why it matters to her."

Up front, Noble approached the register where Shelby stood. Her back was pressed against the dividing wall behind her as a man he didn't immediately recognize leaned over the counter in a way that caused Noble to bristle.

Whoever it was, was clearly ogling her, and he felt the urge to grab one of the John Deere fleece throws from the nearby display and wrap it around her.

"—wouldn't mind having a piece myself someday."

Noble heard the man's words slide out of his mouth like slime. "A piece of what?"

The man startled and stepped back, and Shelby stared at

Noble blankly as if in shock. Then Noble recognized him. Cade Canady's father, Silas Canady.

"You talkin' to me, boy?" Silas's bottom lip was swollen full with chewing tobacco.

"I wasn't talking to myself." Noble turned to Shelby. "He bothering you?"

She shook her head and Noble noticed the color had drained from her face.

Noble, surprising even himself, shoved the cart into Silas's knees, causing him to stumble and knock over a stand of beef jerky with a clatter.

"Noble, don't—" Shelby said.

"Don't, Noble," Silas mocked. "'Sides, whatcha gonna do with that goon of a brother by your side?"

With that, Noble knocked over the cart between them and was on top of Silas, holding him by the neck of his shirt so tight he was gagging.

"You know you want a piece of that too," Silas choked out, nodding toward Shelby and spitting tobacco juice in Noble's face.

Noble felt his arm rear back as if it was working on its own and saw his fist fly into Silas's face, the tobacco and spittle flying back into his own.

Shelby came around the counter and tried to put herself between the two men. "Stop it! Just stop it!" she wailed, then shocked Noble by turning to him and hissing, "I don't need you or anyone else protecting me. Mr. Canady was just checking out. Weren't you, Mr. Canady?"

Silas scooted away from them both and rubbed his jaw, which was split open and already swelling, and a trickle of blood oozed out of his nose. He stood and brushed himself off. "That's right, sweetheart."

Noble felt himself tense again, but out of the corner of his eye he saw Eustace, his arms flapping and face contorted with worry. When he turned, he saw that at least a half-dozen customers had gathered around to stare.

"Everything alright up here, Shelby?" Brock was breathless from running up from the back of the store, along with a couple other employees. "Noble?"

"It's fine, Brock," Shelby said, and Noble thought she appeared unusually composed. "It was an accident. Stand got knocked over by a cart."

Silas slunk out the front doors while Noble and Eustace cleaned up the packs of beef jerky and began to set all the little plastic animals in their rows.

Shelby came beside them and helped.

"Why'd you do that?" Noble said to her. "Why'd you protect him?"

A tear slipped down Shelby's face, and she shook her head. She looked over at Eustace, white hat crooked on his head, lost and jittery as he tried to fix the display that held the miniature tractors and farm machinery. Then, barely moving her lips, she whispered, "I'm so sorry."

Noble sat back on his knees. "It's Cade, ain't it?"

She kept on picking up plastic farm animals and beef jerky and didn't respond.

"You're afraid if you stood up to Silas, you'd have to stand up to Cade." He put a hand on her shoulder and she jumped. "Shelby, what's he doin' to you?"

She stood briskly, brushed off her knees, and tugged at the shirt as if now self-conscious about her bare midriff. She met his eyes, and in them Noble saw flashes of fear and pain like lightning on the horizon. "You better mind your own business, Noble."

"I think I can be the judge of that."

"You think you know everything, don't you?"

"I know what the eyes of a woman look like when she's bein' treated wrong by a man." He thought about how Mama's eyes had gone from green to gray, to match the bruises on her arms and face, whenever Dad beat her. "I know what a girl looks like when she's bein' beat and is too scared to talk about it."

"You have no idea."

"Neither do you. But if you've got any sense left in you, you'll leave him. Or—"

"Or what, Noble? This ain't pretend anymore like when we were kids. You don't have a magic sword you can wave and make it all go away."

She started to head toward the register, where Brock had temporarily filled in for her and eyeballed the two of them, concerned.

"Wait," Noble said.

She stopped but didn't turn around.

"Listen. You come out to our place tomorrow. We're

transferring those cows of Frank Whitmore's to our place and could use some help."

She turned her head toward Noble. "I—"

"That's what I thought." He wasn't about to let her finish. "Ten a.m. sharp. The girls and I don't take no for an answer."

23

James sat in his office at the church, a desk lamp brightening only the corner of the dark room. He'd only planned on spending a couple of hours cleaning out his office after Gertrude left, but it was 10 p.m. and he still had a couple of boxes half-full of files he wanted to go through before he went home. The file drawers were like scrapbooks of his twenty-some years—old sermons, bulletins from baptisms and funerals, Christmases and Easters, and flyers from congregational meetings and picnics, youth gatherings and other celebrations. There were folders full of failed programming efforts recommended by online and in-person consultants specializing in preventing the demise of small churches, along with brochures, catalogs, and articles torn out and given to James with lists of things a small-town church should do if it finds itself dying.

What disheartened James most about the church closing was that there was nothing tangible he could blame, and so he could of course only blame himself. There'd been no infidelity or embezzlement. No church split or eschatological divide. But then he knew enough from two decades of Indiana weather that it wasn't necessarily the big storms that ruined a pasture. It was day after day, week after week of rain and overcast that killed the spirit of the farmer and caused the flock to get stuck in the mud or the seeds to drown before they could sprout and take hold.

Folks had left slowly, and guilt poked at his heart as he was reminded again of Dr. Wilcox and Ezekiel 34, of his call to seek lost sheep. He'd never gone after the ones who left. For a while, he had a piece of paper torn from a yellow legal pad taped on his desk where he'd recorded names of people who hadn't been attending. He'd pray over the names every morning when he came to the office. But he'd stopped when the page was filled, the names representing failure rather than faces. He knew he should have torn up the town running after them like missing coins. He knew he should have stopped them when he'd seen them in town. But instead, he'd begun avoiding them in the grocery as much as they avoided him. He couldn't bear to hear another reason—ridiculous or not—why someone left or wouldn't or couldn't come.

"Do not be slothful in zeal, be fervent in spirit, serve the Lord."

"I hear you, Lord. But how?"

He put a few more files in a box and a few framed pictures from the shelves behind him, including a large, two-sided one which had a picture of him with Tilly at the church barbecue celebrating Tilly's retirement and the commencement of James's tenure, and on the other side a brief letter of encouragement from Tilly:

Dear James,

Never forget your calling. When the storms and trials of the pastorate come, keep these things in mind:

A crisis doesn't mean the end. More often than not, it signals a beginning.

Critics usually aren't heretics. They are, however, usually hurting.

You're not in this alone, so don't try to do this alone.

The grass isn't greener at the church down the road.

Culture changes.

The gospel stays the same.

God never leaves.

Your friend,
Tilly

He set the frame aside and turned to the folder in his lap. He'd been avoiding this one most of all, since it contained all the details of Molly's funeral, including a stack of photos someone had scanned to make a video for the service. There was Molly in her wedding dress, Molly and him at their wedding, on their honeymoon on the Alabama Gulf Coast, at their engagement on the Furman campus. A photo of Molly standing sideways, pregnant with Shelby. Photos of Shelby, just learning to walk and running to Molly's outstretched arms. Photos of the three of them on hayrides and in pumpkin patches, at Shelby's concerts and Christmas. Of an anniversary spent in Savannah. Tears in James's eyes blurred another picture of Molly with a paintbrush in her hand, her cheeks flushed with joy and life.

Where are you, God?

The thought that had been shadowing every other thought and prayer for as long as he could remember became clear. He wondered if the realization had been the same for Frank Whitmore.

He couldn't do it anymore.

His chest and throat tightened and he pushed himself away from the desk, away from the files and stacks of memories, and stepped outside. The moon was high and the night was cool and still so that he heard his heart pounding in his ears. He opened the trunk of his car and felt for the leather bag he kept tucked in the wheel well. He'd bought it in case coyotes came too close to the house, and he had only shot it at a practice range a couple of times. It was a small gun, but it felt heavier than he remembered. He tucked it between his belt and pants and walked toward the back streets of town, where the last row of homes stood at the edge of the corn and soybean fields surrounding Sycamore.

Along the way, James could not think, could not pray, could not rationalize the steps he took any more than he could rationalize why he'd removed the gun from his trunk. He was beyond the point of praying. He stepped carefully along the sidewalk and avoided an entire section of concrete upheaved by the roots of an enormous oak tree. The leaves on the branches above seemed plastic, cold, unmoving.

One out of every two or three homes he passed was well cared for, yard trimmed neat, black-eyed Susans and daisies blooming, planters bursting with bright-red geraniums and a flag flying above the front stoop.

The rest of the homes were terribly dilapidated. Town folks struggled as bad as the farmers. The big auto factory which had, in the late twentieth century, helped build many of the homes, had been through nearly half a dozen layoffs in as many years. The homes that hadn't been built during that era were relics from the Sears catalog. Fewer and fewer people chose to live far from malls and hospitals and convenience. Fewer and fewer wanted to live the rest of their lives with people they'd known all their lives.

After two decades, James knew which homes contained shut-ins and which ones contained drunks, which ones had young, struggling families and which ones contained folks who had once attended his church.

He slowed his pace as he reached the last street on the back edge of town and stopped when he reached a driveway bordered by a rusted wrought-iron fence tangled with brown and viny weeds. Beyond and up on a hill stood an abandoned, worn, two-story house, windows black and without signs of life.

The place must have been majestic in its prime, but now the curved driveway was overtaken with scraggles of bushes. Most of the windows had lost at least one shutter, and the shutters that remained were missing slats or hung crooked, reminding James of rotten, crooked teeth. Alongside the once-gated entry stood a sign erected by the Indiana Historical Society indicating the home had once been a site of the Underground Railroad. Partially because of its history, and partially because of the cemetery that took up the plot of land next door, residents of Sycamore had long been passing down stories of ghosts of the original owners and the slaves who'd died there of dysentery or typhoid or exhaustion before fully realizing their emancipation. Some of that was true, and many were buried in wind-worn graves which were only sporadically maintained. The place was notorious for Halloween pranks, teens driving by or bullying some unsuspecting classmate into their trucks, blindfolding them, and leaving them on the property to find their way back alone.

James stared at the home, which held no significance to him except that he felt as worthless as it looked. The palm of his hand was damp against the handle of the gun, and he felt sweat drip down the middle of his back. He leaned against the granite top of the old gatepost on the right side of the driveway, the same gray granite that marked Molly's grave a quarter mile down the road at the Sycamore Cemetery. The tightness in his chest and throat turned to sobs as he slid to the ground, let the gun fall to the ground at his side, and held his face in his hands.

What good would it do to shoot himself?

Shelby would be an orphan.

Then again, what difference would that make?

Shelby's grandparents, Molly's parents in Atlanta, would take her in and give her everything he never could. It'd be her ticket out of Sycamore. She'd have college and freedom and money, plenty of money. The town wouldn't miss him, and the church was all but dead anyway, so they wouldn't need a pastor.

He straightened and wiped his face with his sleeve. The sweat on his back had soaked through his shirt and he shivered from the chill.

As he began to reach for the gun again, the lights of Sheriff Tate's cruiser turned the corner onto Maple Street and shone on him. Tate pulled his car up to the curb. James could see him speak something into his handset, and then he turned the car off and got out.

"Reverend?" Tate stepped toward him. "You alright?"

"Sheriff." James's voice cracked with emotion.

"What's goin' on here?" Tate crouched down next to him in the grass, already damp with dew.

"I'm not sure I know."

"That a gun?"

James followed Tate's gaze to the spot in the grass where he'd dropped the gun.

"Why you got a gun, Reverend?"

James sighed. "Not sure I know that, either."

"How 'bout you give that to me for safekeepin', and I'll give you a ride home?"

James considered the sheriff's offer, and he began to understand it was more of Tate's kind way of telling him what was going to happen than a choice James had.

Tate was a large man with a round face and ruddy complexion, broad shoulders, and a wide middle indicative of many hours behind the wheel. His knees crunched as he jimmied himself down and sat against the granite post next to James, so close their shoulders touched. Tate moved the gun from between where they sat, made sure the safety was on, and tossed it toward the grassy edge of the road beside his cruiser.

James felt the warmth, the life, of the sheriff even through his thick, stiff uniform shirt.

"Wanna talk about it?" Tate took his hat off, extended his legs, and crossed them at the ankles as if prepared to stay awhile.

James rolled the hem of his shirt between his fingers and shivered again, lacking the energy and willpower to reply.

"It's alright. You don't have to say nothin'. I think I understand."

Tate had never been a member of their congregation, but he'd always been a friend. He'd been a first responder to Molly's accident. He'd been a pallbearer for her funeral. He was the sort of person James counted on not because of conversation and time spent together, but because he was the sort of person who was always there. The two of them sat silent for a long while, bugs zapping against the streetlight nearby, their breath thick and illuminated as it caught on the damp night air, until eventually James broke.

"I'm a pastor," James said finally, laughing.

"Yes," Tate said, in a voice that sounded as much an attempt to confirm James's obvious statement as it was a question about why James was laughing.

"How is it, then—" the laughter caught in his throat—"that a pastor of over two decades cannot . . . feel . . . God?"

He felt Tate eyeing him.

The emotion in his throat turned into a sob. "All these years I've been telling people God is with them, that he makes a way, that he never forsakes us, that everything works for good if we love and trust him. He feels so absent I'm afraid I've lost my faith."

Tate turned his hat in his hands in a way that indicated he knew James needed a soft, empty place for his words to land more than he needed attempted answers.

"Is it a lie, Sheriff? Have I been lying to these good people all these years? Is that why the church died? Is that why Molly died? And if it is, then what reason do I have to keep on living? What use am I to anyone now?"

"You know," Tate began, his eyes lifted to the stars, glimpses of them visible through the leaves of the ancient oak above them. "I'm a Baptist, so I can't be sure what I think is worth much."

James wiped his face with his sleeve and chuckled through his tears. "I won't hold that against you."

"Would it be trite to mention Job?"

"Maybe so."

"David?"

"Ahhh, the consummate manic depressive."

"Paul?"

James shook his head. He was so tired of platitudes about proverbial thorns in the side. "Don't bring up Romans 8:28, either."

"Okay then, what about Balaam and his talking donkey?"

James looked at Tate. "You serious?"

Tate pushed gently against James's shoulder. "Nah, I'm just playin'. Trying to lighten the mood. Although—"

"Don't say it. I know . . . I'm acting like a donkey."

"No, it's not that. But you know, if God wants to do something, or wants something done, there ain't a whole lot anyone can do to stop him. And if he needs to use a donkey to talk some sense into us . . ."

"Oh, so you're the donkey."

"Let's forget about the donkey, okay?"

They both chuckled.

Tate drew in a long breath. "Whole town knows you've had more than your fair share of hurt, Rev. No one blames you for anything—not Molly, not the church."

James shot him an exhausted look of skepticism.

"Look, I don't know what I'm trying to say. All I know is I've seen a lot of bad things happen to a lot of good people over the years. Wasn't anything any of them did or didn't do that led up to it. But I've also seen God with them in ways they never would've realized if the bad hadn't happened. It took a while, but once they figured out there was still some good in the world, they started looking for it, and the more good they saw."

"So I just need to look for God? Is that it?"

"No, no . . . all I'm saying is you can't see God if you're too busy looking at yourself."

"Now wait a minute—"

"Judging from the looks of things here this evening, I don't have a minute to wait. If no one's told you before, you need to be told now: you got a lot to live for, Reverend. A daughter who needs a father to walk her down the aisle someday. Neighbors and friends who love you. Congregants who are looking to you to help them through the next couple of weeks."

"That's just it, Sheriff. I'm supposed to be a shepherd, but I need one of my own."

Tate shifted his weight so he was facing James and looked him straight in the eye. "You have a Shepherd. He's with you now, and he's never left. Even if you can't feel him, he's right here. Right now. You know . . . before I turned down Maple Street, I was headed out to the TA. I'm technically on my break, and I was really looking forward to a nice cup of coffee and a donut. But I heard the good Lord telling me to turn instead of going straight on out to the interstate. Believe me, I had that chocolate-covered donut pictured so clear in my head I could taste it. My mouth was already watering. But he told me to turn, and by golly if I didn't run right into you. Now what do you make of that?"

James's eyes filled with tears again. "I guess I owe you a donut."

The two men sat awhile longer under the old oak tree talking about faith and doubt, Baptists and nondenominationals, and the sweet, sweet goodness of wives and donuts. Finally, before they were tempted to drift into a discussion of predestination, James climbed into the passenger seat of Tate's car and let the sheriff take him home.

He rolled the window down and let the cool night air and the scent of freshly mown alfalfa rush across his face. He thought about his gun and wondered whether, if Tate had not shown up, he would've really used it. Funny, he couldn't answer that question better than any of the others he'd asked Tate. He was, he felt, at the end of himself. Or just plain exhausted. Or both.

The tires of Tate's cruiser crunched against the gravel driveway and he could see the glow of the small lamp they kept on in the kitchen at night, in case he or Shelby woke and needed a snack. On the second floor, Shelby's shades were drawn and her lights off. James etched the still peace of their home on his heart as he imagined Tate arriving there alone, or perhaps with a deputy, to wake Shelby and tell her that her father . . . that he . . .

Dear God, forgive me. For my blindness. For my despair. For my unbelief.

Tate shifted the car into park, then rubbed his hands on his thick thighs as if unsure how to go about ending their evening.

"I think I'll be okay, thanks to you," James offered.

Tate nodded toward the house. "Take care of that baby girl, Rev."

"I will." James pushed the door open and started up the sidewalk but then hesitated, turning back to Tate. "Thanks . . . for being there tonight . . . for . . . *listening*."

Tate appeared to understand that James referred to the fact that he'd turned down Maple Street instead of going to the TA. He hung his head out the window. "You bet. . . . Oh, and I think I'll hang on to your gun for a while if that's okay with you."

"Keep it." James turned and went inside. And as he did, he felt something hard in his pocket. It was the Purple Heart he'd forgotten to take out the day he'd visited Jack McGee.

24

Noble fell fast asleep after finishing the 4:30 a.m. milking and woke again at nine to the sound of hay mowers in Stuart Granger's neighboring fields. He hadn't meant to stay in bed so long with all the work ahead of them that day bringing Whitmore's cows over.

His phone buzzed. A text message from Cass Dinsmore flashed on the screen. Everything's set. Looking forward to seeing you!

They'd arranged for him to fly out from Indianapolis Wednesday afternoon, arriving in time for dinner with Cass and his wife. Then first thing Thursday morning he'd have a tour of the studios, followed by other meetings and introductions. He'd be able to get home by Thursday afternoon.

Noble pulled his pillow over his head and stifled a giant yawp and holler. This had the potential to be every dream he'd had coming true.

Downstairs, he found Eustace sitting at the kitchen table eating a sugary cereal with marshmallows.

"Checked the electric fencing yesterday to make sure things would be set today to bring Whitmore's girls over."

Eustace munched on without a response.

"Found half a dozen of the girls across the road grazing on Granger's alfalfa. They stopped and stared at me when I drove up like they'd done nothin' wrong. I got out and shooed 'em back over and fixed the busted wire. Good thing I checked. No telling how far Whitmore's woulda roamed if they'd found that opening. Still, it's gonna be some work training them. They're used to barbed wire."

Eustace added a green clover-shaped marshmallow to the line of other colored shapes he'd been arranging on the table next to his bowl. Then he slurped down a full glass of orange juice.

"Aren't you gonna eat those?" Noble nodded toward the marshmallows in front of Eustace.

Eustace threw his head back and laughed like Noble had told the funniest joke he'd ever heard.

Noble playfully pulled Eustace's white ball cap over his eyes as he walked to the sink for a glass of water. He squinted at the sun, glaring against the bright-blue sky. "Wind is starting to pick up. Weather's s'posed to turn pretty ugly in the next day or two. I'd like to have those cows over here and at least started on their fence training in the corral by this evening so we can get the rest of the chores done around here between now and then."

The doorbell rang.

"Who is it, Noble?" Mama hollered from her sewing room, which doubled as the laundry room.

Noble peered into the front room and saw the figure in the front door window. He hadn't thought she'd really come. "It's Shelby."

Mama emerged, eyebrow raised.

"Don't start, Mama."

"Mmm-hmm. I saw the way you had your eye on her at church on Sunday."

Noble ignored her and opened the front door.

"Well, I'm here," Shelby announced. She wore cutoff shorts and a tank top, the fluorescent-pink bow of a swimsuit top peeking out from underneath it. Her neck glistened in the heat, already rising fast. She'd pulled her black curls up in a mess of a knot, and he wished he were brave enough to reach out and brush a few of the stray, damp tendrils away from her face.

She sashayed right past him, through the front room and into the kitchen before he had a chance to invite her in, making Noble wonder how someone who carried herself so confidently one minute could stand being with someone so controlling—and he suspected so abusive—as Cade the next. What did she see in him?

"Hey, Shelby. Nice to see you," Mama said.

"Thanks, Mrs. Burden. Nice to see you, too." Shelby looked over and smiled at Eustace, who was in fact eating all the marshmallows he'd so carefully lined up. "Hey, Eustace."

As if Noble needed another reason to admire her, she was one of the few people who acted even remotely like Eustace was a regular human being. She always had, from their earliest days of playing together. For Shelby, at least, Eustace was another regular old important character in their adventures. No more. No less. He just was. And he mattered. Noble had noticed this again that day at the Tractor Supply when she'd patiently helped him straighten the toy tractors and plastic animals Canady had knocked over.

"Would you like a Coke?" Noble pulled open the refrigerator.

"Thanks, I would." She held the cold bottle against her neck before popping the cap off to drink it.

She was driving Noble crazy. And he was beginning to suspect she knew it. If only he could get her to forget about Cade and remember what they had—if not in recent years, then at least what they'd had as kids.

"Brock will be here soon with the truck and the livestock trailer. Hope you brought some boots." He eyed her flip-flops, then her toes painted pink and decorated with hand-painted daisies. She had always been one to be notoriously underdressed for farm work.

Noble had been out to Frank Whitmore's place a few times to feed the fourteen cows, three of them babies, that remained. He'd made sure they were in the corral the day before. The mud and manure in there was deep, but he'd rather have muddy cows than have to waste time that day shooing them in from the pastures. They were Holsteins, and though he wouldn't have chosen to mix their milk with his Jersey girls' milk, he wasn't in a position to refuse a way to make a little more money and add to their herd. And while the Holsteins weren't quite as docile as the Jerseys, they were nice enough. It was apparent that Whitmore had been good to his girls because they were accustomed to people.

When they arrived with the trailer—Noble and Shelby, Eustace, Mama, and Brock—the cows had sauntered up to the fence and were staring at them, chewing their cud, their ears twitching at the flies and the breeze. Whitmore hadn't named his cows like they had. Instead, each of the bright-yellow tags on the Holsteins' ears had numbers on them. They nudged and shoved against and around each other, part afraid and part curious.

"They're so cute," Shelby laughed. "They look like they're a bunch of fans, jockeying themselves to get the best spot at a rock concert."

"Hey, yeah!" Noble glanced at them and laughed too. "I'd never thought about it that way." He nodded in the direction of the cows. "Go on, Eustace." He and Mama opened the long metal gate. The cows startled and a couple of them moaned as the gate creaked wide, forcing them to bump and jostle into each other some more.

"What do you want me to do?" Shelby said, standing on

the second rung of the fence, her toes curling around her flip-flops as she worked to keep her balance.

Noble looked at her feet and grinned. "Get your boots on for starters. Then I s'pose you can go help Eustace herd them into the truck once Brock gets the ramp lowered."

She clambered into the cab of Noble's truck and came back, looking down sheepishly at her feet.

"You call them work boots?"

Shelby glanced at Noble, then down again at the shiny black fashion rain boots with pretty, multicolored polka dots all over them, her eyebrows furrowed with concern. "What's wrong with these? It's wet, right?"

He shook his head and laughed. "I s'pose they'll have to do."

"They'll be fine, honey," Mama echoed, her amused smile not convincing.

Brock lowered the ramp of the transport trailer as Shelby joined Eustace, who'd already made good friends with half the herd standing around him. He petted first one nose and then another, as one of the calves nuzzled in close to his side. Frank's old sheepdog—another survivor—ran around the knobby legs of the cows, more excited than anyone.

Noble stood on the fence rail. "Y'all ready back there?"

"Alright, let's bring 'em in," Brock hollered.

Wasn't trouble at all getting those cows to follow each other right into the trailer, especially with the unexpected help of Whitmore's dog running back and forth and keeping them lined up and following each other, and Eustace and Shelby following up the back. Cows would follow each other off a cliff one right after the other if they were herded that way. All but one calf filed into the trailer. When the straggler got close to the metal ramp, the sound of the others' hooves banging against it spooked her. She started running the opposite direction, and Shelby took it upon herself to run after her.

"Wait—Shelby!" Noble hollered but soon realized the girl was determined to catch the calf, who behaved like a greased pig. The two of them ran circles around the corral until Shelby hit a particularly thick patch of muck. One boot sank deep. Then the other. But her feet kept moving, and before she knew it, she'd landed face-first—and bootless—on the ground.

At first Noble thought by the look on her face she might cry.

"Get on out there and help her, Noble." Mama elbowed him hard in the side.

He started toward her as she rolled over and tried to push herself up, but the mud and manure were slippery and she fell facedown again. Her chest and shoulders shook, and Noble moved quicker, concerned now that she might be hurt. But when she looked up at him, she was hysterical with laughter.

He held out his hand to help her, and she yanked him right down in the muck with her, and the two of them doubled over and laughed right along with Mama and Brock at the fence. Eventually, they managed to help each other up by holding tight to the other's arms for balance. When they finally stood upright, face-to-face, Noble couldn't contain his affection any longer. He pushed a hunk of manure-covered hair back from Shelby's face, freckles more pronounced than ever against her cheeks flushed with laughter, and he kissed her.

"Well, I'll be," he heard Mama say behind him.

Shelby pushed back at first, then leaned in close and kissed him back, which made them both weak-kneed enough to fall into the muck all over again, and they sat there unable to move for some time, tears of laughter falling down their faces.

Eventually they got the calf into the trailer, and Brock drove off, back toward the Burdens'. Laurie and Shelby waited in the pickup as Noble pulled the gate shut and made one more inspection of the property.

The bank would be offering it up for auction, and it was doubtful that anyone would take a risk on trying to make it a fully operational dairy again. Noble felt his stomach clench at the thought of this place, so familiar, shut down and empty. The hum of cicadas, flies buzzing over the manure, and the solitary call of a field sparrow were all that was left of decades of Whitmore's hard work. Already the house, white clapboard and not unlike theirs with a saggy front porch roof and dormers on the second story, showed signs of abandonment, the weeds and thistle high as the windowsills, newspapers—delivered before anyone realized Whitmore was dead—piled up and yellowing along the threshold of the front door. How quickly a lifetime of sweat and hard work could be erased from the world, as if it never happened.

"He lets me rest in green meadows; he leads me beside

peaceful streams. He renews my strength. He guides me along right paths . . ."

Noble recalled the words, cross-stitched by Mama into a framed picture beside his bed. He used to ask her to recite the whole psalm to him, along with the Lord's Prayer, every night before she turned off his light, before he stopped asking her to pray with him.

What would happen to their pastures, to the stream on the back part of their land, if they left?

"Hey, Noble, there ain't no paint drying out there! C'mon!" Mama hollered from the truck.

"I'm comin'!" he hollered back, taking one long, last look at the overgrown pastures and the blown-out transformer next to the giant old walnut tree, charred and split in two by the lightning bolt.

>>> ——— <<<

Shelby, freshly showered and dressed in a T-shirt and shorts, sat next to Mama on the fence of the Burdens' corral, and they watched as Noble and Eustace worked on training Whitmore's cows to the wire, electric fencing.

"So explain to me what y'all are doin'?" Shelby said. "Y'all had barbed wire last time I knew."

"For a girl who's grown up in the country, you sure know next to nothin' about cows," Noble said.

"No, but I've forgotten more than you've ever known about the Bible."

"Touché." Noble tipped his hat at her and winked.

"I can't hardly stand to watch it," Mama said, looking out at the new and skittish cows. "I don't care what you say, it's gotta hurt 'em some."

The corral, which was about the size of a basketball court, was surrounded by a sturdy white PVC fence. On one end was an enormous trough of water. On the other end was a concrete pad where a couple bales of alfalfa were set and a second trough full of feed. In the middle of the corral was a length of electrical fence, which required the cows to go around the end of it to get from the food to the water. If any of them tried to take a shortcut through the middle, they got shocked.

"The barbed wire was a mess. Couldn't go a week without having to replace a post or the wire or something. We had to acquire a little debt to switch it out, but it's making up for itself in repairs and the sores the cows got from the other. 'Sides that, it doesn't take long for the cows to learn what the wire looks like, to know not to go near it," Noble explained as he and Eustace gently nudged the cows from one side to the other, encouraging them to learn the fence. "And once they're trained, they'll stay away from it, even if it ain't turned on."

"So even if the power goes out, they stay?"

"Once they're trained, yep. They only have to get shocked once or twice before they learn. Plus, they can sense the current with their bare noses. Can't see to save their lives, but they can sense the fence."

"How long will you leave them in here?"

"A couple days is all it should take. There may be a couple who test it, but they should be fine once we let 'em out to pasture. Haven't had time to look at Frank's records to see when we can breed them, get them milking again."

Eustace stood near the feed trough, three of the cows mesmerized by him as he moved among them, bending down to look into their eyes, stroking their necks. If any one of them made it around the electric fence, he'd offer it a munch in a bucket of sweet feed he held.

"He's amazing." Shelby nodded toward Eustace.

Noble, who'd come alongside the fence where she and Mama sat, turned and watched his brother for a long minute. Whatever language he spoke, those cows understood it. They were probably the only ones besides God who understood him.

I know the plans I have for you, Noble. I know the plans I have for your brother, too, he heard the Lord whisper.

"That don't mean we have to have the same plans," he blurted out.

Shelby looked at him, clearly bewildered.

"Never mind," he said. The afternoon sun angled against her eyes so they shone a blue like Noble'd never seen before. He was tempted, were Mama not right there next to her, to kiss her again. Instead, he stepped back and leaned against the fence, watching Eustace and the heifer going crazy eating grain out of the bucket in his hands.

Later, after they finished settling the cows, Noble walked Shelby to her truck. He could feel her pull away from him, not exactly physically, but the way he'd said the cows sense the current when they get too close to the electric fence.

She reached for the door handle, and he put a hand gently on her shoulder. "Shelby—"

"Noble, stop." She took a step back. "It's complicated. I shouldn't have let you kiss me."

"Oh yeah? Then why'd you kiss me back? Why'd you even bother coming out here today?"

She got in her truck, slammed the door, and put the keys in the ignition. "I don't know."

"I think I do. You don't love him—Cade." He could barely bring himself to say the name.

She turned toward him. "I do. I mean . . . I have. He's not all that bad, Noble."

Noble stepped closer to the truck. "Not *that* bad? Really? Then why do you act afraid of him? Why'd you act afraid of his daddy?"

She stiffened, and Noble could see her eyes dampen. He kicked an old can that'd been left out in the yard as hard as he could, causing Shelby to jump. It went sailing into the field across the road.

"You don't have to put up with that. You can't let yourself put up with that. It only gets worse, you know."

She wiped a tear but did not acknowledge him either way. She just clenched the steering wheel harder.

He ran his hands through his hair and sighed, looking up at the line of feathery cirrus clouds. Whatever storms were supposed to have come in must've burned themselves out. "It's just as well, I suppose, considering I'm going to Nashville."

She straightened her shoulders and pushed the hair away from her face, which had gone from soft to hard as stone. "So you're really going?"

"I'm gonna check it out, yeah. The guy's legit, Shelby. And it's *Nashville*. You wanted to go there once, too, remember? You used to want a lot of things."

She opened her mouth as if to say something but closed it and began to drive away. Then she stopped and leaned out the window. "Things change, Noble Burden."

Stones flew from the gravel drive as she floored it onto the dirt road toward her home across the fields before Noble could argue with her.

Problem was, she didn't get far.

25

James, having gotten his car back from a deputy who'd been kind enough to return it quietly before dawn, rolled to a stop in front of Shelby's stalled truck alongside the road in front of the Burdens' home. Still raw from the night before, James hadn't wanted to see anyone today. He could feel the memory of the cold metal of the gun in his hand. A headache behind his eyes throbbed, and the sight of Laurie's place up close sobered him. Her struggles over the past years showed in the wind-worn, chipped siding, the sag of the yellowed curtains in the front windows, the ailing front-porch swing. They had no doubt spent much of the past years recovering from the drought of the previous years, and now too much rain this year, which probably wiped out some of their feeder fields like everyone else in the area.

Steam rose from the open hood of Shelby's truck. She leaned against the side, her chin high and shoulders tensed the same way Molly used to when she had been furious with him. Noble sat on the front steps of the porch looking like a puppy who'd been reprimanded for straying.

James knew better than to say anything to Shelby as he approached her.

She rolled her eyes. "Stupid truck."

"Yes, well, she might get angrier if you start calling her names."

"Whatever, Dad. Can you fix it?"

"I told her it's probably the cooling hose or a gasket." Noble came down the drive toward them. "I coulda fixed it, but she wouldn't hear of it. Wouldn't even let me take a look."

"Just like her mama," James laughed, and memories of Molly like old, faded Polaroids flashed through his mind. She had been quite a pistol, too. The ache of missing her pressed against his gut. That's the way the memories were, the way the ruthless pain of grief worked, coming on sudden and unexpected. "Don't worry about it, son. Appreciate you being willing."

"Ugh," Shelby groaned at both of them.

James walked back toward his car and rifled around in the trunk, cringing when he saw the empty leather gun cover. He found a cooling hose and a gasket and some fluid, which he handed to Noble, who stood near the hood.

Noble covered his hand in an old rag and took off the radiator cap. "Which one do you think?"

"I'll bet on the hose," James said.

Sure enough, it was, along with an empty water compartment, and the two men replaced it while Shelby pretended to ignore them. A half hour later and the truck was up and running, and James and Noble watched as Shelby picked up where she left off and drove home in a flurry of dust.

James shook his head. "Sorry about that."

"She's upset with me. Can't say I blame her, I guess."

James studied Noble and wondered at how fast the unshaven face and broad shoulders had replaced the lanky droop of youth he'd remembered. His features were relaxed, even in his distress over Shelby's abrupt departure, and James appreciated the calm resignation of the lad, who had every reason to act more like a Cade, cocky and rude, after being raised by a father like Dale and having to take on too much manhood too soon. It occurred to James then how much of a choice it was whether to let pain take hold of your heart and harden it, or whether to press on through it, whether to pick up a gun or let it rest, whether to pull a trigger or live.

"Wanna talk about it?" James thought about how Tate had asked him the same question a few short hours before as they sat together at the end of Maple Street.

Noble kicked a stone around the ground with the toe of his work boot. "I don't know." He met James's eyes. "I got a chance to go to Nashville."

"Nashville? That's great!" James tried to sound enthusiastic despite the heaviness hanging over his own head and the obvious hesitation in Noble.

"Yeah, you'd think. Always wanted to get out of this place. Now I have a chance, and I feel like . . . well . . . I guess it's not crazy to say this to you since you're a pastor . . . but I feel like all of a sudden God's hintin' at me that I need to stay."

"No, that doesn't sound crazy."

"You know what's funny about it is that all these years, with Dad leavin', all this time I been wondering where God is. And now . . . *now* he decides to show up." Noble shook his head, clearly frustrated. He lifted his eyes to the sky, took off his ball cap, and scratched his head. "I mean, I guess realistically, how could I leave, Rev? What am I even thinking, entertaining the idea? There's this farm, Mama, Eustace—they can't run it without me. And Mama, she's been here her whole life. She ain't gonna want to move to Nashville. Hard enough living around here with half the town knowin' all Dad put her through. I was thinkin' maybe the city'd be good for Eustace, a place where they'd have people who could help him, give him more of a life. But the more I watch him—really watch him—the more I think his place is here. I'm afraid the city would suck the life right out of him."

"But it's your dream, right?"

"It is."

"Then you have to try it. Go and see what it's like. If you don't, it'll rumble around in your soul and you'll always wonder, even if it turns out to be all wrong. At least you'll know for sure." Wasn't that what Molly had told him all those years ago? He wondered where they'd be if he'd tried harder to stay around Atlanta.

"You can fill your mind with *if only*s," Tilly had told him at Molly's funeral. "Or you can fill it with *thank heavens*es. It's up to you how you choose to go on and live from here."

"I suppose you're right," Noble said.

"I can help, talk to your mama, help with the farm. It's not like I've got anything better to do anymore, church closing and all."

Noble shot him a look of surprise. "You'd do that? Help with the farm?"

"If your mama will have me, I would."

"Care for a drink of water? Maybe some lemonade? We can see what Mama thinks."

"That sounds wonderful." James wiped the sweat off his forehead, and the two men walked up to the house. The worn steps creaked as they approached the front door. It was a hundred degrees in the shade, and he was conscious of the sweat dripping down his back between his undershirt and skin.

"Been a while, Reverend." Laurie opened the door before Noble could reach it. She smiled slightly, then raised her hand and tugged at a calico fabric scarf holding back her hair.

James shoved his hands in his pockets, caught off guard at feeling a little nervous around her, the way he tried not to notice the curve of her hip and the gentle angle of her chin, the green of her eyes and the sunlight gleaming against her hair. "I'm sorry. It seems my daughter got herself into a predicament out front."

"Mmm-hmmmm. Mighta been prevented if she hadn't tried to floor it out of our driveway." She stepped back unexpectedly. "Would you like to come in?"

"I already invited him in for some lemonade." Noble walked toward the kitchen, leaving the two of them standing alone.

"I don't want to be a bother. Figured I ought to at least say hello since I spent the last hour in your yard." He took his hat off and ran his fingers through his hair.

Laurie leaned against the threshold and crossed her arms. Her eyes flitted to the road beyond him and back to his again.

"How are you, Laurie?"

Her gaze fell and her hand came to rest on the doorknob. She shifted her weight.

He took in her frame, the slightness of it, the way her fingers looked pale and thin, like a child's almost, the emptiness beneath the oversize T-shirt, the jeans which hung on her thin legs. He was overwhelmed suddenly with remorse and something . . . not pity, but something more that he couldn't quite name.

"I've been meaning . . . ," he started. "I'd like to tell you I'm sorry."

She looked at him again, tilted her head, and sighed. Her eyes focused again on some unknown spot on the horizon. "Sorry for what?"

"For not being here more. I should have . . . could have offered to help. Not as a pastor, but as a neighbor. As a friend."

"I suppose you could've. But it's a little late for that, don't you think? 'Sides that, you've had enough of your own tragedy, haven't you? Anyway, I would've refused."

"Yes. Yes, I suppose you would have. You've been intent on handling everything yourself before, and I guess I was trying to honor that. But . . . would you still? Refuse my help?"

She sighed again. "I'm not in any kind of mood for being preached at, if that's what you mean. And I don't anticipate that changing anytime soon. I only came to church Sunday to see Noble play."

"Like I said, I don't mean as a pastor. Clearly that's not working out for me anyway." He felt heat rising up his neck, surprised to hear himself say that out loud.

"I don't need you feeling sorry for me either."

"Laurie—"

"I'd make a great project, right? Lonely woman with the hard heart. Washed-up, newly widowed pastor comes along and fixes her."

James straightened. "I beg your pardon, but I don't need feeling sorry for, either."

Laurie's eyes widened, appearing as surprised as James felt abashed at his response.

He shoved his hands deeper in his pockets and was glad when Noble returned and handed him lemonade, condensation already forming on the sides of the glass.

"It's getting close to milking time," Noble said to Laurie. "Rev says he'll help with the milking and Eustace while I'm gone to Nashville."

She raised her eyebrows at them both.

"I'm a fast learner," James offered. "Besides, it's like riding a bike, isn't it? That's what Molly always said."

Laurie's eyes flickered at his mention of Molly.

"Of course I'll need a refresher."

"Of course. You better go on and show him, Noble." She turned and disappeared into the cool dark of the house, and James heard her snigger, "Just like riding a bike."

James stayed to watch the milking, even though the weight of his exhaustion from the night before caused his body to ache and feel twice as heavy as it ever had. He wondered why he had been so quick to offer to help.

Once James and the boys were out in the milking parlor, Eustace flipped on the radio and a country singer crooned across the room. Noble taught James to close the stanchions around the cows' necks and hook the teats up to the machines, which were much improved compared to the ones James remembered helping them with years ago. The claw devices sensed when the udders had given all they could and dropped off automatically, a spring contraption pulling them up toward the ceiling, ready for the next cow to come into the stall for the process to repeat. When each cow finished, James dipped their teats in the cleansing iodine mixture like Noble showed him. Around the corner, Eustace tossed hay and sweet feed into the concrete trough, and the heads of the cows hung over the side and munched contentedly as they gave their milk.

The job wasn't as hard as he'd remembered. He was

amazed all over again by the way the cows filed in and chose their stalls, then waited patiently for Noble to hook them up. They scooped manure if the cows pooped, cleaned their udders, and sent them on their way. It wasn't unlike a church service, he thought, just twice a day compared to once a week.

File in.

Give them something to eat.

Clean them up.

Send them on their way.

Same stalls, same pews.

Salve their souls to prevent chafing in the harsh world.

Later, as James walked to his car to go home, he turned back to the house and saw someone let go of the curtain in the front window. He grinned to himself, considering that maybe he shouldn't have been so frank with Laurie, but she was feeling as sorry for him as he was for her. He drove away, and the road he'd traveled a thousand times looked different, the rise of a hill he hadn't noticed before, the cry of a whip-poor-will, the groan of frogs as he crossed over the stream. Tilly had said endings can bring beginnings, and he began to wonder if that's what the Lord was doing with him now.

26

The following Sunday, Noble set a high stool in the chancel and began tuning his guitar. He paused for a moment and looked at Shelby, who sat in the second pew scrolling on her phone. They were the first and only ones in the sanctuary, as James had retreated to his office to put the finishing touches on his sermon.

"C'mon, Shelby, are you really going to pretend we're not in the same room together?" Noble's voice bounced across the emptiness of the high-ceilinged room.

She didn't respond.

He began to strum his guitar hard, then louder, diving into a hard rock riff that eventually got her attention.

"Cut it out, Noble," she yelled.

He turned his ear toward her and continued to play. "What's that?"

"I said, cut it out!"

"Huh?" he teased.

"What is goin' on in here?" Myrtle Worley walked in from the narthex.

Shelby smirked as Noble tried to muffle the last chord echoing through the sanctuary.

"Sorry about that, Mrs. Worley."

"I should say." She straightened her skirt and approached the chancel and her seat behind the organ.

Noble excused himself and nodded toward Shelby to step outside with him. Thankfully, she did, although he suspected only because she probably didn't want to stick around and listen to Myrtle warm up the organ. He turned to her as the heavy doors closed behind them. "Now that I have your attention . . ."

"You had my attention." She stared out at the park, the street, obviously avoiding his eyes.

"Look, I'd like to be able to play through this service without wondering how long you're gonna be mad at me and why."

"I'm not mad at you."

"If stormin' off the other day and pretending I don't exist in there ain't your version of mad, I'd hate to see what is."

She sighed and finally met his gaze. "Can we not do this?"

"If you could define *this*, I sure would appreciate it. Because I don't know what *this* is. It sure ain't what we used to have, back when we did everything together. Back when you asked if we'd be together forever. Remember when you asked me that? Besides that, I ain't the only one who's noticed you changing. You haven't hardly talked to me since your mom died, and you're determined to push away everybody in this town who cares about you. Watching you with Cade's like watching a train headed toward a cliff. In the meantime, it's the second-to-last service before your dad has to shut the doors to this place forever."

"I'm well aware of what's happening with my dad."

"Really? 'Cause you sure fooled me. Seems you're more concerned with giving me a hard time about a decision I'm making, which by the way is hardly any of your business."

She furrowed her brows and crossed her arms.

"Look, Shelby, I'm going to Nashville to see what it's all about. I can't know if it's even worth considering if I don't go. Don't know why you care anyway," he mumbled under his breath. Times like this he thought about how nice it would be to get out of Sycamore, to move them all into a nice house in suburban Nashville, Eustace getting in some kind of program allowing him to work and interact with people like himself, Mama with better access to jobs or even going back to school like she used to talk about, but Dad had never let her. He sat on the top step and wiped the beads of sweat off his forehead. The humidity was already thick, another set of weekend storms doing nothing to chase it away, but instead fueling the damp heat.

Shelby plopped down next to him and brushed a damp

strand of loose curls off her neck. Sweat glistened on her forehead and arms.

"What happened to you?" He nodded at her arm, bruised all the way around. He knew she'd been out with Cade the night before.

She cringed and put her hand over the spot. "Nothin'. I was carrying something up the stairs and stumbled. Caught myself on the railing."

Noble said nothing, just looked at her as she held his gaze. Something between vexation and pride replaced what had been tears in her eyes the other day at the Tractor Supply, and he suspected she was trying hard as she could not to give anything away.

He remembered the way Mama kept hanging on to Dad, even when Noble'd gotten old enough to beg her to leave him. He remembered the way Dad drank and hit and Mama cried and cowered and Dad apologized and brought her flowers and the same thing repeated itself like a movie on replay week after week after week. He wondered if that was what Cade did to Shelby, if the wooing outweighed the pain . . . although it was hard to imagine Cade wooing anybody.

James stuck his head out the door. "You two getting hot out here? How about gathering up some fans from the basement or wherever you can find them and setting them up in the sanctuary? It's not any cooler in here."

"Be glad to," Noble said.

Shelby pulled her cardigan over her arms despite the heat, and the two of them went inside.

James preached and the couple dozen folks who'd come to church that day sat and nodded at his assurances of life going on after Sycamore Community Church closed, about the determination to keep on following God even when the way got cloudy and the waters got rough, about God being outside of time and space and about the Holy Spirit not requiring bricks and mortar to do his saving work. He said the amen and the people sang the closing hymn in a collection of flat vibratos, while Mrs. Worley swayed in her organ seat, patches of sweat growing wider under her bosom.

Noble slowly joined in with his guitar in the key of G, all the time wondering about the reason God had him playing here again and going to Nashville that week:

*"Some bright morning when this life is over, I'll fly
away . . ."*

When his life was over, what would he have to show for it if he didn't go to Nashville? The same hills rolling past their sagging home, the same Mama hiding in her sewing room, the same Eustace preaching silent benedictions over the same brown cows? What harm would come in getting away from all of this, from the memories of Dad's beatings that still stung and memories of Mama curled in bed for days after he left, from those shadows he couldn't hide from, but maybe he could fly from, to Nashville, to lights and music and the stage . . .

"Like a bird from these prison walls, I'll fly away."

Thoughts of the possibility of playing in front of real crowds with real bands swelled in his chest, and for the first time since he could remember, he let himself feel excited. He saw Mama watching him from her spot in the back row of the church; he saw Eustace sitting beside her, bent over his phone. The stained-glass windows caught and splattered hot sunlight across the sanctuary, a beam of it illuminating Eustace's white ball cap like a halo.

Noble recalled stories of prisoners who got out of jail and didn't know what to do with themselves after they'd been stuck there so long, the blue of the sky too blue, the freshness of the air near bursting their lungs, and them winding up right back in jail because they couldn't handle the freedom. But he'd heard of others who'd made it out and gone on to live, and live well and live right.

His family had not only been stuck in Sycamore, they'd been born into the pattern of the small town and the small ways that come along with it. Even if Mama and Eustace didn't know what they were missing, Noble would go and find out. Maybe their lives were fine, the familiar safety of the creek running through the backyard, the embrace of the dirt- and crop-quilted countryside. But if Nashville were better . . . Well, like the reverend had even said, they'd never know unless he went and saw for himself. If he could get a good job there, they could all have a new start. Lord knew they deserved one.

As the service ended, James reminded the attendees that they had only one remaining service and that Shelby and

Bonnie were collecting memorabilia for scrapbooks to document and preserve church history. The people shuffled to their cars, which had turned into saunas in the blistering heat. Noble bent to put his guitar in the case and felt a hand on his sweat-drenched back.

"Not now, Eustace. Let me pack up." He turned and saw Reverend Horton there instead.

"That was great, Noble. Truly."

"Thanks."

"You ready for your trip this week?"

"Ready as I'll ever be. Cass said there won't be any formal auditions. He's got some CDs with my demos on them he's had some friends listen to. Says this is just a meet and greet to see how I like things and to give folks a taste of what I can do."

"Try not to worry while you're out there. I'll take care of your mama and Eustace."

"Means a heck of a lot," Noble said.

"I know it does."

Noble tried not to watch Shelby as she adjusted the knot of hair on her head and reapplied lip gloss.

"Still won't talk to you much, eh?" James asked.

Noble flushed.

"You wear it on your sleeve." James laughed as the two of them walked down the aisle and out to the front steps of the church. "And everywhere else for that matter. I wouldn't recognize it so easily if I hadn't been so in love myself when I was your age."

"Rev—"

"Call me James."

"Okay. James. I . . ." He paused, unsure for a moment how to proceed with the conversation, then sighed, exasperated. "I mean, anyone else. Anyone besides *him*." He threw his arm in the direction of Cade's car, Shelby climbing into the front seat like they were headed to a fire, taillights flashing as it tore out onto Main Street.

"She's so much like her mother." James sighed. "Beautiful and stubborn. Precocious and proud. All of which add up to a woman who can't be told a thing and has to figure it out on her own or, sadly, learn the hard way."

"I'm worried about her."

James put a hand on his shoulder. "Me too, son. Me too."

27

The last time James had set foot in the Methodist church was a few weeks after Molly died. They'd had enough casseroles to freeze and feed the two of them for months, partially because of the sheer number of them he and Shelby had received, but also because it was awfully hard for a man and a teenage daughter to finish a whole one at all. James understood that casseroles were the equivalent of condolences for congregants. But casseroles weren't enough. James needed someone who didn't place him on a precarious pedestal, who saw beyond his reverend mask.

And so he had turned to Charlie Reynolds. Now he found himself seeking out the counsel of his fellow pastor once again.

The Methodist church had advantages, not the least of

which was that it was built in the 1950s at the height of the Eisenhower years. The floors were solid and did not squeak. The windows were not drafty. The roof was straight and intact. And although some aspects of the building—such as the heavy, odd-angled trim work—were a bit Googie-looking, at least nothing was falling apart.

Charlie's office was at the end of a long corridor of offices, and James nodded at the folks he recognized, a woman using a die-cut machine and colored construction paper, probably for a Sunday school craft; an associate pastor talking to a couple facing away from the door; the church secretary, who smiled as if to say, "Go right ahead," as James knocked on the frame of the open door.

"James!" Charlie's voice echoed down the hall as it might have across the sanctuary on a Sunday morning, and he scurried to the door to shake James's hand.

James felt his face grow warm and he regretted that he had not thought to ask Charlie to meet him somewhere less conspicuous. Then again, there were few if any places either of them could go without being recognized. The only thing worse than the scrutiny of someone in the community suspecting something was wrong with the pastor were church staffers thinking something was wrong with the pastor.

"Come in, come in! Have a seat." Charlie motioned to one of two overstuffed chairs across from his desk.

James was grateful when Charlie sat in one of them instead of behind his desk, which would have made him feel like a congregant rather than a peer.

"How are you? How's Shelby?" Charlie crossed his legs and leaned back.

"I'm okay . . . alright . . . I'm not okay, really. And I'm concerned . . . Shelby's still distant—she won't hardly talk to any of her old friends, and now on top of her grieving . . . Well, I assume you saw the headlines last week." James slouched back in his chair, his long legs poking out in front of him like a praying mantis, he thought.

Charlie leaned forward, resting his chin on his steepled forefingers. "What can I do to help?"

James shook his head, then cursed under his breath. "Sorry. You're the only one I can talk like that in front of without thinking I ought to be disrobed . . . Then again . . ."

Charlie laughed. "What's said in my office stays in my office."

James glanced at the door, still open, and was grateful when Charlie got up to close it. He looked around the room, noting the books on the shelves, many they'd shared back and forth over the years. There were various paperweights and trinkets with Scriptures and platitudes engraved on them, probably gifts from congregants, and a large Thomas Kinkade painting hanging on the wall behind his desk, the windows of a church glowing as evening fell—or was the sun about to rise? He couldn't tell.

"What would you do?" James asked as Charlie sat down again.

"Well, I—"

"If you didn't have any of this anymore," James interrupted

and waved his arm around the room. "What would you do then?"

Charlie sat back and looked around the room then, too, as if noticing his office and all that was in it for the first time.

"You know," James continued, "the other night, Sheriff Tate found me sitting at the end of Maple Street out by the old mansion. Said he was on his way out to the truck stop for donuts, but God told him to turn, so he did. And because of that, he saved my life."

"How's that?" Charlie leaned forward again, brow raised.

"I thought . . ." James closed his eyes and massaged his temples, trying to decide how much to confess to his friend. But that's why he'd come to see Charlie, wasn't it? To confess? "I had a gun."

"Lord, have mercy . . ."

"Well, that he did."

"I know you've had more than your fair share of pain . . . and you'd mentioned before about the church's financial troubles . . . but I didn't know you were feeling that desperate."

"Is that what I'm feeling, Charlie? Desperate? Because it feels a lot more like failure than desperation."

"Did he take it?"

James cocked his head, confused by the question.

"The gun. Did Tate take the gun, or do you still have it?"

"Oh yes, the gun." James let out a nervous half laugh. "You're good to ask. Tate has it. I told him to keep it. The thing is, I don't even know if I had the courage or the ability to have really shot the thing anyway. I think . . . after all these years . . . I think my father was right."

"Your father?" Charlie relaxed slightly, probably relieved to know about the gun.

James hesitated again as he considered talking about his father, this time because he knew Charlie had his own inferiority complex when it came to his father, the great Chuck Reynolds Sr. He'd started a church in Texas with 150 people and turned it into the biggest megachurch in Texas. Chuck Sr. had not even tried to hide his disappointment when Charlie opted for a position in Sycamore, and at a Methodist church, besides.

"Don't you ever get frustrated . . . ?" James started. "You know, there've been nights I lay awake thinking about the church, the ministry, what God's called me to, and I admit, the worst kind of jealousy comes over me. I wonder what it'd be like to have a great big stage and parishioners pouring through the doors . . . big, hot lights and sound boards and worship leaders and backup musicians with perfect segues between service elements, rows of people raising their hands, alive with passion, electric with the Spirit. Don't you ever feel that way? I mean . . . between my dad telling me outright I'd never amount to anything by being a pastor and my pews being sparsely filled for a while now . . . Whatever those other churches are doing . . . whatever I've been missing . . . maybe my dad was right."

Charlie scratched his chin, and the two sat in silence for a while. Finally Charlie spoke. "It is a conundrum, that's for sure.

And yes, I think about those things every time I think about my dad too. I've struggled with it. Wrestled with God about it. Shaken my fist at him about it. Wept about it. I still do, sometimes. We clergy, we like to quote C. S. Lewis and Eugene Peterson. We applaud the clarion words of Henri Nouwen, the simplicity of St. Augustine, even the apostle Paul himself. But the bigger and better, the *me* of ministry, is what we're really smitten with. Or at least, if we're not careful, we are. We can't help it. Everything in our world shouts at us to be more to more people, to not offend but to be relevant. But Jesus . . . he talks about the meek and the small, the tired and the poor, the unsightly and the overlooked, and the eye of the needle."

Charlie stopped for a moment, walked to his desk, and picked up a stack of booklets and brochures. "All this is what I've gotten in the last week alone, mailings about growing a church and discipleship programs that will knock the socks off small groups—"

"My entire congregation is a small group."

"Right." Charlie laughed and tossed the pile back on his desk. "Am I making any sense? We've got Higher Ground sucking people away from our church, too. I've even considered investing in a couple of fog machines."

"Don't do it." James grinned.

"We won't." He laughed again. "But here's the thing. A couple of things. First of all, like the old hymn says, the church's one foundation is Jesus Christ, and big or small, he uses them all. Second, no pastor ever feels like he's enough. And third—"

"A three-point sermon," James taunted, holding up three fingers.

"I can't help it," Charlie laughed. "Anyway, third, I think we forget that as much as grace is for our congregants, grace is for us—you and me—too."

"His strength is made perfect in weakness," James said wistfully.

"It's not a cliché."

"Sounds like one. Lately every Scripture sounds cliché. I've heard them all too much."

"Don't I know it." Charlie grabbed a worn copy of the Bible off his desk. He flipped through the pages until he found one to settle on. "Even so, do you recall the story of the Jews building the wall in Nehemiah? When all they had was a pile of rubbish, and the Samarians were making fun of them for trying to make something out of the little that they had?"

James frowned slightly, vaguely recalling the passage, but unsure of what Charlie was getting at.

"It's in Nehemiah, chapter 4. Nehemiah brought other people to surround the workers so they could carry on their work. Some men worked, and others stood guard and encouraged the workers to remember the Lord. It was quite a rescue effort, because the wall covered a very large area. And the workers, they were exhausted."

"Alright. Your three points and a conclusion, Reverend?"

"Sometimes we're like the workers, sometimes we're like the guards, and sometimes we're like Nehemiah. There's a place and a time for all of us—"

"Now you're quoting Ecclesiastes."

Charlie laughed. "Look. You've been laboring a long time, friend. There's no shame in what happened with your church. There's no shame in taking a break from the ministry, maybe even making a total change in your career. And to answer your question, I don't know what I'd do if I were you. Except to say that I do hope after the doors close, you'll consider this a safe place for you, or if not here, then with the Baptists."

"That might be a stretch," James laughed. "Kidding, of course. Well . . . sort of."

"'It is through God's kindness, then it is not by their good works. For in that case, God's grace would not be what it really is—free and undeserved,'" Charlie quoted.

"Ahh, there we go. Romans 11. Always could relate a little better to Paul. 'For who can know the Lord's thoughts? Who knows enough to give him advice?'"

"Verse 34," Charlie said.

"Can we just agree that I'm a horrible pastor?" James rubbed his temples again, weary of the effort to try to sort out where and why and how things went so wrong.

Charlie leaned forward, resting his elbows on his knees, and looked hard into James's eyes. "I will not agree to that. I will instead insist that you are one of the greatest pastors, because you are here doing the hardest, most courageous thing of all, which is admitting that you can't do the job yourself. The rest of us, whose doors will remain open for the foreseeable future, have a lot we can learn from that."

James considered this, and even as he did, he felt his face relaxing a bit.

The two men talked awhile longer, arguing over translations, wrestling with God's grace, even cursing a little about the taking of a wife too soon, the state of the church in Sycamore and at large, and because they could in the privacy of that office. They could be plain men in front of each other. That in itself was a blessing to James, for it had been too long since he felt the robes of his calling lift enough for him to come out from under them and breathe.

>>>———<<<

Back at home, James stopped as he was about to pass by the doorway of Shelby's room. Surrounded by scrapbooks she and Molly had made together, she sat on the braided rug in the middle of her hardwood floor.

"She was so pretty."

The page she was looking at featured Molly laughing, covered in paint, as James surprised her refurbishing an old dresser she'd found at a yard sale.

"Yes. She was."

When Shelby looked up at him, James saw that she had been weeping. "Do you think she'd be proud of me?"

"I'm sure of it."

"Dad, how did you and Mom know you were right together?"

James took a deep breath. He'd felt so unable to reach her

lately and now was a chance. Now she had asked him about something. Now he could say something and she might actually listen.

"Hmmm . . . well . . . that's a hard one."

He sat on her bed and picked up the pink stuffed bear Molly'd packed in the hospital bag all those years ago. The fur was rubbed off in places, the seams showing on the edges.

"I mean, I guess it wasn't hard for us as much as it was for her parents. I didn't come from much, and I certainly didn't have the professional and financial ambitions they were expecting for her."

"Why did money matter so much?"

"At the time, I wondered the same thing. Didn't seem fair. But now—"

"Now that you're a parent . . ." She rolled her eyes.

"Well, yes, now that I'm a parent, I can understand." He smoothed the frayed strings down around the bear's embroidered eyes. "There's a lot of things I understand better now. They wanted her to be cared for. The way I hope you will be cared for . . . better, I think, than the way I think Cade might be treating you."

She sighed and focused back on the scrapbook page. "He treats me *fine*."

"Does he?"

She met his eyes and looked hard into them. "Yes."

"Folks around town have mentioned—"

She held up her hand. "Wait. Let me guess. They've told you he hangs with a bad crowd and he's like his dad."

"Well, yes. And there's concern for physical harm, too."

"Just because someone looks one way on the outside doesn't mean they're like what people think they're like." She shut the cover of the scrapbook and slammed it on the floor.

"All I'm saying is I'm worried about your safety. Apples don't fall far, and Silas has hurt a lot of folks. There were reasons his wife left him years back. And Cade has made his own reputation for himself." The newspaper printed the police blotter, and everyone knew about the day Silas's wife reported a domestic disturbance and had filed for divorce and eventually left town. Cade and Silas both had been listed for traffic violations and multiple other runs to their house for various reasons. Besides that, folks talked about how Cade didn't measure up to Silas, who'd been the town hero when he'd gotten a full-ride scholarship to play for Indiana University back in his day.

"I suppose you think I should be with a nice guy like Noble Burden, right?"

"You two were close . . . before the accident. I do worry about why you're not close anymore."

She sighed, and her shoulders drooped. "He's going to Nashville. He's leaving. Just like everyone leaving the church and others leaving town altogether." Her shoulders drooped and the hardness in her face softened as tears began to fall. "Just like Mama."

He watched Shelby, shoulders shaking as she began to weep. She sat there cross-legged like a little girl but looking all grown up and on the verge of so many big decisions. So many changes. Too many changes.

"I think after Mama died, I . . ." She hesitated as if bracing herself and him for what she was about to say. "It feels scary to be close to anyone anymore—" she tried to hold back a sob—"'cause what if they die, too?"

A picture on her bedside table caught his eye: the three of them, James, Molly, and Shelby, hair windblown and cheeks pink as they stood on a Lake Michigan beach. He remembered that day clearly. They'd gone up there for spring break and spent the day flying the kite Shelby held in her hands. He got down and sat on the floor beside her. "You know, Shelby, the hardest thing about living is realizing dying is a part of it, and I'm so sorry you've had to learn that this way, too young, too soon."

She rested her head on his shoulder and sniffed again. "What's gonna happen to us, Dad? I mean, after the church closes and all."

James rubbed his eyes, wondering about the answer to that question as much as she was. "We're not moving, I know that much. I promised to see you through your senior year."

"I know. But can you be a preacher someplace else?"

"Maybe . . . I don't know . . . I have a few folks I could ask . . ." He thought about Dr. Wilcox, friends he still kept in touch with from college. He thought about Hank's offer to give him a job at the hardware store. He tried to hold in the tears he felt puddling in his own eyes now. The last thing Shelby needed right then was to see her dad have an emotional breakdown. He was relieved she spoke up next.

"Do you remember how you used to tell me the story about Gideon?"

He kissed the top of her head, still resting on his shoulder. "I do. I kept wanting to read you other stories from that old children's Bible, but you insisted we read that one every night."

"He thought because all the bad things kept happening to them that God had abandoned them. And his clan was the weakest one in the land, but God told him to go and fight the—who was it?"

"The Midianites."

"Yeah." She wiped her eyes and grinned at him. "God kept making the army smaller and smaller, and in the end it was three hundred guys blowing their trumpets and breaking clay jars and they scared the Midianites into fighting themselves to death. You said God did all that so that when Gideon won the battle, everyone would know that God had made it happen. So he'd get the glory."

"Did I? I was so wise back then."

She laughed and gently elbowed him in the ribs. "Do you think that's what God's doing with us?"

James considered this for a moment, then pulled Shelby closer. "If he is, I think he can stop whittling us down now. We don't have much more to spare."

28

Being in Nashville hardly seemed real to Noble. Just hours ago he'd seen to the milking of sixty cows and now he was walking up the driveway of the mansion of a respected country music professional. He tried not to stare as he entered the pristine home of Cass Dinsmore on the top of a high hill in Brentwood, Tennessee. He felt like every bit the hick that he was against the dining room's coffered ceiling and the exquisite trim work on the walls. He kicked his worn shoes off and felt the thick carpet and padding under his feet. He tried to keep his chin from dropping at the sight of the fireplace in the front room, which was large enough to set a couch in and made from one solid piece of limestone carved with intricate Gothic patterns. He took in the view from the two-story picture windows.

Mama would love this, he thought. *And Eustace. It'd sure give him a lot of new places to go to find more butterflies.*

"Welcome to Nashville, Noble. I've heard so much about you. Can I get you somethin' to drink?" A woman he assumed to be Cass's wife appeared from the kitchen. Her glossy blonde hair was pulled back into a neat and smooth chignon. He caught the scent of her perfume and couldn't help but notice her pressed clothes that looked fresh off a clothing rack at a high-end store he'd seen in a mall in Indianapolis.

He remembered enough manners to extend his hand toward her and was grateful he'd stopped to wash them in the airport bathroom. He cleared his throat. "You must be Mrs. Dinsmore. I'll have some water if that's alright."

"Well, we've got plenty of that," she laughed. "And please, call me Azalea. Mrs. Dinsmore is my mother-in-law. Sure you don't want a soda? We've got some good craft beer?"

"No thank you, ma'am. Water's fine."

Cass put a hand on his shoulder. "Make yourself comfortable. Azalea's cooked us a fine supper, and we can sit in here or out on the veranda if you'd prefer while she's finishing it up."

The two of them settled on the veranda, which was surrounded by a generous limestone banister and canopied by Southern red oaks and magnolias. The patio furniture featured thick black scrolled iron and thick, weatherproofed seat cushions. One thing for sure, it sure wasn't any cooler in

Nashville. Noble held the glass of ice water, beads of moisture dripping down the sides. "You have a beautiful place here, Mr. Dinsmore."

"Please, as I've said, call me Cass."

Noble felt his face flush as he laughed a little louder than he'd intended.

"Look, Noble," Cass said, taking a sip of his bourbon from a crystal tumbler. "I'm sure this isn't what you're used to. But I wouldn't have brought you here unless I thought you really had something special. We hear all kinds play in auditions, and so many of them can move their fingers and carry a pitch, but it's forced, anxious. When I saw you playing at that bar—"

"The Purple Onion."

"That's it. The Purple Onion. When I saw you playing there, I said to myself, 'There's somebody who's a natural.' And you know what's so great about natural talent?"

"What's that?" A red-tailed hawk caught his eye as it flew from the red oak to a willow across the expansive backyard.

Cass leaned forward and swirled the bourbon in his cup. "Gives us something to work with. Gives bands what they're begging for. We're gonna find you an agent and then a contract, Noble Burden. What do you think of that?"

>>>———————<<<

Welcome, Noble Burden!

The slide lingered for a few seconds before flashing to the

next announcement on the flat screen mounted on the wall above the welcome desk inside the entrance to Mountain Top Studios. The seventeen-thousand-square-foot building was the recording home to some of the biggest names in country and western music. The lobby was enormous, and the walls were covered with gold and platinum albums, signed guitars and photographs of artists Noble had admired since before he could walk. He realized Cass had been talking to him.

"—six giant recording studios, all updated with the best and most advanced technologies. There's a fitness center, additional studios for TV and video productions, a conference center for education—I could see you leading some sessions there—and plenty of greenrooms for hanging out."

"Impressive." Noble's voice cracked as he struggled to comprehend and believe where he was in that moment. Before he'd gotten to Nashville, and despite Cass's assurances and all he'd discovered to be true about him on the Internet, he'd half assumed the whole thing was a joke and that he'd come back to Sycamore with his proverbial tail between his legs.

People in cowboy hats, reptile-skin boots, and pricey suits walked by, each of them greeting Cass. Noble knew from his Internet research that Cass was a highly respected scouter, but the full meaning of that only now had begun to register.

He gripped the handle on his guitar case tighter.

This was the real deal.

He could say yes and sign a piece of paper, if they offered one, and this life could be his.

"Mountain Top Studios is home to several of my main clients, and I've got a few people I'd like to introduce you to today," Cass said as he led Noble down a wide hallway to a collection of offices with oversize mahogany doors.

Noble noticed a man dressed in navy-blue work clothes sweeping the floor, the sort of job many of Noble's old high school friends had back home. The man stepped back as they approached. Noble met his eyes and nodded and was slightly troubled when the man looked away. Noble wondered if he had assumed he wouldn't greet him in kind. *I'm no better than you,* Noble wanted to say.

A beautiful girl, long blonde hair contrasting with her black dress suit, and who appeared to be no older than Shelby, sat behind a mahogany desk. She wore an earpiece and gazed into the screen of a high-end computer. When she looked up at him, she smiled, her white teeth sparkling against a lightly suntanned face. He figured it must be the girl named Michelle who'd answered the phone when he first called. "This must be Noble Burden."

"It is," Cass affirmed. "Noble, this is Michelle Hatfield. Michelle, would you get us a couple of waters, please, and three copies of the papers I drew up last week? And did you confirm with Mr. Thomas?"

"Absolutely," Michelle said, a little overly cheery in Noble's opinion. "And yes, Mr. Thomas's secretary confirmed he'll be here in about five minutes."

"Great."

The view outside Cass's office window was no less

spectacular than the one in his home, the hills of Nashville and blooming azaleas all around them, and a courtyard shaded by locust and persimmon trees where a couple of other groups of people gathered in apparent business meetings. But Noble's mind was stuck on the name Thomas.

"Do you mean *Mack Thomas*?"

"That's the one." Cass grinned.

"You didn't tell me—"

"It's a surprise. He's been looking for a guitarist to rep for a while now. I gave him your demos and he wanted me to bring you in ASAP."

Noble's throat tightened with emotion. Mack Thomas was one of the biggest agent names in country music, and his artists had won at least half a dozen Grammys, probably more. Getting signed by him would be like winning the lottery. People worked for years and years to get to where Noble was sitting, and he'd done nothing except play at the Purple Onion on Rosie's tenderloin night. He'd heard fairy tales of this sort of thing happening to people, but not to people like him.

Cass had been going on about some introductory paperwork and Noble had been too shocked to listen until Michelle knocked on the door. "Mr. Dinsmore? Mack Thomas is here."

Cass stood and Noble after him as Thomas entered the room. He was much shorter than Noble had imagined, and looked like he'd come from a hipster magazine ad shoot, wearing skinny jeans, a T-shirt that mentioned something about peace, a leather jacket, and a pair of thick-rimmed black glasses.

"Is this our prodigy?" Thomas grinned at Noble and extended a hand.

"It is," Cass said.

"Have you shown him a studio?"

"No, we were waiting on you."

Noble picked up his guitar and followed the two men to a studio featuring enormous sound boards and state-of-the-art acoustics that left Noble speechless.

Thomas must've sensed the intimidation he'd been trying to hide. "Don't worry about all that stuff. We just want to hear *you*."

The three of them sat together in a circle on tall wooden stools and made small talk as if trying to put Noble at ease as he took his guitar from the case and adjusted the strap around his neck.

"Alright, then." He plucked and strummed the strings until they were in tune. "I hope what I got for you is okay. It's not fancy or nothin'. But it's what I got."

> *"Well, the blue's still in the water and the blue's still in the
>   sky
> And way beyond the blue there's someone watchin' from on
>   high . . ."*

Whatever nerves Noble'd had when he'd begun were lost as he focused on the beat of the music, the way it felt when his voice blended in with the melody and he couldn't tell where his singing stopped and the chords began. He nearly forgot where he was, in a real studio, in front of a real agent, in Nashville, Tennessee, until he finished improvising and got to the end of the song:

"He'll be there
Like he always is to answer when I call him."

He strummed the last chord and the two men stared at him. Noble couldn't tell if they were stunned, abhorred, or impressed. He knew the style was chancy, but it wasn't any different from what he'd played the night Cass had come to the Onion. And it did lend itself to showing them some pretty good riffs and improvisation.

Cass had been pressing his fingers like a church steeple against his chin the entire time Noble played. "Johnny Cash."

"Yessir."

Thomas didn't say anything.

Anxiety roiled inside Noble. He must've blown it. Of course he'd blown it. Who in the world would sing old Johnny Cash in front of a potential agent? He shoulda picked something more modern . . .

"Hooooo-ey, son!" Thomas finally said and turned to Cass. "How in the world could he be better in person than on that demo?"

"Told ya," Cass said.

Noble caught himself as he swayed a little on the stool.

"Tell me, Noble. Can you read music, or do you play by ear?" Thomas asked.

"A little of both. I can play bass, too, if you need bass. But I prefer acoustic." He shifted his weight.

Thomas got up and set a music stand in front of him and set a piece of sheet music on it, the notes—not uncomplicated—written by hand. "Play this. Then I'll have you sight-read some vocals."

Noble obliged and watched as they each scribbled on their papers, which appeared from his vantage point to be score sheets of some kind.

"Noble Burden," Thomas said when he was done.

"Yessir."

"I am quite impressed."

"Sir."

"Tell me. We'd like to know a little about you personally, why you want to be part of this." Thomas waved his hand around the studio.

"Well . . ." Noble considered the question and tried to be as honest as he could. No use putting on airs in front of them at this point. "I guess you could say I do the best I can with what I got. And I believe if God's given you a gift, it's your duty to use it."

They appeared to be studying him, and he felt more heat rise and prickle around his neck. He adjusted his guitar strap, which didn't really need adjusting. Clearly that wasn't the answer they were looking for.

"What I mean is, I've been dreaming about Nashville as long as I can remember. At night, on my front porch, I look out into the fields and pretend all that corn's an audience.

And when I sing in front of folks and they start moving and swaying and singing along with me, well, there's somethin' pretty special about that."

The two men continued to exchange looks Noble couldn't interpret; then they focused back on him. Thomas glanced from Noble to Cass and back to Noble again. "I think I can speak for all of us at Mountain Top Studios. You've got a spot here if you'd like one."

Noble whistled long and loud. "You kiddin' me?"

"Would I kid about something like that?" Thomas grinned and extended his hand.

29

James pulled up to the Burdens' home in plenty of time to help with the evening milking the day Noble went to Nashville. He watched the golden cows move lazily across the pasture, seemingly unaware of the approaching thunderclouds. Humidity had been building all day and would no doubt result in another late-afternoon storm. Paint curled and cracked, revealing raw gray wood around the frame of the front screen door, which rattled as James rapped.

"Coming!" Laurie called from far inside, and he watched as a butterfly, blue like the sky and trimmed with black and white, flitted across the tips of the last remaining lupine growing beside the front porch steps. He swatted at what he thought was a larger insect as it swooped beside his ear, only to see that it was a hummingbird when it slowed to sip from the pink hibiscus at the corner of the house.

He startled when Laurie swung the door open.

"Just in time, Reverend. The girls don't like to wait." She waved her hand toward the cows already sauntering single-file toward the barn. "Come on and have a drink before we get started."

Eustace sat at the kitchen table working on a butterfly collection.

"I didn't know you collected butterflies, Eustace."

Laurie raised an eyebrow. "There's a lot folks don't know about him."

James watched as Eustace worked his blocky fingers carefully to remove a blue butterfly from between two pieces of paper where it must've been drying. He took a silver pin and pierced the middle of the butterfly's body, then pinned it to the velvet-covered display.

"Teachers said he'd never be able to do anything involving small motor skills." Laurie looked at her son adoringly. "Teachers said he wouldn't be able to do a lot of things, didn't they, buddy?"

"What kind is that one he's working with?" James asked.

"It's a Karner blue. Unusual for these parts because they like to live where there's more water, sand, and such. Noble looked it up and said my lupine must've attracted them somehow. Maybe they followed Sugar Creek down from the north. I don't know. But it's endangered. One to be proud of, for sure."

Eustace, who held his face awkwardly close to the display case, closed the cover and latched it. Then he sat back and began flapping his arm, staring off into the distance, his countenance smooth with something like satisfaction.

Laurie put her arms around him and squeezed, then kissed the side of his face. "I'm so proud of you."

James noticed the chipped edges of the Formica countertops, the avocado-green stove, and the worn veneer of the cabinets as Laurie stood at the sink making lemonade. Nothing had changed in the many years he'd known the Burdens. The breeze coming through the window above the sink blew Laurie's hair back off her shoulders to reveal her long, suntanned neck. James didn't realize he was staring at her until she turned around.

They both blushed.

Laurie dried her hands on a stained dish towel and stuffed it over the handle of the stove. She grabbed two glasses from the cabinet and handed one to James. "I do appreciate you coming to help. What I said the other day about not feeling sorry for me, well . . ."

"I get it. Really. Although I must admit that not taking notice of your needs ranks right up there at the top of my list of guilts." James studied her fingers, long and soft, and felt a long-dormant urge to reach out and put his hands around them. "Anyway, I'm happy to help."

Her eyes met his and she smiled in a way that put him more at ease. "Well, we could both stand to be a bit more neighborly."

Out in the barn, Eustace shoved a couple bales of hay from the hole in the floor of the mow to near the door to the milking parlor as Laurie called outside the sliding door to the cows. Several were already waiting at the gate to the holding area.

"In a hurry, ladies?" Laurie patted them on their rumps as they moseyed past. "Basil, Ginger, and Paprika. Since birth those three have always been inseparable."

"Where's Thyme and Rosemary?" James said jokingly, only to see those very names appear on the ear tags of the next two cows to come in the barn. "Must've been a spicy year."

Laurie didn't reply, either too focused on the work or finding his attempt at humor ineffective. She shoved a spray bottle with brown liquid into his hands. "Here. You clean the teats."

He felt himself blush, scolded himself for thinking like a middle school boy, then approached Ginger, who'd claimed the first empty stall.

"Don't stand right behind her. She behaves like a lady most of the time, but not if she doesn't know you're behind her."

James walked gingerly around to the side of the cow, knelt, and cleaned each teat, then stripped them as Noble had shown him before he left town. Then he moved on to Basil.

Laurie came behind him and attached the milking unit, then turned the radio on to a country station out of Lafayette and grinned at James. "Cows give more milk if there's music."

Eustace moved along the outside of the stalls, securing and opening the stanchions as each cow came and went, and tossing an occasional armful of hay into the trough in front of them.

"Have you heard from Noble?" James asked as he came out from under Rosemary's belly.

"Yeah . . ." She leaned over the top of Thyme. "He called when he landed. Texted a couple times. Says it's pretty fancy down there."

"I bet. Chance of a lifetime, yeah?"

"I guess."

He heard her mumble something he couldn't distinguish and saw her frown.

"Mind if I ask you something?" he asked.

"Not at all."

"How has Shelby seemed to you lately? When she comes to pick up Eustace?"

The two of them stood back as the machines drew the milk from the cows, content, even relieved, to give it.

"She doesn't visit as much as she used to. I figured she's been in a hurry, although I noticed she and Noble haven't been as friendly as they used to be. He, of course, won't talk about it. I wouldn't blame her for needing space to grieve. Why do you ask? Somethin' wrong?"

He was grateful to see the soft spot Laurie'd always had for Shelby did not appear to have lessened. "Seems to be taken with Cade Canady."

Laurie's eyes widened. "No wonder Noble's been a little

out of sorts about her. Paces the room before she comes to pick up Eustace in the mornings. And he was awful bothered when she was here the other day. 'Course he doesn't tell me a whole lot. But things haven't been the same between those two for a while now. Ain't no girl around here he's ever looked at the way he looks at her."

"So I've noticed. She hasn't been herself since the accident of course . . . but lately she seems worse." He hesitated, not wanting to reveal too much to Laurie out of respect for Shelby, but he knew Laurie had always been someone Molly had turned to for advice. And since she was a woman, he suspected she might have more insight into the way Shelby's mind might be working. "The more I've tried to put my foot down about Cade, the more she thinks she's in love with him."

"I remember that feeling." She crossed her arms and rubbed them as if suddenly feeling a chill. "All kind of folks tried to tell me not to see Dale, but I wouldn't listen. There were warning signs, even back before we were married. He was so . . . jealous."

"Do you know what happened between Shelby and Noble?"

She paused and watched as Eustace let the last cow out of the stanchions. "Eustace? Why don't you go on and take some hay out to the troughs outside. Make sure the water tanks are filled."

When he'd left the barn, she went on. "I don't know, James. Before the accident, they were gettin' real close. Molly and I . . . we used to kid around about them getting married someday. . . . I will say times when I'm hurting the worst is when I go running toward the worst thing for me. Or maybe . . . maybe I don't think I deserve any better."

He frowned, then noticed the radio playing one of his favorites. He fiddled with the tuner until it settled in clearer, then turned up the volume. He extended his hand toward her. "I know you at least deserve a dance."

She hesitated, wiping one hand on her jeans, and reaching up—as if by habit—with the other to cover the side of her face as if it still showed bruises.

Stepping toward her, he reached for her hand, which felt small and fragile in his. He could feel the curve of her back beneath his hand, her warmth against his chest. The oversize dungarees and work shirt cloaked her slight frame, and as they moved in three-quarter time, he inhaled the sweetness of her silky hair. He felt the ache of guilt in his gut as he thought about Molly, but then he remembered what Susan had said to him about deserving to love and be loved. While so many memories and blessings had been buried with Molly, his capacity for love had not.

"You sure you aren't feeling sorry for me, Reverend?"

He gazed at her, trying to memorize the green-and-blue pattern of her eyes. "And what if I was? Would it matter now?"

She leaned her head against his chest. "No, I s'pose it wouldn't. It wouldn't at all."

He felt the moisture from her tears against his shirt and kissed her gently on the top of her head.

"It's been so long," she said, pulling back to meet his eyes. "So long since I've felt like a man wanted to look at me, let alone touch me."

"Well, then, there's a lot of men out there who've been missing out."

The storm that'd been threatening blew in as they danced to that song and then to another. Underneath flickering lights, they both quit forcing themselves to survive and gave in to the grace of surrender. The thunder clapped above and around and then beyond the small white barn, until finally the sun broke through and they walked back to the house, the heat of the day gone and the dance still warm between them.

30

"You gonna tell me about it?" Laurie set a plate piled with strawberry rhubarb pie in front of Noble. The scoop of vanilla ice cream on top was already dripping down the sides.

Brock had been kind enough to pick Noble up from the Indianapolis airport and bring him back home, and he'd arrived early in the afternoon, but late enough that lunch had been done and put away. Eustace was at work. The house was quiet. And somehow, it seemed smaller than it had before he left, disappointing, the old drapes, the smell of fabric softener and leftovers, along with the perpetual faint trace of manure.

"I will, Mama. I've got a few things left I gotta work out with them and then—"

"And then what?" She pulled a chair out and sat across from him and held her face in her hands. "You're gonna leave us? Or you're gonna expect me and your brother to leave with you?"

"It was just a visit, that's all. I didn't even audition." He didn't have it in him to tell her everything, not yet. Truth was, he did have a few things left to settle with Cass and Mack, and she didn't need to be worrying about anything until it was all said and done.

"Well, can you at least tell me what they thought?" She sat back and crossed her arms.

"They loved me." He sat up straighter and grinned, taking another huge bite of pie.

"Of course they did."

He frowned at the sound of resentment in her voice and the way her brow was knotted up like it always was when she was worried. Then he took another bite of pie. "You know, you could be a little happy for me."

"Don't talk with your mouth full. And to be sure, I am proud that they like you. But I'll be happy when you tell me exactly what's going on." She glanced at the ceiling, where Eustace's room was above them. "I don't have to remind you that you're not only making decisions for yourself."

He stuffed the last bite in his mouth and took his plate to the sink, stopping to kiss Laurie on the top of her head. "I love you, Mama. You're gonna have to trust me on this."

Noble grabbed his guitar and headed outside. He'd only been home a couple of hours and already felt like he had to get out of the house. He didn't blame Mama for wanting to know details, but he was still trying to sort it all out for himself. The plane ride and drive home hadn't offered near enough time for him to sort through all he'd experienced and been offered.

Noble took his time walking across the yard. He noticed the pale-blue chicory growing near the road, the bright-orange trumpet vine blooming up the sides of the silo, and the fact that their yard had more clover than grass. He walked out to his favorite spot to think, on the far side of the barn, in the field where they put the older calves who were weaned from their mothers but too young still to be bred.

Their ears perked up, then their heads, one at a time, as if one of them had issued some sort of inaudible warning signal that a human was nearby. Stepping toward each other, they pulled themselves into a tighter group and stepped closer, like a single unit, to inspect him. Noble settled himself on a concrete ledge that was a remnant of an old outbuilding from long before their family owned the place.

As he began to strum, he observed the fields beyond, the gleaming silver tops of silos on neighboring farms, the clumps of clouds growing thicker, darker, in the sky above.

"My hope is built on nothing less . . ."

The old hymn was the first song that came to his mind, as bits of chords and lyrics sometimes did when he simply let his heart, through his fingers, wander along the strings.

> *"Than Jesus' blood and righteousness;*
> *I dare not trust the sweetest frame,*
> *But wholly lean on Jesus' name."*

He fiddled around with the G chord the line ended on and began to improvise loosely with the melody as he contemplated all he'd seen and felt in Nashville. If he accepted the contract Mack offered, they would certainly have to move to Nashville. He'd explained to Mack in detail all of Eustace's needs and about Mama's potential desire to go back to school. Mack had told him they'd pay for the first month's rent in a house downtown, where there were shops and restaurants and all kinds of places for Mama to work. He knew from other friends with special-needs relatives that there were caseworkers who really cared about and could help Eustace with everything from finding a job to getting access to good rehabilitation services Noble hadn't even known existed.

And as for Noble, Mack had some ideas of country bands he knew needed a guitarist right away and others who would soon. He'd have plenty of commercial studio work lined up for him as soon as he arrived. And the pay was more than he'd ever imagined.

What he hadn't expected was the sense of pressure he'd felt when money became attached to something that always, until then, had risen freely and on his own terms from his heart. He hadn't decided if that was necessarily a bad thing, which was part of the reason he didn't know what to say to Mama yet. The studios and the people he'd met there oozed a confidence and security that he knew came from money, knew this because no one in or around Sycamore carried themselves like that. Most of them probably never would.

He thought about the janitor in the hall outside Cass's office at Mountain Top Studios and how he'd felt more of a camaraderie with him in the few seconds their eyes had met than he had with most of the industry professionals he'd met. And after all the fine dining and compliments he'd been treated to, he'd been unprepared for the knot that had formed in his gut by the time he got on the plane to go back home.

"On Christ the solid rock I stand . . ."

"Mind some company?"

The sweet voice behind him startled him, and he turned to see Shelby. "Where'd you come from?"

"I brought Eustace home. Brock let us go early. Things were slow. Your mom said I could find you here." She held her flip-flops in her hands and fixed her eyes on her toes as she dug them into the soft, cool dirt. "It's nice to hear you playing out here."

"Thanks." He wasn't sure how to read her, considering the last time they saw each other. He thought she seemed tentative. Definitely not the ornery Shelby he'd last encountered.

"I wanted to tell you I'm sorry," she said, pink rising to her cheeks.

He could barely hear her and knew it probably killed her to say it. "What was that?"

She sighed and rolled her eyes. "Noble Burden, you heard exactly what I said, didn't you? You're just tryin' to make me say it again."

"Maybe."

She swung her legs over the ledge and sat down beside him. "So?"

"So . . . what?" he bantered. Her tanned skin, so close to his, made his head swirl. He'd never stopped caring for her, and if she asked him again what she had on the waterfall that night that seemed like forever ago, he'd surely tell her yes.

"I was thinking, maybe if you forgive me for . . . well, for the way I've been . . . and . . . that maybe we could sing together properly at Dad's last service." She fiddled with several homemade bracelets on her wrist.

Her fingers were slender, so much softer looking than his, and they were so close Noble felt the need to reach out and hold her hand, but he resisted. As much as he cared for her, Cade was still in the picture. Besides that, he needed to talk to her about Nashville, and he needed to keep his wits about him.

"Wait—did you say you wanted to sing on Sunday? Together? You haven't sung since—"

"I know. I haven't sung, not really, since Mama died."

Noble turned thoughtful and studied her. "You sure you want to? Did you tell your dad? What'd he say?"

Color pinked her cheeks. "He doesn't know."

Noble sat back so he could get a good look at her. "That's a pretty big step. You sure you're ready for that? There'll probably be more folks there than usual, being the last service and all."

"I thought about that. Then I thought about Dad. I thought about what Mama'd say if she were still here, how she'd handle the church closing and all. I think she'd try to make it a special day. Bonnie and I have been working on putting together a couple of scrapbooks with the last few years of bulletins, photos from events, newspaper clippings folks have collected, past sermons. There were a bunch of pictures of me singing . . . and of you and me singing together, too."

"Yeah?" He raised his eyebrows, pulled off his ball cap, and ran his fingers through his hair. "How did I look?"

She elbowed him. "You are so full of it, Noble Burden. You looked just fine."

He watched her face fall. He could see her chin begin to tremble even as she turned her head away from him.

"After Mama died . . . This is so awful . . ." She covered her face with her hands. "I hated God. Noble . . ."

"It's alright. I don't think you're the first person who's felt that way. 'Sides, I think he's big enough to handle it." Noble hoped this was true, since he'd experienced the same thing himself when Dad left.

"But I've loved God my whole life, and then all of a sudden I hate him. It feels so awful."

Noble put his cap back on, unsure how to respond to that.

"I'm so mad. I mean, why'd he have to take her from me? From Dad? I didn't want to have anything to do with God or church or who I was before the accident."

Noble wanted to tell her it was alright, to put his arm around her, to fix her pain. Trouble was, he asked God the same questions himself. All the time. He didn't know how to pour into someone else what he didn't have himself.

"Dad always says at funerals that God's close to the broken-hearted, that God saves those whose spirits are crushed, but I haven't felt any of that. I can't feel him. But when I saw all those pictures, started looking over all the baptisms and funerals and weddings Dad had officiated at, read pieces of his sermons, I began to see all the good things God's done—not only for me, but for Dad and Mama and the church over the years, for Sycamore. Even though I can't see where he is in my life, I started to see that he has been here, with other folks, anyway. Does that make sense?"

Noble nodded, although in many ways he wasn't sure at all. He looked out at the young cows who'd gone back to grazing and spread themselves out across the field, their curiosity about him and Shelby evidently satisfied.

"I think I'm realizing God's been wanting to comfort me, but that he can't if I don't let him. If all I'm doing is running from him, I ain't gonna find him because I'm looking in the wrong direction."

"Nothing can ever separate us from God's love . . ."

It was a Bible verse Mama or a vacation Bible school teacher or someone had made him memorize when he was young. "Maybe I don't think of God as someone who'd chase after me, since all my own dad ever did was run away."

Shelby met Noble's eyes. "So I'm running from God, and you think God's running from you. We're a real mess, aren't we?"

"So maybe we oughta stop running from each other and figure it all out." Noble couldn't help himself any longer. He leaned in and felt Shelby's breath against the side of his face, then ran his hands down her arms where he knew the bruises he'd seen were still healing. He pushed stray hairs off her forehead and brought his mouth close enough to hers to brush against the softness of her lips and held himself there, savoring the faint smell of coconut sunscreen and the energy that'd been dormant between them, until finally he kissed her.

"Does that mean you'll sing with me?" she whispered.

They both jumped at the sound of a car door closing hard behind them.

Shelby's face turned pale and no sound came from her mouth as she formed the word *"No . . ."*

Cade's jacked-up truck idled on the road, and he hot-footed, both hands clenched in fists, toward Shelby and Noble. He homed in on Shelby. "What are you doin' here?"

"Cade, wait—"

"Wait for what? For you to sleep with this piece of farm trash?" He motioned toward Noble.

"It's not like that, I swear!" Shelby scrambled to her feet.

Noble set his guitar aside and stood up to step between them. "You're on my property, Cade. Either mind your manners or go on your way. You ain't got no business here."

Cade, militant, pointed his finger at Shelby. "She's my business. And I ain't going anywhere unless she comes with me."

"You'll not be taking Shelby anywhere, Cade." Laurie marched toward them from across the lawn.

Noble couldn't remember the last time he'd seen Mama move so sure and strong.

Cade, who clearly hadn't expected to see Laurie there, sucked in a breath and clenched his fists tighter.

"Mama, I can handle this." Noble shot her a look of warning.

"Now, Mrs. Burden, I wouldn't want you tangled up in this. Shelby was just leaving with me. Weren't you, Shelby?" Cade approached Shelby and put a hand on her shoulder.

Noble could see he was squeezing her a little too tight, but she didn't show signs of resisting. Could she *want* to go with him? Didn't the last few minutes they'd shared mean anything to her?

"Shelby, you don't have to go with him." Laurie's shoulders had slackened and her voice sounded pleading, weak. Noble remembered she'd sounded that way when Dad got riled up.

"Why don't you let her decide." Cade shifted his grip on Shelby's shoulder to her upper arm.

"Shelby—" Noble stepped toward her.

"Noble." Shelby looked at him and then at Laurie, color fading from her face. "I have to do this."

Noble used every bit of willpower he had to keep himself from climbing on top of Cade's truck and beating the lights and windshield out with a bat. But something in the way Shelby had looked at him made him think he should trust her, give her whatever space she seemed to indicate she needed. Still, as Shelby climbed into the front seat of Cade's truck, Noble felt like she was taking part of him with her that he'd never get back.

Cade revved the three-ton engine and tore off down the road, dust and gravel spewing out, creating plumes of dust, and somewhere in the pasture behind them a cow mooed, sad and long.

31

Roiling with fury and concern, Noble took his guitar back into the house, then threw himself into chores he'd fallen behind on while in Nashville. The cows would need to be milked in a couple hours, and so he took the time to mow and trim, fill water troughs and feed buckets, and spread a fresh layer of straw in the pole and calf barns. The skies darkened along with his mood, and he noticed the milker cows standing together near the old oak—the only shelter from sun or weather in the pasture—on the slope of land that dipped before rising toward the barn and silos. Their tails swished, beating back incessant flies and gnats. The air felt like a furnace, and even from this distance he heard the window units on the house struggle and chug. Branches of the nearby silver maple groaned, the pale-white underbellies of the leaves blowing upside down.

The still-sunny eastern sky intensified the threatening gray and billowing white of the cumulonimbus clouds moving in from the west. Bolts of lightning flashed along the horizon. Within an hour, black clouds covered the sky, and it felt more like nightfall than midafternoon. Strange patterns played in the clouds. Great sections swirled and dipped and licked toward the ground. Noble didn't need a meteorologist to tell him conditions were right for tornadoes. They'd be fine if one came close. The cellar would offer them protection, but the barn and the cows might not be so lucky. The same storm that shut down Whitmore's power had spawned a tornado that destroyed a beef farm down the road, the winds heaving a dozen cows plumb off their hooves, nine of them never accounted for and three of them landing upright and very much alive in Viola Dean's backyard.

Noble rushed into the house and found Eustace with his nose pressed to the window in Mama's sewing room. He was already flapping his arms with worry. Mama, lost in her work, continued to push fabric through the determined needle of her machine.

"C'mon, you two. We gotta get to the cellar."

Mama paused the machine and looked up at him over the rim of her reading glasses. She glanced at the window where Eustace stood. "My land, I didn't even realize—"

She stood so fast the metal folding chair fell over.

"Stay close to me, 'kay, Eustace?"

In order to get to the cellar, connected to the side of the back porch, they had to leave the house. As Mama opened the back door, the wind snatched Eustace's white ball cap off his head, and he left Noble's side to chase it across the yard. The wind tossed the hat every which way. Each time Eustace grabbed at it, the hat blew out of his reach.

"Leave it!" Mama hollered.

The sides of the old metal silos near the barn creaked. The screen door smacked back and forth, worn spring hinges not strong enough to hold it closed. Lightning cracked and a transformer popped a few miles in the distance.

"Lord, have mercy," Mama prayed.

Noble tried to assure himself lightning wouldn't strike, now that he'd gotten Frank Whitmore's herd settled. The cows of his they'd brought over had quickly learned the electric fence and would be safe from that standpoint as long as the power stayed on. Even if the power went out, he knew their own Jersey cows would respect the wire and stay well within its borders. More worrisome was if the power stayed out and threatened the milking.

"Wait here while I get the doors open!" Noble called over his shoulder as he ran to the cellar alongside the house. He fumbled with the latch, then fought to pull the doors open as the rain and wind pelted him.

He smelled electricity in the air. Everything appeared tinged with green. The wind roared and the siding rattled. Marble-size hail and giant raindrops splatted sparsely before ushering in cascades of rain that looked like curtains of water billowing across the yard and fields beyond. Eustace pulled his hat—which he'd finally caught—back on his head and scrambled back to the porch, crouching against the gusting wind.

"Let's go!" Mama grabbed Eustace's arm and pulled him toward the cellar. Noble braced the doors as they climbed in, then followed behind them into the dark hole that smelled of earth and must. He closed the doors and latched them, and the coolness of the underground surrounded them.

Laurie pulled the chain on the one lightbulb on the ceiling, illuminating rusty cans of paint and empty shelving once used for storing root vegetables. One shelf had a case of bottled water, a box with a lighter and candles, and a couple of old wool Army blankets belonging to their dad when he'd been in the service. They didn't use the cellar hardly at all but for occasions like this.

"We can't lose power," Noble said.

"I know it." Mama shook her head. She sat on a long-abandoned, bright-orange plastic milk crate and wrapped her arms around Eustace's shoulders. He sat on the floor next to her and rocked back and forth. With his fist he rubbed the calloused spot behind his ear. It was the third time they'd used the cellar that summer. Noble began to wonder if the storms might be worse than the three previous years of drought.

Thunder crashed and the lightbulb above them flickered.

Eustace rocked harder, and Laurie moaned a little. Noble noticed she was weeping.

"Mama?"

"I'm so sorry, Noble."

"Sorry for what?"

"Sorry for this." She nodded at the cellar and the house above them. "I never meant for you to grow up and be so burdened with this. I didn't want farming for you and Eustace. Didn't want the uncertainty and vain life that it is, us hemmed in behind these fences right along with the cows. I wish I could do it all myself. I wish I could be less selfish about this whole Nashville thing and tell you that you don't have to be a hero for us . . . that we could sell and leave all this behind."

Noble hesitated, then figured there wasn't any use in hiding anything from her. "Are there times I wonder and wish about getting out of here? 'Course there are. Anyone with half a brain in this town wonders that. But taking care of you and Eustace ain't a chore."

He needed to tell her about his decision about Nashville, but not in the middle of all this.

Another crack of thunder sounded like it hit right above their heads.

Thunder pealed and rolled.

The lightbulb above them sparked and blew.

32

Power's out, we need help.

James read the text from Noble and scurried to pull on his old jeans. The storm had passed, a fast-moving squall that lit up the radar on his phone's weather app, triggered the storm sirens, and sent him to crouch in the basement, which he rarely went into but was grateful for, especially with the number of storms they'd had this summer. He'd wondered how the Burdens had fared, and he was grateful Noble thought to ask him for help. James wasn't sure he would have a month ago.

When James arrived at the Burdens' barn, he found the three of them, along with Brock, already working in the milking parlor. Sunlight streamed through the filmy windows, making the fast-moving storm seem like a bad dream. The room was strangely quiet, except for a rhythmic *whoosh-whoosh* of milk hitting the bottoms of the large plastic feed buckets.

"Grab a bucket." Laurie nodded toward several lined against the far wall.

Each of the stanchions held a cow in place; each of the people sat on a bucket and began milking by hand.

James's cow was named Harriet, and he jumped—nearly falling off his bucket—as she stomped her back leg.

"Careful there, Rev." Noble grinned from around the end of the cow named Lucy.

James nodded back nervously, then began milking Harriet again. When Noble was in Nashville, they'd used the machines, so it took him a few tries before he remembered how to hold the teat, pull and squeeze, pull and squeeze, until a stream of milk sprayed into the bottom of the pail.

"How do you know when to stop?" he asked.

"When the udders are soft," Laurie replied.

"How long is that?"

Laurie chuckled. "What's wrong, James, your arms hurtin' already?"

"No—I just—" He thought it better to focus on the milking. After about fifteen minutes, he felt the udders, which were noticeably softer and less full.

"Most will give a couple of gallons, if that helps," Noble offered.

Eustace finished milking his cow and began cleaning her udders and throwing hay into the trough before releasing the stanchions of the cows as they were done being milked. He released Harriet and Lucy, then Roseanne.

James wiped his hands on a towel he'd tucked in the side of his pants. "How many do you have again? Sixty-some?"

"Yep," Noble said. "Should be quite an evening."

"I spoke to Sheriff Tate on the way here," James said, his hands moving in an even rhythm now as he milked his second cow, Daisy. "He said it was a tornado. Plus over three inches of rain in less than an hour. Power's out all over Sycamore, in town and out here. Our house, too. Rivers were already swollen from all the other rain we've had. Flash flood warnings everywhere."

Laurie sighed. "We'll lose every penny from this milking, and every one after this until the power comes back on. No way to keep it as cool as it needs to be with the tank not running."

The muscles in James's forearms tensed, and he knew they'd be cramping and burning by the time they got all the cows milked. If the power wasn't on by morning, they'd have to do it all over again, and again that next evening. No wonder Frank Whitmore had succumbed to despair.

"Did you happen to check how long the power company said it'd be?" Noble hollered at James from beneath the great belly of Opal.

"I called . . . got a recording that listed the outage areas and said they're working to restore power as soon as possible. No time frame."

They milked and milked and poured bucket after bucket down the drain in the cooling room. During one break, James took a moment to step outside.

"Hank?" he said into his cell phone. "Hey there. I need some help out here at the Burden dairy."

He didn't ask Laurie before calling Hank. With himself and Brock already there, he doubted she would've approved, but they couldn't do this by themselves. Besides that, they'd have to figure out a plan for the morning, too, if the power stayed out, and Hank was great at organizing people. Hank said he'd be there within the hour, and James went back into the barn and resumed his spot under the next cow in line, Ethel. Eustace tossed a bunch of hay in front of her nose. Suddenly James realized that if Eustace was back from work, Shelby should've been home, too. "Did Shelby come home before the storm?"

Noble emerged from beneath Gidget in the next stall. "She brought Eustace home early. Cade came by and—"

"She was out with Cade in the middle of that storm?" James felt himself pale, a feeling of panic shooting through him.

The tornado had barely touched the ground, but the flash floods—the storm had dumped inches. Even Cade's big truck could be swept off balance.

James had lost Molly on a sunny day. He'd crumpled to his knees when Tate came and told him, and again when he'd first seen Shelby in the emergency room with only a few cuts and bruises, but irreparable wounds to her soul. He imagined himself doing the same again, tears spilling from Tate's reddened eyes again, the way Tate turned his hat in his hands, fumbling, stuttering, trying to find the words to tell James he'd lost his baby girl . . .

"She's not texting me back, and she won't pick up," Noble said, interrupting James's thoughts.

"I'll go back to the house and see if she's there," James said. The barn and the cows, Noble, Laurie . . . everything around him seemed altered, surreal, as if he weren't really there and the day was just a dream.

Noble appeared helpless as he surveyed the rest of the cows that had to be milked.

Laurie stood and gave Ethel a gentle push on her rump to get her moving out of the barn. "Why don't you go with him, Noble. Eustace and Brock are here. We can get these last ones."

"With our help, you can for sure."

James was relieved to see Hank appear in the doorway, along with a couple of stock boys from his store. "Power's out at the hardware, too. Figured it'd do these boys some good to help."

The two teens glanced at each other and then at the cows, apprehensively.

"You sure?" Noble asked.

"I'm sure. Now you two get going."

"I've got this, Noble," Brock encouraged. "Go on now."

33

"I think Shelby's missing," James said into his phone to Sheriff Tate.

As James steered toward his home, Noble strained to see if he could catch a glimpse of Shelby's truck in the driveway. At the same time, Noble's cell phone rang.

"Are you sure?" Noble's stomach felt like it was falling to the ground. He turned to James, who still had Tate on the line. "Tell Sheriff Eustace is missing, too."

Noble listened as Mama explained to him that after they'd left, she thought Eustace had gone to get more hay, but the tractor was still parked and he was nowhere to be seen. "Maybe it's too soon to panic," Mama said. "But I'm worried he mighta got the idea in his head that he needed to go look for Shelby, too."

Noble considered this. Eustace was sure to have heard James talking about Shelby. But he wondered if he might've gone to look for a cow, too. "Are all the cows accounted for?"

"That's the other problem," Mama explained. "With doing everything by hand, none of us remembered to record who got milked and who didn't, so I don't know. Seems like they all came in, in order, and that they were all here. But I don't know."

"See if you can get a head count. He might have realized before us that one of the cows was missing, and if so, he could be out looking for her. . . . Hold on a sec, Mama. . . ." Noble held the phone to his chest and got out of the car. No sign of Shelby.

James sat in the driver's seat with the door open. He was still talking to Tate. "I see. . . . Yes. . . . Tell him thank you for checking on that so fast. . . . Right. . . . Okay. . . . Bye."

"What'd he say?" Noble asked.

"He had a deputy check with Silas to see if he'd seen Cade and Shelby, and he hasn't. He said he'd meet us at your place."

Noble kicked the ground and cursed. "Mama? You still there?"

"Yeah—what is it?"

"Looks like all three of them are missing—Cade, Shelby, and Eustace."

"Noble." Mama's voice cracked with concern. "Don't let nothin' happen to my Eustace."

"I won't, Mama." Noble tried to sound calm, sure, in spite of the fear burning inside him. "I won't. Listen, we're going to come back, me and James. Sheriff's going to meet us at our house. We'll figure out a plan when we get there. Stay put."

On the way back, they drove the perimeter of the Burdens' property and discovered part of the electric fence down. Noble got out of the car to take a closer look. The grass and weeds were flattened, and the mud covered with the imprints of fresh hoof marks.

He kicked the ground and cursed again.

>>> ——— <<<

James's car skidded to a stop in the wet gravel of Noble's driveway and stopped short of the bumper of one of the two squad cars. Tate and another officer stood by Mama, the three of them next to the Gator at the entrance to the pasture between the barn and the house. Even from a distance, Noble could see the dark circles of worry under Mama's eyes.

"Reverend. Noble." Tate stood by Mama and tipped his wide-rimmed hat toward them.

"I figured he—Eustace—was out there with Dolly, but I took the Gator out, did a sweep of the pastures, and he's not anywhere. And two cows are missing . . ." Laurie's hand shook as she motioned toward the pasture. Tears filled her eyes and her mouth trembled. "Dolly and the one numbered 46 from Whitmore's herd."

"He may be with them, then." Noble nodded at James.

"We checked the fence perimeter on the way here. There's a break on the far northeast corner, near where Granger's field turns to meadow and leads down to the falls."

"Those falls'll be like rapids right now," Tate warned, nodding to the other officer Noble vaguely recognized from town. "We better get a move on."

"Eustace'd do anything for Dolly." Noble's heart sank with doubt even as he said the words. Why hadn't he checked on his brother and made sure he was safe in the barn before leaving with James?

"It's not your fault." Mama's voice sounded small, defeated. It was as if she'd read his mind.

"The heck if it ain't."

"No use worrying about who's at fault for what," James said. "We've gotta find these kids."

"I'm taking the Gator," Noble said. "Get the gate for me, Mama?"

"I'm coming with you," James said. "You shouldn't be out there on your own."

"But you gotta stay and look for Shelby—" Noble began to argue.

"I sure would if I thought I could help." James turned to the sheriff. "I think we'll do better if we split up, don't you?" He looked at Laurie. "Besides, while I'm less than thrilled at the thought of Shelby out there somewhere with Cade, you have to admit he's got one heck of a truck. Eustace has got nothing."

"I think you're right." Tate took his hat off and wiped

a thick layer of sweat from his brow, then stared hard into James's eyes. "We won't give up until we find them all."

"Careful, Noble," Mama said, unclamping the chains holding the gate closed and pushing it open wide.

James hopped in beside him, and Noble floored the gas on the Gator. He headed toward the patch of woods near where they'd found the busted fence. He saw a hawk circling above the trees. The closer he got, the more he could see the detail of the giant bird's pale-yellow belly, the dirty brown of its wings. Soon another joined it, and another, making three of them circling above the trees. He imagined their beady black eyes focused on a rabbit or a squirrel or worse . . .

Dear Lord, please . . . let him be okay . . .

He drove the Gator as far as he could to where the pasture turned to brush and beyond that, thick woods. The two men pushed past thickets and vines, stepping high over the overgrown grass and goldenrod, following the edge of the woods toward the broken patch of fence.

"Eustace! Euuuuu-staaaace! You here, buddy?"

"Eustace?" James called behind him.

Noble's chest ached; the adrenaline of worry felt like fire running up and down his arms, his spine.

"Euuuuu-staaace!" he called again.

The two men stopped to listen. Noble strained to hear anything, a whimper, a branch breaking, the crunch of brush that might indicate his brother's step. Instead, he heard the chirp of sparrows and the chatter of a squirrel in a high tree.

He was about to push farther into the woods when he heard a sound nearby, something that sounded like a sigh, a moan.

"Eustace! That you? Where are ya?"

"Over here," James said. His expression was grave as he looked down at something near his feet.

"Oh no . . ." Noble approached and saw a newborn calf, still covered in birth fluids and blood from its mother. It was a sickly calf, and he'd seen enough of that kind to know it would not survive the hour.

He bent down on one knee and put his hand on the side of the neck to provide some comfort, but the calf's eyes rolled back until the white edges of them showed, wild and terrified. It wasn't a Jersey calf. It was a Holstein. Whitmore's number 46 must've been pregnant. If she gave birth there, and in the middle of that storm, she most likely would have some injuries herself. The coyotes didn't mess much with the cows, but if there was one in labor, giving birth, they would attack for sure. He'd seen it only one other time, before Dad left. Coyotes tore the whole hindquarters off the mother and all that was left of the calf was bones by the time they found them.

Noble stood and looked around the woods. They had to find Eustace and those two cows. Dolly was a protector—all the Jerseys were. It was their instinct to protect the members of their herd. If number 46 had gotten away and been in labor, Dolly might have wandered off with her. And then Eustace would've gone after her.

But where?

Questions tumbled through his mind as he tried to piece together a scenario that would make sense, that would lead him to his brother. If Eustace had found that calf, Noble couldn't imagine the emotion that would've overcome him. Once when they'd found a rabbit still alive, but barely, after a coyote attack, Eustace had gone near catatonic and crumpled on the ground right there, refusing to move, stroking the bunny's head until it took its last breath. Almost as bad as when the owl got that cat and her kittens.

The only thing that might've made him leave an injured calf was if Dolly was in danger.

Or something worse.

34

"**The tracks seem** headed that way." James pointed. The sun was low on the horizon, and he wished they'd thought to bring flashlights.

"The falls aren't far," Noble said. "And the highway's just beyond them."

James let Noble lead the way. He supposed he should pray, but he couldn't. Foreboding filled his mind. Photographs he'd seen of Molly's wreck. The concrete walls and steel table in the basement of the hospital where he'd had to go and identify her.

"Didn't Tate say the highway was washed out?" Noble asked over his shoulder.

James tried to focus. "Yeah, but I don't know where."

Leaving the calf behind, they pressed on, past the broken fence, down toward the swollen creek, finding occasional hoofprints.

"Hey, look here." Noble stopped and stooped, his fingers on the ground. "These are boot prints. They look about the size of Eustace's."

"Maybe we're on the right track then." James felt a flicker of hope for Eustace, shadowed by uneasiness and a growing dread about Shelby.

"Eustace!" Noble hollered.

James pressed his fingers to his lips and let out a long, earsplitting whistle.

"Sheesh! Where'd you learn to do that?" Noble said, rubbing his ear.

"Years of helping Molly round up Sunday schoolers."

Molly.

Lord, please don't let me lose my baby girl, too.

They plodded on. The swollen creek roared louder as they followed the broken and trampled brush they hoped was from Eustace and the cows.

"Can't remember the last time I've seen it so high," Noble said. The muddy water roiled, large limbs sweeping past them. They passed the falls, walls of water coursing over the craggy rocks, landing in foamy rushes of rapids. "We should be getting near the bridge."

James felt the mud sucking at the soles of his tennis shoes. He struggled to keep up with Noble without tripping or losing a shoe at the same time.

Noble stopped so suddenly James almost ran into him. "Oh no . . ."

James looked up and gasped, and his gut wrenched inside of him as he struggled to process the scene in front of them.

》》》 ————《《《

Noble froze when he saw the pickup truck balanced precariously on top of a boulder in the middle of the river. The top was smashed, and the back end of it was filling up with water.

"Help!" a short man yelled from the riverbank.

It was Cade. "Shelby's in there!" he yelled.

Beside Noble, James started to run, but Noble grabbed his arm. "Wait, James! It's not stable!"

The truck teetered, growing heavier by the second, the back end sinking fast and threatening to capsize onto the passenger side, where he could see the outline of Shelby's head and shoulders through the cracked glass of the back window.

Another movement caught Noble's eye in the raging water.

"Eustace! What the—?"

This time, Noble started for the water, and it was James's turn to restrain him. The reverend grabbed his arm with one hand and fumbled for his phone with the other. "We can't risk losing you, too. We need Tate."

"We can't wait for Tate." Noble fought him. "Eustace can't swim!"

Noble could see every muscle in Eustace's broad shoulders

and back tensed through the wet T-shirt as he ran along the riverbank. "Eustace! Wait! Stay there!"

Until now, Noble had always been able to protect his big brother. He nearly choked on the terror in his throat, the adrenaline of wanting—having—to do *something* shooting through his limbs.

He stepped into the water, the current so forceful it knocked him to his knees.

"Noble, you can't go in there!" James grabbed his shirt from behind.

Noble lurched back onto the bank. He noticed how still Shelby was through the window.

Dear God, help us . . . help them . . .

Metal creaked and groaned, and the truck tipped farther, the water nearly halfway up the side of the cab doors.

"Eustace!" Noble shrieked as his brother lost his footing and struggled to keep from going under.

⟫⟫⟫———⟪⟪⟪

"Shelby!" James screamed. He saw Eustace grasp a large limb of the tree stuck against the rocks. It was the only thing keeping the truck—and him—from toppling into the water.

"James? You there?" Tate's voice crackled from the cell phone.

"Sheriff! We found them—all of them. But we need help. They're in the river . . . under the Bethel Road bridge. . . . Shelby's stuck. . . . You gotta hurry!"

"We're close. Hang tight."

By this time, Cade had joined them, shivering, on the riverbank. James thought he looked like a child, nothing left of his haughty, brooding attitude. He'd been so focused on Shelby and the truck, he hadn't realized the implications of the fact that Cade was safe and Shelby was still in the truck.

Noble must've realized this at the same time, because he pushed past James and grabbed Cade's shirt, lifting him off the ground. "You creep! You left her!"

Cade's face reddened as his shirt tightened around his throat with Noble's grip. "Door . . . wouldn't . . . open . . ."

Noble let go of him, shoving him to the ground.

James was afraid he might not have been so kind. Up the bank a ways, he noticed Dolly and the other cow munching on grass as if still in the pasture with nothing at all awry.

Metal screeched against rock, and the sound of shattering glass turned their attention back to Eustace, who had just punched a hole through the passenger window. He leaned into the cab, and the truck pitched farther toward the water.

"Stop! Eustace, it's gonna go!" Noble yelled.

James held tight to Noble's arm as he struggled to go into the water. He could hear the faint sound of sirens approaching. But what he saw in the water amazed him.

"Wait," James cautioned. "Watch."

Eustace pulled and fought with the stuck door, even as Noble fought against the hold James had on his arm.

Finally the door opened, but Eustace lost his footing in the current.

Again the truck hitched and doddered.

He couldn't keep hold of Noble, who leaped into the water, but again the current knocked him over.

James grabbed the back of his shirt again, pulling him back to the bank.

Eustace regained his footing and paused until the truck steadied. James could tell Eustace was using all his strength to stay upright and move toward Shelby in the truck.

Dear God, she's not moving. Please, Lord . . . not my baby girl . . .

>>> —— <<<

Noble watched, helpless, as Eustace pulled Shelby from the truck cab. Her blood soaked Eustace's T-shirt. She didn't move as Eustace cradled her limp body.

"Lord, not Shelby," James mumbled, falling to his knees next to Noble. "Not my baby girl, too. Please, God, no . . ."

Sirens sounded and emergency lights flashed from the bridge above as Eustace lurched and plodded through the water toward the shore.

Noble reached for Eustace, grabbing him to steady him as soon as he was close enough.

Eustace kept going until he reached a grassy patch and laid Shelby gently on her back.

"Shelby," James said, stumbling toward them and falling to his knees again when he reached her side. He ran his hand across her forehead, her face.

Paramedics and firemen had already scurried down the embankment and rushed in to attend to her.

"Stay with us, darlin'," one of the paramedics said.

Noble heard James let out a cry of relief.

She was alive.

Noble went to his brother, who had found a stump to lean on nearby. His countenance reflected the same satisfaction as when he pinned a new butterfly to its mounting board, a look so gentle, so peaceful, Noble hesitated to disturb him.

"You saved her life," he said softly.

Eustace didn't move but continued to watch the emergency workers as Cade's truck slid silently beneath the water.

35

Red and yellow lights from the emergency crews above flashed, almost like firelight, as James knelt, his face pressed close to Shelby's. He could see the condensation of her breath on the inside of the plastic oxygen mask as she inhaled and exhaled, inhaled and exhaled.

Alive.

"Thank you, Jesus." Tears streamed down his face. "Thank you, thank you, thank you, Jesus."

"Daddy?" Her voice was weak, muffled, under the mask.

"I'm right here, baby. You're gonna be okay. Everything's gonna be okay."

>>>———《《《

Before he shut the door to Sheriff Tate's cruiser, Noble met Cade's eyes and almost felt sorry for him. His letter jacket lay in a soaked heap at his feet, and he looked as if he wished he could disappear as a couple of deputies and an accident investigator surrounded him, questioning him, after paramedics determined he was fine.

"I'm sorry about all this," Noble said to James, who sat in the front next to Tate. Lights flashed and the police radio crackled with news and updates of other problems around the area. They followed the two ambulances, one carrying Shelby and the other Eustace, on the way to the hospital in Lafayette. "I shoulda stopped her from going with him somehow."

"Nothin' you could've done, son. I know how stubborn she is. She would have gone with him, strong-armed or not." James's voice sounded thin and bone-weary.

Noble knew the pastor side of James was trying to make him feel better. It was bad enough he'd let his brother down today. His heart broke over letting Shelby down, too.

"Did you see that Granger came and took the cows back for you?" Tate said.

"Oh, wow—thank goodness. I'd nearly forgotten about them."

"Can't imagine why," Tate said.

As they pulled along the curb near the hospital's ambulance bay, Noble saw Mama hovering over Eustace's stretcher as the paramedics wheeled him into the hospital. Someone in a white lab coat showed Noble to the small treatment room where a nurse helped Eustace onto a gurney.

"What's your name?" the nurse asked. She glanced at Noble and Mama when Eustace didn't answer.

"He doesn't speak," Mama said matter-of-factly, as she had a thousand times before in their lives. "His name is Eustace."

The nurse raised her eyebrow, then turned to Eustace and patted his knee. "Okay, Eustace. We're going to help you out of these soaked clothes so we can make sure you're alright."

Noble considered his brother, raising his brawny arms like an overgrown child as the nurse pulled the bloodstained T-shirt over his head. She helped him stand, and Eustace held on to her shoulders as he stepped out of his drenched jeans and skivvies. He stuck his hands into the holes of the mint-green hospital gown, and the nurse tied the strings behind his neck.

"There you go. I bet that feels better," she said.

Eustace sat back down on the bed, and the nurse put a blood pressure cuff on his arm and proceeded to take his vital signs.

Mama told the nurse about his brother's medical history,

about how he never did talk, never did play much with other kids, never did much of anything.

"But he saved Shelby's life."

Mama and the nurse turned and looked at Noble, while Eustace smiled, focused on something on the wall—a spot, a seam in the wallpaper, no one ever knew exactly what—and let out a raucous yawp.

"Some folks might think he never did much of anything, but today he walked through a raging river, pulled an unconscious girl from a pickup truck as it was slipping under the water, and saved her life."

A doctor came and examined Eustace, listened to his lungs, looked closely at his eyes.

"You're a lucky man," he said, patting Eustace's leg. "We'll finish up the paperwork and we'll let you go."

"Mama—do you mind if I go check on Shelby?"

She smiled. "I think you'd better."

Noble peered around the corner into the next room where Shelby lay, James sitting beside her and holding her hand. Her head was almost entirely wrapped with gauze, and blood caked in chunks of the dark curls of hair spilling across the white pillow. Her eyes were closed, and the room was dark except for the horizontal lines on the monitor which seemed to compose a steady cadence of life.

"Reverend . . . may I?" he whispered, his attempt not to disturb Shelby in vain.

"Noble?" She lifted her head, then threw her arm over her eyes and groaned. "Oh . . ."

"Go on and visit, you two." James winked. "But not too long. They're getting ready to move her to a bed upstairs."

Noble took James's seat. "Shelby—"

"I can explain." She winced.

"Shhh . . . You don't have to say anything." He grabbed her hand, warmth surging through him as she ran her fingers over his, thick and calloused. "And anyway, before you talk, I want to tell you about Nashville."

She opened her eyes a crack, shielding them from what little light came into the room from the hall.

"I said no."

"What?" Her eyes popped open and she tried to sit up again, without success. She groaned.

"I'm not leavin'."

"If it's because of this . . ."

"It ain't. Not exactly."

"What do you mean?" She put her arm over her eyes again.

"Look. Nashville, it's . . . well, it's amazing. Incredible. Unbelievable. They have everything and more than I could've imagined. They offered me a job, help with moving, resources for Eustace, everything. But I told them no."

"Noble Burden," she said as forcefully as she could without moving her head. "Are you *stupid*?"

"Well, I—"

"You can't . . . turn that down. . . . You'd be a fool."

"Then maybe I'm a fool." He moved the chair closer to her and grabbed hold of her hand. "The farm, the fields,

I know 'em by heart. They're a part of me, as much as my music is. The smell of the haymow and fresh-cut alfalfa, the sound of the barn swallows and bullfrogs, that music moves me as much as anything I could ever play myself."

"But it's not the same. You can't give up playing."

"I'm not going to give up playing. Not entirely. It's just . . . I can't fully explain why . . . but I know I'm supposed to stay here. It's like knowing a ring around the moon means rain . . . that thunder in February means frost in May . . . that it's time to plant corn when the oak leaves are the size of a squirrel's ear, and that a red sky in the morning means you better take cover because a storm'll roll in by midafternoon."

"I do believe you're a poet, too." She grinned.

He laughed and gripped her hand tighter. "There's plenty of time for writing and playing songs. And Mack said he could get me freelance work, so I only have to travel to Nashville once in a while, when it works for everything here at the farm. But I can't turn my back and leave this and all it means to me . . . all *you* mean to me."

"Noble—"

He saw a tear run down the side of her face and his heart sank. "I know you're with Cade, but I can give you more than he can. I ain't giving you up without a fight."

"Stop—" she whispered.

"I won't stop—"

"No, I mean be quiet a minute."

"Alright." He sat back, bracing himself and preparing to argue with whatever she had to say.

"We broke up."

"What?"

She lifted her arm and looked at him, squinting through the pain. "That's why I got in the car with him. I went with him to break up with him."

"What?"

"I'm beginning to think you got your ears blown out by all that music in Nashville."

"But . . . Did he . . . ? He didn't hurt you, did he? Before the wreck? He was so angry."

"Oh, he was angry. Mad as a hornet. But I knew if I didn't go with him and finish us right then and there, it'd drag on till who knows when." She paused and gingerly put her arm back over her eyes. "He was driving like a maniac, and when we hit those flash flood waters by the bridge, he lost control and we flipped right over. But he didn't hit me."

"Thank you, Jesus," Noble said, lifting his eyes to the heavens.

"Give me your hand again," she said.

He did.

"So . . . ," she began, trying to open both her eyes. "You chose Sycamore . . . and I choose you."

Noble stood and reached across her, careful of her bandaged head as he pulled her close and kissed her. Any doubts he had left about where his home was fell away.

He pulled back and ran his hand down the side of her face, then kissed her again.

No, he wasn't a fool at all.

»»»———«««

Back at the house, the power was still out, so Noble and Mama lit some candles, dug through a couple of junk drawers, and found a few flashlights. Eustace went right to his room, pulled on his pajamas, and curled onto his side under the covers. Tears stung Noble's eyes as he sat on the bed, then regarded the Bible verse Mama had cross-stitched and put into a frame above the nightstand: *God blesses those who are humble, for they will inherit the whole earth.* Noble pulled the frayed-edged blanket up under Eustace's chin and brushed the hair back off his blockish, sunburned brow. He leaned down and picked up Eustace's ratty white ball cap, then hung it on the bedpost.

"You really are a hero . . . you know that?"

Eustace replied with a soft snore.

Downstairs, Mama sat at the kitchen table illuminated by candles and the glow of her cell phone in front of her.

"He asleep?" she asked.

"Soon as he hit the pillow," Noble said. "Any more word on Shelby?"

"No. I imagine she's asleep, too."

"Thank God she's alive."

"Yes, thank God they're *both* alive," Mama echoed.

There was a knock on the front door.

Noble answered it. "Reverend. Sheriff Tate. How's Shelby?"

"She was fast asleep when I left. Sheriff here was good

enough to bring me by here to get my car. Thought you might want an update. They're still giving her fluids, and they gave her some pain medication and something to help her rest. The CT scan shows she has a pretty good concussion, in addition to the couple dozen stitches on her head. They hope to release her tomorrow, though."

"Tomorrow—that's great."

"Yes. Yes, it is."

36

The next morning, James knocked softly on the Burdens' front door, and this time a sleepy Eustace answered. James pulled the screen door open with one hand and grabbed Eustace's shoulder with the other, pulling him in for an embrace. "Hope you don't mind. This is something I shoulda done last evening, saving my girl like you did."

Eustace stepped back and dropped his head, then, with a barely perceptible grin, lifted his eyes to James's.

Laurie came through the dark living room, hopping as she pulled a rubber boot on her one still-bare foot. "Thanks for coming. We're all still a little shell-shocked. How's Shelby?"

"Nurse said she slept well. Said she'll be ready to come home late afternoon."

"Thanks to the Lord. And this guy." Noble came from behind Laurie and put his arm around Eustace.

"Thanks to the Lord and this guy, indeed," James replied.

"Can you believe they don't have the power up yet?" Laurie headed down the front steps toward the barn, the rest of them following her.

"Hold up," James said. "Don't be getting ahead of me now."

When they reached the barn, he stepped ahead of all of them and stood in front of the door.

"What's goin' on?" Laurie asked.

He pulled back the barn door nice and slow, and Laurie and Noble gasped.

Eustace guffawed and started clapping his hands.

Inside were at least two dozen people holding glow sticks and flashlights.

"What the—?" Noble said. His friend Brock came alongside him and put his arm across his shoulders.

"We knew there was a chance the power wouldn't come back on right away," James explained, stepping toward Laurie and taking her hand. "So yesterday, even before the accident and all, Hank and Brock and I went ahead and organized more help for today."

"We used the prayer-chain phone numbers. Hope you don't mind," Hank, sheepish, confessed to James.

"Not at all," James laughed. "I'm glad to see there's one

part of the church still functioning." He turned back to Laurie. "After what happened to Frank Whitmore and his herd, we couldn't stand by and not help."

"Why, Reverend Horton." Laurie stepped toward him and put her arms around his neck. James felt his knees weaken as she placed her hand against his cheek and pored over his face, his eyes. "You shouldn't have."

As they kissed, everyone inside the barn cheered, even Eustace.

Bonnie stepped forward. "We came to help, for as long as it takes. Even after the power comes on, if that's what you and your boys need. The ladies here, they brought brunch and casseroles. And the men are prepared to help clean up the storm damage and do the milking. Whatever you need, darling, you just tell us what to do."

Acknowledgments rumbled through the folks behind Bonnie, and the tears that had been puddling in Laurie's eyes let loose.

James put his arms around her and pulled her closer. "'If one part suffers, all the parts suffer with it, and if one part is honored, all the parts are glad.'"

"'All of you together are Christ's body, and each of you is a part of it.'" Charlie Reynolds, whom James hadn't noticed was there, finished the passage from 1 Corinthians.

"Charlie. Thanks for being here." James surveyed the folks in front of them. Dr. Lawson and his two older boys had come, along with his wife, Angie, and their daughter Sara Beth with her baby.

"I was up anyway," Sara said, smiling, the baby wide-eyed in a sling across her chest.

Mark Madsden from the Baptist church was there, and he'd brought extra flashlights. George Bogan and Frank Dean had come, as well as Stephen Lee, who greeted Laurie by setting a large plastic deer in front of her.

"Olive said to bring you something for your yard. This one here was an extra."

Myrtle Worley and Ella Cox were already fussing with setting up folding chairs and tables, putting tablecloths over the tops of them.

Gertrude Johnson huffed past James but smiled wholeheartedly at Laurie. "Brought three of my special egg casseroles for you, one with sausage, one with mushrooms, and one plain. My husband requires the plain one. Oh, and I brought flowers, of course. Every party needs flowers."

Mike Crawford set up a couple of lawn chairs near the cottonwood for Jersha Pittman and Jack McGee.

Jack waved at James and put his hand over his heart, and James responded by giving him a big thumbs-up.

Rosie Fancher and Pete Moore had brought barbecue from the Onion. "Never too early for pulled pork." Rosie grinned.

And Julie Shaw, from the newspaper, had brought her camera.

"My church might be closing," James said to her, "but be sure to take a bunch of pictures of this, because you're looking at the body of Christ right here."

"Well, alright then." Laurie straightened and addressed the group. "Noble, teach the ones who need to know how to milk, how to milk. Brock, could you take a group around and cut up all the downed branches and debris? And, Hank, could you make sure and keep an eye on Eustace?"

"Sure thing, Mrs. Burden." Hank stepped toward Eustace. "I heard we have a hero on our hands."

"Yes, we do," James said. "We surely do."

"I don't know how we'll ever repay you," Noble said to James as they walked side by side into the milking parlor.

"That's the thing about grace, Noble. It's not something that can—or needs to—be repaid. It's something you simply accept."

As he spoke the words, James realized, as Charlie had mentioned days earlier, that this was the truth he'd been thirsting for as much as Noble. Perhaps even more. God had been setting grace before him in the midst of the church closing, with folks who loved him and Shelby, with a roof over his head, with a Savior who'd never abandoned him. He'd just been too proud to accept it.

Inside the barn, James stood back as Noble let the first group of cows in from the holding pen. The men who hadn't been around milking before shuffled their feet nervously as the cows pressed and pushed against each other, vying for positions as they came inside. Diamond and Reba clomped in first, then hesitated when they saw the men. They weren't used to anyone besides Noble and Eustace and Laurie, and the group of strangers made them prick up their ears and turn their heads; their eyes rolled back so the whites of them showed. They kept their heads low, fiddle-footing into the walls and each other as they passed the strangers and ran into their stalls. Noble let six more in after that who acted as spastic as the first group but eventually found their stalls.

"Would you look at that?" Rich Orwell said. "They're trained."

"And then some," James said.

"You first, Pete." Noble motioned to his friend the bartender and sat him alongside the cow named Crystal. He grinned at his friend. "Grab a teat. Rest of y'all come and watch."

James closed the stanchions as Noble told them how to clean the teats, how to milk and how to know they were done, and how to dip the teats to protect them before letting the cow go.

"Guess I'm a bit rusty." Pete chuckled as he struggled to find a rhythm to getting the milk out of the teat.

"A little easier getting beer from a tap, eh?" Noble teased.

"Sorta fun when you get the hang of it," Mike Crawford said, his voice muffled by Loretta's great belly in his face.

"If you can say that, then you haven't been at it long enough," said James, who'd begun to milk Opal. She unexpectedly shifted her weight and James pushed her back into place, her giant head rattling against the sides of the stanchions as she balked and then grabbed another mouthful of alfalfa.

After all the cows were milked, the group filed cafeteria-style along the tables of pastries and casseroles that the ladies had set up. They were serenaded by Noble, who'd brought out his guitar and sat on the stump of an old tree nearby. The sun was well on its way to being up, the clouds golden as they hung along the turquoise eastern horizon. Sore arms made everyone hungry, and they wolfed down the food but lingered awhile over coffee and to listen to Noble play.

That's the church, right there, James thought, prayed, sitting on the tailgate of Shelby's blue pickup truck. *That's what you've been trying to show me, isn't it, Lord? That walls and buildings come and go—some grow too large, some get too small, some join together, some split apart—but the body of Christ and your purposes, your will, never fail.*

Laurie came to join him on the tailgate. "Think the power'll come back on by this evening?"

"We can pray," he said.

"Looks like we're gonna need prayer and then some." Noble set his guitar down beside them, then stormed toward the tricked-out truck kicking up dirt on the road.

James recognized Silas's truck and walked out to where Noble stood.

"What do you think you're doing here?" Noble said to Silas as he jumped down from the cab.

Silas, shame-faced, put his hand up in defense. "I don't mean any harm . . . and . . . well . . . I sure didn't know all these folks would be here."

James swallowed hard, furious. He hadn't given much thought to Cade, since all his focus had been on whether or not Shelby was going to be alright. "Your son—"

"My son . . . ," Silas interrupted, avoiding their eyes and looking almost as shrunken and defeated as Cade had on the side of the river, "my son is a coward."

"Lucky for you, Shelby's gonna be okay," Noble said.

"That's good to hear." Silas adjusted the bill of his ball cap.

"Don't rejoice when your enemies fall; don't be happy when they stumble."

I'm trying, Lord. Really, James prayed silently, then said to Silas, "So . . . what *are* you doing here?"

Silas glanced at the back of his truck, then met James's eyes. "Cade knew better than to show his face around here today. And I know you don't really want to see mine either. But he's right sorry about what happened last night. We both are. The deputy told me it was Laurie's boy who saved your girl . . . so when I heard about the power still being out here and that y'all were lookin' for some help . . . well, I figured finding a generator was the least I could do."

"A generator?" Laurie joined them.

"Yes, ma'am." Silas studied the ground for a moment and tugged his hat down again. "It's not a rental. It's yours to keep, if you'll have it."

James wasn't sure if she was going to accept it or not. He wasn't sure whether he would've either, even though neither of them could've afforded even to rent—let alone buy— one. He thought about Shelby still at the hospital, her head wrapped and sutured, how he'd thought she was dead when Eustace laid her on the riverbank the night before.

And he thought about Cade, shivering and frail, watching everything at a distance, safe.

Laurie reached for Silas's hand, her face grim but not unkind. "Much obliged, Silas."

Silas's timorous expression softened into a gratified grin. "Alright then. We'll need a few men to get this unloaded."

James kept an eye on Silas as several of them helped unload the generator and set it outside the cooling chamber of the barn, where all the electrical connections were for the milking machinery. He considered how much pride the man had to set aside to not only apologize, but offer a sort of peace offering, too. He considered how it could have been Cade who'd been stuck in that truck and how any one of their three children could've died last night. But they'd all been spared, children and their parents alike. They all still had futures. They all still had hope. And in that moment it occurred to James that God could use any situation, even the impossible and unlikely, to make all things new.

37

"Feels like the old days, doesn't it?" Noble said to Shelby, sitting next to him with her feet propped up on a footstool. Before her mom's accident, they'd often rented movies or watched TV together at her house on Saturday nights.

She glanced at him sidelong and grinned. "Almost."

The power had been restored to all of Sycamore by midafternoon. The evening milking had been a success and a relief to the sore arms of everyone who'd come to help that morning, as well as to the nerves of the cows.

"You sure you're gonna be up to singing tomorrow? Did the doctors say it was alright?" Noble said.

She'd only been home from the hospital for a couple of

hours, and Noble had come over after milking to welcome her home, to sit with her while James went to the church, and to practice singing with her for the last service the next day, if she still felt up to it.

"I didn't ask the doctors. Dad was right there the whole time, and it's supposed to be a surprise."

He studied her for signs that she might not feel well.

She'd been dizzy when she'd gotten up to make popcorn, and the dusky gray of fatigue circled her eyes.

"I don't think he'd appreciate the surprise of you passing out on the stage," he said.

"I'll be fine. Really. Another good night's sleep . . . I'm not saying I'd be ready for hard-core worship, but Sycamore Community Church worship? I think I can handle that."

"If you're sure. How long did your dad say he'd be at the church?"

"He said not to wait up for him, that he'd be late."

"So no chance of him hearing us practice?"

"Nah—I think we're good."

He stood and tucked the quilt in snug around Shelby's feet before going to the car to get his guitar. "Be right back."

When he came back inside, she was right where he'd left her.

"My people will live in safety, quietly at home. They will be at rest."

Noble recalled the verse from Isaiah. Where he'd heard it exactly, he could not say. Perhaps in Sunday school, perhaps a repetitive prayer or plea of Mama's.

He set his guitar down and unlatched the case, running his fingers along the smooth cool of the wood, the tension of the finely ribbed strings. He thought about the studios, Mack, Cass, the big homes, the way the hills around the music city seemed to rise up around it, a perfect sanctuary, as if to say, "This! This is what you've hoped for all your life!"

He grabbed the neck of the guitar and turned to Shelby. "I thought we could start with—"

He stopped and caught his breath as he took in the sight of her, the bandages around her head, the bruising on the side of her face, the dark curls she'd braided and which rested against the side of her lithe, pale neck.

She rested her head on the back of the couch, eyes closed.

You're safe, darlin', he thought.

We're home.

38

As it often is with the finishing of a time or a place, there were more folks in attendance than usual on the last Sunday of the existence of Sycamore Community Church. Although some folks were not present, such as George Kernodle, plenty of others were. Jack McGee. Rosie and Pete from the Purple Onion. Brock and Tiffany even made an exception from attending the Methodist church to be with them this day.

James smiled when he saw Silas and Cade slip in late. They took a seat in the back row on the left. He couldn't honestly say that he liked Silas or Cade any better than he had the day before, but he could say with a clear conscience he didn't hate them, either. Because when the lights came on in the Burden barn, he realized there was something that could transcend hate and bitterness, something that could rise above loss and failure. He realized then that everything changes when someone who is lost is found and when things that look a lot like endings become beginnings after all.

The service commenced with a short sermon, one James had spent twenty years thinking about, but only fifteen minutes writing.

"The other day, my daughter . . ." He looked at Shelby in the front row, head in bandages, albeit finagled to look like a headband. He fought back a tightening in his throat. "Shelby brought up one of her favorite Bible stories when she was growing up, the story of Gideon and his battle against the Midianites. You may recall, in Judges chapter 7, that God asked Gideon to do more and more with fewer and fewer men. Gideon doubted but went to battle anyway with the few men he had. He trusted God. And he won the battle."

He looked out at Laurie, sitting in her place on the right side of the church, near the back, with Eustace at her side.

"If we've learned anything over the past twenty years, even in the past few days, it's that we can do a lot with a little . . . that few of us end up where we hope to be, but somehow we all end up where we ought to be. In the same way, no one can say why a church dies or why a life ends. But we can say that no matter what, God is faithful, and faith keeps on going."

He prayed, and when he gave her the nod, Myrtle Worley revved up the organ. With Noble on guitar, they sang a rousing rendition of "All Creatures of Our God and King." James had told them he didn't want the service to feel like a funeral, but a celebration. Because that's what everyone who'd ever crossed the threshold of Sycamore Community Church deserved.

When James began the benediction and dismissal, Shelby approached the pulpit.

"We've got one more thing, Dad."

She took her place next to Noble, like she had so many times before Molly died, and unclamped the microphone from the stand. She steadied herself on a stool and nodded at Laurie, who got up and began passing out papers to all the rows.

"We've got one last song we'd like to do for y'all, one some folks might think is about death, but we think it's about the start of something new," she said as Noble adjusted the frets and tuning pegs on his guitar. "It's an oldie, but if you can't remember it, the words are on the paper Mrs. Burden's handing out."

James felt for the chair behind the pulpit when he realized Shelby was going to sing. For the first time since before Molly died, she was really going to sing.

Noble began to fingerpick the notes softly, and Shelby began to sway, then sing:

"Precious Lord, take my hand,
Lead me on, let me stand,
I am tired . . ."

Shelby's voice cracked and her face flushed. She lowered the microphone and shook her head, using her arm to shield her face from the congregation. James feared her concussion would cause her to have to stop.

In an instant, Noble stood and began to fill in. James watched through tears as she glanced at Noble, who smiled and nodded her on, as he continued the next line:

"Through the storm, through the night . . ."

Finally Shelby took a deep breath, then stood and joined him:

"Take my hand, precious Lord,
Lead me home."

Shelby wiped away tears as Noble's fingerpicking turned to strumming and as the song rose to a crescendo. Shelby's voice soared as it always had, perfect and free, and the whole room brimmed with joy as the congregants and Myrtle joined in.

James held his arms out as she finished and came to him. "Are you okay? Your head—"

"Couldn't be better." She nestled herself against his chest.

He couldn't remember the last time they'd really embraced since Molly's funeral. He kissed her damp forehead, which still smelled faintly like hospital antiseptics, and he was overcome with love . . . for her . . . for the time God had given him at this place . . . for whatever he had planned for them next.

A second feast in as many days awaited them all after the service, as Bonnie had set up tables in one of the children's rooms off the sanctuary. Soon they were topped with casseroles and covered dishes, salads and pies. Another table displayed several scrapbooks chock-full of decades of memorabilia from not only his ministry, but also Tilly's and even a few relics from generations before that. Programs of Sunday services and funerals, baptisms and weddings, snapshots of potlucks and newspaper clippings of vacation Bible school, and a pair of old, yellowed gloves someone had worn when they'd had a bell choir.

James sat in one of the chairs—meant to hold a child— his long legs splayed out as he balanced a plate of food on his lap.

Across the way, Noble and Shelby talked to each other and carried on like they were the only ones in the room.

"Mind if I sit here?" Laurie nodded toward the small chair next to James.

"Please."

Laurie pulled a third little chair over for Eustace, who plopped down next to her, knees bent awkward nearly up to his chin.

Posters of Bible timelines and the Ten Commandments, a cartoon of a soldier wearing the armor of God, and giant cutouts of fruit—each one representing gentleness or kindness, peace or joy, love or patience or self-control—hung all around them. People piled corn casserole and baked beans and cheesy potatoes and apple pie high on their paper plates.

Jersha Pittman cut the cake, and Jack McGee doled it out, along with Dixie cups brimming with lemonade to wash it all down.

It was one of the finest Communion services Sycamore Community Church had ever had.

EPILOGUE

TWO YEARS LATER

"You need anything else, Mrs. Johnson?" James tucked the last two pots of red and yellow mums into the cart and handed Gertrude the receipt. James had come to love his work at the hardware store, which was unusually busy for a Friday evening. He thought he might even have a sort of gift for helping folks find the right sizes of bolts and washers, deciphering what sorts of drill bits were required for certain jobs, and mixing paint.

"No. Thank you. I'll see you tomorrow."

If he didn't know her, he'd say her smile was almost congenial.

The next customer placed several packages of string lights, landscaping burlap, and outdoor votive candles on the counter.

"Did you find everything you needed today?" James asked, focusing on the computer behind the register.

"Everything 'cept the bride," the customer chuckled.

"Noble! How's everything going?" James came around the counter and embraced Noble, patting him heartily on the back.

"The barn's cleaned out, tables and chairs delivered this morning, and Shelby's a nervous wreck. Aside from that, everything's great," he laughed.

James stood back and took in the sight of him, the young man who'd be his son-in-law in less than twenty-four hours. "I'd expect nothing less from her. She's like her mother was about how things look. Wants it to be perfect. I guess I can't blame her."

"Me either. I keep telling her it'll be perfect, even if it rains all day and the only guests who show up are the cows."

"Cows are enough," James chuckled, reminiscing about the vows he and Laurie had exchanged under the big cottonwood the previous spring. Charlie Reynolds had officiated. Shelby, Noble, and Eustace had been the attendants. Laurie had carried a bouquet of blush-pink peonies, freshly cut from where they blossomed along the fencerow. And they'd been serenaded by the piping and warbles of chickadees, mourning doves, and sparrows. He could almost feel again the warmth of her small hands as he'd taken them into his, the trembling of his heart as he promised to love and cherish her as the dew rose up from the meadows all around them. Everything under that ancient tree that day was enough.

But Noble needn't have feared. More than cows did show up for his and Shelby's wedding the following afternoon.

Seemed like most of the town of Sycamore was there. James officiated; Eustace was the best man. Gertrude Johnson had done a beautiful job arranging the mums, along with sunflowers and bright-eyed daisies, on the burlap-covered tables and in the bouquets and boutonnieres. Lizzie Bailey had done Shelby's hair up in loose braids, accented with sprigs of baby's breath. Shelby had chosen to wear Molly's wedding dress, which Laurie lengthened and tailored so that the sleeves were capped instead of long.

As the ceremony proceeded, James scanned the crowd and was pleased that he had not lost his ability to speak and notice the countenances of his audience at the same time.

Do you love me? James heard the Lord whisper, even as he read the vows from his worn and dog-eared prayer book.

Lord, you know I do, James replied silently.

Then feed my sheep.

James knew then, as he spoke the promises ushering in the future of his daughter, that his calling to minister had been and always would be real. He would continue to preach the gospel and heed the gospel. At times he would doubt it and be furious with it; at other times he would revel in the ecstasy of its certain truth—whether in the pews of the Methodist church, in the aisles of Hank's hardware store, in the interminable silence as he knelt alongside Molly's grave, or in peaceful moments spent with Laurie on the front porch swing, watching the sun set gold, then pink, then blazing orange over the rolling fields.

When it was time for the ring, Brock, a groomsman,

nudged Eustace, who reached and fumbled around in his jacket pocket. As he held it out to Noble, a blue Karner butterfly drifted down from the barn rafters above as if someone had orchestrated it. The tiny wings shuddered and the antennae twitched as it lit upon Eustace's wrist, batted its wings three times, and flew away before anyone but the wedding party could notice.

"Maybe—" James leaned in toward Noble and Shelby, their faces flushed and stained with tears—"the promise of Jeremiah 29 isn't as much about deliverance or success as it is about finding hope right where we are."

He straightened and said in his best preacher's voice, "Noble Burden, you may now kiss your bride."

Afterward, they feasted on Rosie's barbecue and danced under the strings of lights until well after midnight, when the cows moved like shadows in the far pasture and meteor showers began to shoot and glisten across the sky.

A Note from the Author

Each of my books begins with an idea, and most often, from something broken in the world that moves my heart. In the case of *Lead Me Home*, my heart was (and still is, in many ways) broken for small churches, small towns, and the overlooked among us—like Eustace. A second major inspiration for *Lead Me Home* was my cousin's dairy farm. Just like the Burdens, my cousin and his family have a sustainable dairy farm with about sixty cows they've been milking twice a day, every day, without fail, for decades. The county next to them once had more than a dozen farms just like theirs that have gone out of business because of suburban sprawl and giant, industrial dairy farms with which they could not compete. This drastic decline of small, sustainable farms continues today.

It's not easy being small these days. It's not easy being the church these days, either. Many small towns, independent farms, and churches are dying, just like in the fictional town of Sycamore, Indiana. Many folks like James and Noble wonder how they could possibly be in the right place. Many feel insignificant—even invisible—because of how they compare to the bigger churches, farms, and dreams all around them. This feeling isn't limited to small towns, either. In the suburbs and the cities and indeed everywhere, folks struggle to feel like they matter when every sound bite, every social media outlet, everything that saturates our senses says that bigger, louder, stronger, smarter, more beautiful, more independent, and more trendy is better.

The gospel of Jesus Christ stands in contrast to all of that. Jesus came for the weak and the small. For the widow and the orphan. For the deaf and the mute. For the blind and the lame. He came for the poor and insignificant. He whispered into the ears of sinners and made them new. He shook the crowds and moved the masses and fed the thousands with truth and gentleness and peace. He did not demand allegiance but allowed questions. He did not deny thieves but embraced them when they repented. He loved the unlovable, spoke to the unspeakable, moved the immovable, and justified the unjust. And Jesus, in his holiness, was—and is—the furthest thing from trendy in this broken world.

If I could sum up this story with two verses from the Bible, they would be Revelation 2:4 (AMP), "But I have *this* [charge] against you, that you have left your first love [you have lost the depth of love that you first had for Me]," and Psalm 16:6 (NIV), "The boundary lines have fallen for me in pleasant places; surely I have a delightful inheritance." I hope that after reading this book, you will look at the town, home, and family where God has put you with new eyes, that you will see that the sunsets are beautiful right where you are, and that you will realize that no matter how big or small your church, the one foundation is Jesus Christ our Lord. And I hope you will realize that when God seems to say no to a specific dream, he may be saying yes to the ones that matter most. As James says, "Few of us end up where we hope to be, but somehow we all end up where we ought to be." The boundary lines we come up against in our lives are there for a reason, because God loves us and knows the deepest desires of our hearts.

And about the little blue butterfly, the endangered Karner blue, three of which appear in the story: I came across the details of the Karner while researching Eustace's butterfly-collecting hobby and learned that, according to the US Fish and Wildlife Service, "Over the past century, the number of Karner blue butterflies has declined by at least 99 percent across their historic range." The report goes on to say, "The single most important factor causing the decline of the Karner blue butterfly across its range has been the loss of habitat. . . . The Karner blue butterfly's habitat is very specific, and the butterfly is unable to adapt to these changes in its environment. Habitat loss, isolation of populations, combined with the extremely small size of many of the remaining population, puts these populations at high risk of 'winking out.'" I believe we would be wise to look at the way nature reacts to changes in the world, not only because we have a responsibility to our environment, but because perhaps the demise of certain species mimics the demise of certain aspects of our culture, and indeed, the spread of the gospel itself, were it not for the ultimate sovereignty of our God.

And finally, above all, there is grace.

Grace for James and Shelby.

Grace for Noble and Laurie.

Grace for Eustace.

Grace for Gertrude and Jack, Silas and Cade.

And there is grace abundant for each of us who chooses to believe.

Discussion Questions

1. Sycamore Community Church has a long and vibrant history, but by the time our story opens, it is in its final weeks. Do you have any experience with a small, struggling church? What do small churches have to offer that larger, wealthier churches do not—and vice versa?

2. James and Shelby are both struggling in different ways to recover after Molly's death. What are some of the coping mechanisms you see them using, either healthy or unhealthy? What are some of the ways you have tried to cope following a major loss or disappointment in your life?

3. James has distanced himself from people, both friends and church members. What problems does this cause? In what ways is this more or less challenging for him as a pastor than it might be for a layperson?

4. Shelby has refused to sing since her mother's death, believing that her singing contributed to the accident that claimed her mother's life. What finally makes Shelby decide to sing again? Do you think she will continue singing in public after the story has ended? Why or why not?

5. Noble has struggles of his own, trying to run the family farm, care for his mother and brother, and put his own dreams on hold. How does his struggle parallel James's? Shelby's?

6. Do you have—or have you ever had—a dream similar to Noble's dream of singing in Nashville? What obstacles have stood in your way? In what ways have you tried to pursue your dream, or for what reasons have you chosen to set it aside? Do you feel Noble made the right choice?

7. Noble's friend Brock tells him, "Sometimes leaving ain't the answer for our pain. Sometimes the dreams God has for us, the biggest difference we can make in the world is right where we are." Tell how both Noble and James come to realize the truth of this statement. Is there a situation in your life that you are tempted to run away from, but you feel God may be asking you to stay where you are? How can we know whether forging ahead or staying put is the right thing to do?

8. Dr. Tom Lawson asks James, somewhat rhetorically, "Where and in what church is it really okay to be

broken anymore?" Do you agree that many churches have lost the ability to welcome the broken and help them heal? What are some ways we can address this need in our faith communities?

9. Why does Jack McGee give James his Purple Heart? In what ways can ministry be compared to military combat? Can you think of any Scripture passages that use this imagery?

10. Eustace's butterfly collection—and specifically, the endangered Karner blue butterfly—play a small but significant role in the story. What do you think the author is trying to communicate through the various ways the butterflies show up?

11. After the storm and the accident, Eustace saves the day. Can you think of any Bible passages that relate to the way Eustace steps up and does something no one else could do—and which no one thought he could do?

12. Despite James's best efforts to save Sycamore Community Church, it eventually does close. Have you ever been involved with a project or ministry that "failed," despite all the time and work you poured into it? Why do you think God allows things like this to happen? What lessons did James learn, and how can you apply them to your own situation?

About the Author

Amy K. Sorrells is an award-winning author whose diverse writing has appeared in medical journals, newspapers, and an anthology (*Indy Writes Books*) benefiting literacy in central Indiana. A lifelong Hoosier and registered nurse, Amy makes her home on the outskirts of town with her husband and three sons. *Lead Me Home* is her third novel. Connect with Amy at amysorrells.wordpress.com.

TYNDALE HOUSE PUBLISHERS IS CRAZY4FICTION!

Inspirational fiction that entertains and inspires

Get to know us! Become a member of the Crazy4Fiction community. Whether you follow our blog, like us on Facebook, follow us on Twitter, or read our e-newsletter, you're sure to get the latest news on the best in Christian fiction. You might even win something along the way!

JOIN IN THE FUN TODAY.

 www.crazy4fiction.com

 Crazy4Fiction

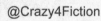 @Crazy4Fiction

FOR MORE GREAT TYNDALE DIGITAL PROMOTIONS, GO TO WWW.TYNDALE.COM/EBOOKEXTRA

CP0021

2116